"Amanda?" he whispered her name like a question because he had no idea what the answer was. Except he knew that he wanted her closer. She was so, so close already, but he wanted more.

That felt like the wrong answer, too. He didn't know which way was up right now, his heart felt like it was pounding in his chest, and there was that smell of lavender again from the other night. Everything about this woman was floral, and he didn't want to move away.

"Dominic," she replied in a breathy manner that felt like an answer but only created more questions for him. Her chest was already against his, but she pushed up on her tiptoes until her mouth was also at the same level as his.

Sunflower Cottage on Heart Lake

Other Books by Sarah Robinson

Queerly Devoted Series
Baby Bank
Les Be Honest

Heart Lake Series
Dreaming of a Heart Lake Christmas
The Little Bookstore on Heart Lake Lane

Women's Fiction
Every Last Drop

Nudes Series
NUDES
BARE
SHEER

At the Mall Series
Mall I Want for Christmas Is You
Mall You Need Is Love
Mall out of Luck
Mall American Girl
Mall-O-Ween Mischief
Mall Year Long: The Box Set

The Photographer Trilogy
Tainted Bodies
Tainted Pictures
Untainted

Forbidden Rockers Series
Logan's Story: A Prequel Novella
Her Forbidden Rockstar
Rocker Christmas: A Logan & Caroline Holiday Novella

Kavanagh Legends Series
Breaking a Legend
Saving a Legend
Becoming a Legend
Chasing a Legend
Kavanagh Christmas

Standalone Novels
Not a Hero: A Bad Boy Marine Romance
Misadventures in the Cage
One Night Stand Serial
Second Shot of Whiskey

Sunflower Cottage on Heart Lake

SARAH ROBINSON

FOREVER

NEW YORK   BOSTON

Forever
Hachette Book Group
1290 Avenue of the Americas, New York, NY 10104
read-forever.com
@readforeverpub

First edition: December 2024

Forever is an imprint of Grand Central Publishing. The Forever name and logo are registered trademarks of Hachette Book Group, Inc.

The publisher is not responsible for websites (or their content) that are not owned by the publisher.

The Hachette Speakers Bureau provides a wide range of authors for speaking events. To find out more, go to hachettespeakersbureau.com or email HachetteSpeakers@hbgusa.com.

Forever books may be purchased in bulk for business, educational, or promotional use. For information, please contact your local bookseller or the Hachette Book Group Special Markets Department at special.markets@hbgusa.com.

ISBNs: 9781538755150 (mass market), 9781538755143 (ebook)

Printed in the United States of America

BVGM

10   9   8   7   6   5   4   3   2   1

To my daughters, Norah and Ava.
Always turn toward the sun.

Chapter One

Amanda

You left a toilet in his yard?" her cousin and best friend since childhood, Nola Bennett-Dean, asked as she stood with her arms crossed and her eyes wide.

"Three toilets," Amanda clarified, lifting her gaze from the Adirondack chair that she had been sanding down enough to be able to put on a darker stain later. She'd scored the two of them at a garage sale of a neighbor down the road who clearly had no idea the value of these things. They were timeless and, when handcrafted correctly by a skilled artisan, they cost a good buck. She'd gotten them for five dollars each, but after a quick touch-up, she was pretty sure she'd be able to get at least two hundred per chair. Or she could use them as an add-on item for an outdoor living concept that she was selling as part of her next design project. The art of the upsell was a tactic she was still working on at her job, and her boss was adamant that she always had at least two or three add-ons for every design sold. "All used, but empty. I even put them in a cute circle, like a toilet party. Don't worry. I'm not a monster."

Nola blinked slowly, like she was trying to put her

words in order or something. "You can't just leave toilets in people's yards."

Amanda stood up straight and feigned innocence. "He left me in a pile of crap, so I left a pile of crap on his lawn. Fair is fair."

Nola was clearly unconvinced by the way she tilted her head at Amanda and turned on her mom voice. "He backed out of the Heart Lake Boat Parade. That's hardly toilet worthy."

"It is when he's the one who started the entire thing two years ago and then left me holding all the responsibility at the last minute," she countered.

Nola finally let the smallest of grins slip. "The poor boy only started the Boat Parade to have an excuse to work with you on something. You know he likes you."

"Well, at least he's finally given up on that goal, because the answer is still going to be no." Blake was a nice guy, but one of those nice guys who wants to make sure that every woman knows he's a nice guy and that if they don't appreciate that... well, then he's not so nice.

It was transactional at best, and Amanda had no interest in dating him or anyone like that.

"At some point, you know, you're going to have to actually get out there and date. You never open yourself up to anyone," Nola started, and Amanda immediately began to tune her out.

Dating was not on the agenda for her right now. At least, she couldn't imagine getting out there and trying to date given where she was at in her life right now. It was nice to think about coming home to someone or having company for once, but that also came with a lot of strings attached that she wasn't sure she'd ever be ready for.

"Or I can keep focusing on my work and get out from under Clayton's thumb soon." Being a designer was her whole life's passion, and it drove her crazy that she was still working under a senior designer at a local firm rather than being out on her own. But she just didn't have the client reach herself yet to start her own firm, so until then, she ran around and completed Clayton's grunt work and made his designs come to life instead of her own. "He did say he might let me work solo on a project this summer."

"Really?" Nola's concerned look vanished and was replaced by a wide smile. "That's amazing! Did he say which project?"

Amanda shook her head. "No, but he's bidding on the remodel of the old Culver farmhouse at the end of Main Street. I've been dropping not-so-subtle hints about all the ideas I have for turning it into an event space and venue."

"Ooh, can you imagine having a wedding there or something? Once it's fixed up, it could be absolutely magical." Nola reached out and gave Amanda's arm a squeeze. "Well, keep me updated. That's so exciting. I'm glad Clayton is finally putting you out there, because it's insane how he's been hiding your talent. Anyway, I have to go grab Kate from her jazz class."

Nola had her four-year-old in a different activity every day during the summer, and Amanda didn't blame her one bit. She loved her goddaughter with all her heart, but Kate was the embodiment of energy. If she wasn't busy doing something at all times, it was just a chance for her to get in trouble—or, more often, give her parents a hard time.

"And it looks like you have company," Nola added as she was walking away.

Amanda glanced in the direction that Nola was gesturing and saw a large pickup truck making its way down the driveway that she shared with the neighboring property. It paused slightly at the fork between her house and the old Murphy place, then made its way up toward Amanda's.

"Have fun!" Nola waved goodbye and wiggled her brows, which was definitely code for _There's a hot man in that truck_. She got in her giant SUV that she insisted was imperative for parenthood and was off before the truck came to a full stop. Sure enough, a very handsome, tall gentleman with thick, dark brown hair and a trimmed beard stepped out of the cab. He had on a black T-shirt that was snug around his biceps and jeans that hugged his hips in a way that felt purposeful.

Keep your eyes north, Amanda, she reminded herself. _Why am I even noticing this in the first place? I am not that type of person!_

"This place looks nothing like the picture," he said in a gruff voice that was almost a growl as he stared up at the front of Amanda's house. "Why the hell is it so yellow?"

Her hands rested squarely on her hips as she marched over to him. "Excuse me?"

He gestured up at her house, not even giving a moment of eye contact. "It's yellow. Like, _bright_ yellow."

"Congratulations on having eyeballs," she replied. "Yes, my house is yellow. Is that a problem?"

The man seemed to finally realize that she was standing there and turned his gaze away from the bright yellow house—which matched the rows of sunflowers Amanda had carefully planted in front, very proudly—to look down at her. "This is *your* house?"

She waved her hands in front of his face. "Are you lost or are you on something? Of course it's my house. Did you think it was yours or something?"

The corner of his lip twitched only slightly into a smile, but he quickly removed it and the deadpan expression of utter disgust toward her yellow house returned. "Yeah. I just bought 33 Lakeside Court from Carl Murphy, and I'm moving in today. The movers are only a few minutes behind me, and Carl said nothing about a yellow house."

"That's because 33 Lakeside Court is next door," Amanda said, pointing toward the house at the other end of the split driveway that he'd driven right past. Luckily for him, that house was a perfect shade of brick and bland. "Carl's house is over there. Or, I guess, your house now."

She hadn't even realized that Carl was selling, but he spent most of the year in Boca Raton, Florida, these days, so it wasn't a huge surprise. He'd been the best kind of neighbor recently—one that is never there. That was much more preferable than when Carl and his wife had been living next door and she'd had to deal with them daily.

And now she had to deal with an entirely new neighbor? *Ugh.*

Tall, dark, and grumpy just stared at her. "Oh. That's 33 Lakeside Court. Not this one."

She stared back.

"Sorry about that," he finally continued. He slowly gestured back toward her house. "It's not bad. It's just...yellow."

Amanda didn't lighten her stare. "I like sunflowers. And I don't like unsolicited opinions."

He chuckled then and put his hand out toward her. "Clearly, we got off on the wrong foot. I've been driving for hours and was moving boxes and furniture before that. It's been a hell of a day, but let's start over. I'm Dominic Gage."

She glanced down at his open palm wearily for a moment before finally loosening her stance and allowing him the pleasure of shaking her hand. "Amanda Riverswood."

"Have you lived here long?" Dominic let go of her hand and stretched his neck from side to side in a way that showed off the definition in his trap muscles.

Honestly, he *was* a good-looking man. A complete jerk, she'd already decided. But still...a good-looking man. Admittedly, that was a little strange to be thinking about at all because Amanda rarely found herself noticing men—or anyone. Something in the way her skin felt prickly when his eyes were on her just felt unfamiliar, but she wasn't about to let Dominic see that he'd gotten to her.

She made sure to stand straighter, crossing her arms over her chest. "I grew up in Heart Lake, but I moved into the Sunflower Cottage about five years ago."

"Sunflower Cottage?" He lifted one brow. "That's an appropriate name for it."

The row of sunflowers that dominated the garden lining the front of her house was a landscape designer's dream, and clearly, he had no taste.

"Do you hate flowers or something?" she shot back. "Where are you moving here from? Some industrial city that never has any sun or greenery?"

He smirked, and it somehow made him even more appealing, and Amanda hated that. "Detroit."

"Oh." Her hands dropped to her sides. "So, yes, then."

"Detroit's got a lot of urban agriculture, to be honest, but this…" he said, gesturing to the small cove of Heart Lake that jutted up behind both houses. "It's like something out of a storybook."

Amanda felt a little bit of hometown pride at the beauty of her town. Heart Lake was all greenery and water and quirky people. There was always something exciting about someone discovering the truth for the first time and witnessing that. Even if it was through this jerk's lens.

"Wait a couple months until the fall. This place is basically a postcard once the leaves start changing colors," she commented.

The sound of a rumbling vehicle caught her attention, and she glanced behind Dominic to see a large moving van making its way up their driveway.

"Looks like your stuff is here," she said, pointing toward the van. "I'm sure I'll see you around."

He didn't respond, but rather tipped his chin to her

before getting back in his truck and reversing down Amanda's drive to get to his own.

She stood there for a moment longer, just watching as the moving van followed him up to the front of the old Murphy place. The van pulled onto the grass beside the house, and Dominic was immediately out of his truck and yelling at them to get off the grass. The drivers quickly reversed, but it didn't matter because there were already two giant tire tracks in his lawn.

Thank goodness that wasn't on the side of the lawn he shared with her.

"Good lord," she muttered under her breath as she walked back toward the Adirondack chairs she'd been working on.

Amanda generally considered herself a pretty nice person—spicy around the edges, especially when pushed—but still, anyone would be lucky to have her as a neighbor. And yet, somehow, she seemed to only attract neighbors that were awful in one way or another. Carl, for example, used to have wild parties all the time until his wife died last year. Amanda was very sorry for his loss, but not at all sorry that he was now never in the state. Before she'd lived in the Sunflower Cottage, she'd lived in a small town house off Main Street, and the neighbors on both sides of her were in a feud over whose dog was louder. Spoiler alert: both dogs were loud as hell, and she was caught in the middle of them.

And now, she had Oscar the Grouch moving in next door.

She picked up the sander, but then had to put it right back down as she felt her cell phone vibrating in her pocket. She pulled it out and clicked on the screen to see her boss calling. Reluctantly, Amanda hit the button to answer his video call and held the phone up in front of her.

"Hi, Clayton," she greeted him.

"Amanda, I'm going out of town." No hello, no niceties, just straight to the point. "Adam booked us a cruise to the Bahamas for our anniversary."

Her brows lifted slightly. "Wow. Uh, well, congratulations."

His husband's face suddenly appeared on the screen. "Amanda, please assure him that you can handle things while we're gone. He's got his anxious pants on, and I need my husband to be present on this trip."

Clayton pushed Adam away and returned to the screen. "For Christ's sake, I'm not anxious. I just want to make sure things are done right because I don't know how much cell service I'll have down there."

"How long will you be gone?" she asked, not trying to sound too excited.

Clayton was a bad guy. He was...he was *okay*. He was just territorial, and never gave her a chance to prove herself. She understood to an extent—he'd built this firm from the ground up, and it was his name on the door. But still. There was no reason to keep good talent down instead of fostering it and allowing it to grow for both his sake and hers.

"I told Brenda to forward my calls to you during the time I'm gone," Clayton continued, referencing the administrative assistant and bookkeeper who really kept the entire operation going. Without her, the firm would come to a crashing halt, and Amanda was glad that she'd managed to get on her good side from the start, thanks to a plate of Marvel's cookies she'd brought in on her first day. "But I need you to only handle emergencies that can't wait until I get back. Don't accept any new projects. Just tell them that I'll get back to them when I return."

"If someone needs something sooner, I could take the project on solo," Amanda interjected. "I'm totally fine with that."

"Absolutely not," Clayton replied. "You're going to be busy enough with the home stagings for the open houses on the schedule. I wouldn't want to put all that on you right now."

Home staging was beginner's work, and she tried to stifle her groan at her disinterest for the task.

"Anything else can wait until I get back," Clayton continued, again pushing Adam off the screen as he started fussing with Clayton's collar. "Do you feel up to that?"

Did she feel up to staging a few houses for the sole realtor in the area? Yeah, obviously.

"Sure," she said instead. "But, um, what if the Culver farmhouse gets back to us about our bid?"

"Just let them know we are honored to accept and that we will staff the project with the best designer we have," he replied. "So I'll take it over when I get back."

Subtle.

"Okay," Amanda agreed, though every part of her wanted to yell up at the sky and throw her phone into the lake. "I'll make sure things are taken care of. Have a great vacation."

"Thanks, doll. I have every faith in you—you've got this!" Clayton cooed in his phony sweet voice before hanging up.

She pushed the phone back into her pocket and picked up the sander, taking her frustration out on the innocent Adirondack chairs. She really needed to get out on her own at some point, but a lot of sacrifices would come with that. Money being the biggest one. Clayton wasn't necessarily her favorite person—hell, few people were—but he paid well, and his reputation meant that business was always steady.

It also meant that she was often constructing his visions, not her own.

But the paycheck had bought her the Sunflower Cottage and a lifestyle that she really loved. Even more than that, the stability was something she had always craved. Growing up with divorced parents, she had always spent half the week with her dad and half with her mom. She had two of everything, and while at first, she'd thought that was amazing, it got old really quick. When her father got remarried and began having children with his new wife, the funds and attention completely stopped coming her way. He ended up missing most of his scheduled time with her, and Amanda's mother became the de facto primary parent overnight. Given that her mother worked three jobs to support them and was never around, this basically made Amanda feel like she'd been on her own since her preteen years.

Having a place, having a single home that she could make exactly the way that she wanted…it meant a lot to her. It was something no one could take away from her, and something she'd earned all on her own.

She gazed up at the front of Sunflower Cottage and smiled, grateful to be in this place. Screw the neighbor's opinion on her sunflowers—this home was perfect.

"Amanda!"

A jarringly loud call pulled at her attention, and she turned to look over to where Dominic was still trying to negotiate with the moving van.

"Was that your mailbox?" He pointed toward the back of the moving van.

She tilted her head to see the yellow mailbox lying on the ground behind the van. "Uh... yeah."

Dominic looked ready to go off on someone, and she immediately felt sorry for the drivers who were about to experience his wrath.

"I'll submit a claim to the insurance company to get them to pay for a new one," he promised as he walked over to her. "I swear it's impossible to trust the online reviews of any business these days."

"I can fix the mailbox myself," Amanda assured him. "It's really fine."

He looked too surprised, and she instantly felt annoyed at his lack of faith in her abilities. "*You* can fix it?"

She lifted one brow and put her hands back on her hips. "Is that really so hard to believe?"

Now Dominic was the one who looked flustered. "I didn't say that. I just meant *I* wouldn't know how to fix it. I'm surprised that you would."

She found herself wishing Nola were here to hear this, because this was at least a partial explanation for why she had no interest in dating. She didn't *need* anyone. She didn't need Dominic's help. She was fine on her own, and anyone else was going to get in the way. "I'll just replace the post. It's not that hard. Looks like it wasn't that damaged, just knocked over. That's an easy fix, as long as they don't run it over entirely."

"Okay, I'll let them know," Dominic said. "Thanks for... being understanding, I guess."

She shrugged her shoulders, because his ego was the least of her problems right now. "Welcome to Heart Lake, Dominic. We take care of our own here."

Chapter Two

Dominic

Well, that was embarrassing.

Dominic walked into the front door of his new empty brick house with the deflated ego of a man who'd just been served his ass on a rustic platter by his handy-woman neighbor.

A neighbor who'd been wearing only a neon green bikini top under jean overalls with the biggest brown eyes he'd ever seen that somehow matched the perfect shade of brown ringlets that fell out of her ponytail. He might be partially blind, but not blind enough not to notice the way her curves hugged her outfit or the blush on her cheeks when she'd first seen him.

He had a detached retina to thank for the increasing partial blindness and his early retirement from the Detroit Tigers. But he couldn't blame a baseball to the face for his inability to hold a normal conversation with...literally anyone. As he'd just proven with his brand-new neighbor who clearly already hated him.

Not that he cared.

Well, not that he *wanted* to care. Ever since his wife left him after she'd decided he wasn't as fun in retirement as he'd been when he was actively playing baseball, he'd promised himself that he wasn't going to let anyone else's opinions dictate who he was. When he'd said his marriage vows, he'd meant forever. Apparently, his soon-to-be-ex-wife had only meant until one of them had a depressive episode. Then she was completely out.

And this depressive episode appeared to be more of a lifestyle choice now.

That wasn't a fair thought, and he knew that. His marriage and the circumstances surrounding his divorce were a lot more complicated than that, but he wanted to sit in self-pity today.

The mover stepped out of the back of the moving van and looked up at the house Dominic had just purchased. "This is it?"

Dominic nodded. "Yeah. Try not to break anything."

"Man, I don't get it," the mover said, this time leaning his weight against the liftgate on the back of the moving truck. "This place is small and out here in the middle of nowhere."

"It's not that small." He wasn't even sure why he felt the need to defend himself to this complete stranger who he was paying by the hour. "It's almost two thousand square feet inside if you include the back porch. You can't beat the view of the lake."

"I'll give you that," the mover agreed as he motioned for the other men on his team to start grabbing boxes. "It's just that penthouse we moved you out of this morning was a thing of beauty. Never seen that much glass that high in the sky before in my life. How did you even find this place all the way out here?"

"My grandfather used to rent a place here for at least two weeks every summer." Dominic wasn't sure how his grandfather had found it to begin with, but he did know that every memory he had here was warm and positive. It wasn't even just the vacation part of it—what kid wouldn't love swimming in the lake, taking the rowboat or canoe out, or going hiking in the wooded areas? That was all fun and amazing, but it had been the quiet nights around the fire pit with his grandfather playing guitar and his mother singing along that had really made things memorable.

His father had never been in the picture, and his mother had picked up all the slack for both parental roles. Because of that, Dominic's grandfather had become the biggest paternal figure in his life, and he really appreciated that his mother prioritized Dominic's relationship with her father. At this point, he couldn't even begin to imagine who he'd be if not for Grandpa Carleton.

Burying him two summers ago had been the hardest moment of his life, and he'd made a vow then and there that he was going to come back to Heart Lake again one day. He hadn't expected a career-ending injury to speed up his timeline, but he was fulfilling his promise all the same.

"That's a nice memory," the mover replied, this time finally carrying a box and walking toward the house. "They still come up around here?"

Dominic shook his head. "Nah."

The man waited for a moment, as if expecting Dominic to say more, but that wasn't going to happen.

Finally, the mover shrugged his shoulders and finished carrying the box inside.

Dominic circled around the house and came to a stop on the back lawn that jutted up to the lake, just staring out at it for a few moments. It had been a while since he'd talked about his grandfather, and being here was stirring up memories he'd been pushing away for a long time.

Two summers ago, Dominic had been in the middle of a game against the Yankees when he saw a messenger run over to his coach on the sidelines and whisper something urgently. The coach's eyes had darted to Dominic immediately, and an unsettled pit in his stomach had burst to life, but then the coach wiped his expression away and the game continued on. He'd tried to ignore it as some sort of weird coincidence, but after they'd finished the ninth inning in the lead by two points and Dominic was headed back to the locker room, his coach had stopped him and given him the news about his grandfather. It had been a heart attack—so quick that nothing could have been done.

His first thought had been for his mother—it had always been just the three of them. His grandmother had passed away before Dominic had been old enough to remember her, so it was just his mother, Grandpa Carleton, and...that was it.

Dominic had already planned that one of the bedrooms in this new house was going to be his mother's room. Not that he expected her to visit often—she had decided to go back to school in her early sixties to get a graduate degree in counseling and was very busy with class work and internships. She had had him when she was barely out of her teenage years, and he was proud of her for getting back out there and choosing what kind of life she wanted for herself.

Her newfound ambition and drive, however, made it glaringly obvious to Dominic that his was completely gone.

Dominic felt his phone vibrate in the pocket of his jeans and pulled it out to glance at the screen. *Speak of the devil.* His mother's name and photo appeared, and he swiped to answer her call.

"Hey, Mom."

"Sweets, I've got the best story to tell you," Ellen Gage began with all the gusto of someone about to spill the latest local tea.

He frowned but kept his eyes on the lake as he watched a bird dive down and snatch something to eat out of the water. "What happened?"

"So you know how I'm doing this internship at a residential mental health facility, right?" she began. "And remember my boss, Jennie? Jennie with an *ie*, not a *y*."

"Mom, I met Jennie less than a month ago at the last fundraising event," Dominic reminded her.

"Right, right." Ellen was not swayed by her dimming memory. "Well, today I walked into the office, and the door wasn't working very well so I kind of had to jam it. Like really put my shoulder into it. It's an old house they lease, so I just figured the wood had warped or something and it had gotten stuck. Turns out, it had been locked."

Now Dominic was frowning, picturing his twig-framed

mother hulking out on a piece of plywood. "You knocked down a locked door?"

"Well, I didn't know it was locked at the time, but that's not the story," she continued. "The story is what I walked in on once the door popped open—barely took a tap, I'm telling you."

Dominic turned away from the view of the lake to look back at the house just in time to see one of the movers drop a box and then trip over it. He tensed for a moment to make sure the guy got back up and was okay, but once he did, all that was left in Dominic was annoyance. "What was going on in the office, Mom?"

His mother continued, "Jennie was playing online poker—on the work computer—but that wasn't even the worst part. The regional manager was doing it with her."

"Bentley?" Interesting development, but he had definitely gotten a vibe from the two of them at the last fundraising event that they were more than just co-workers. "That's weird. How were they playing it together?"

"I don't know," his mother admitted. "I didn't actually see it, but she was sitting in his lap in front of the computer, and they said there weren't enough chairs for them both to see the screen at the same time. How absolutely irresponsible to be gambling on company time like that. Can you believe them?"

Dominic bit his lip because he wasn't about to say that he actually didn't believe them at all, and it seemed quite probable to him that a computer gambling game had a lot less to do with what was happening in that scenario. His mother was the one trying to become a counselor though, so she was going to have to figure out how to read people better and he wasn't giving his two cents. "Wow, Mom. What a wild story."

She clucked her tongue on the other end of the phone. "Some people just don't take work seriously, kid. Not like you and me, you know? I know you're so busy today, but I wanted to check in. How is the big move going?"

He shrugged, even though she couldn't see him at the moment. "I'm not using this moving company ever again, but it's been fine. There's still a lot to do, but the place looks in good shape. The view of the lake is everything the previous owner said it was."

"I can't wait to come up and see it," she commented. "In the meantime, send me pictures. Oh, and your new address. I want to send you a care package as a house-warming gift."

"Thanks, Mom. I will." He could feel the icy edges of his heart melting ever so slightly at the way his mother cared for him without fail. She'd dedicated her entire life to making sure he had everything he needed and wanted—including driving him to baseball practice and away games and trainings so often that she barely had time to do anything other than be his chauffeur as he was growing up. Once he had a driver's license, she still never missed a game—home or away—and was always the loudest person on the sidelines.

There's nothing fiercer than the love and dedication of a single mom.

When he hung up the phone, he found himself

reflecting on his mother's new career journey and considering the fact that he needed to do the same for himself. Up until earlier this year, a baseball career had been the sole plan for his life.

Play baseball. Keep playing baseball. The end.

There was no backup plan, and there was nothing else he found much interest in aside from his secret passion for World War II history. But watching yet another documentary on the invasion of Normandy beach was not going to give him a purpose or path forward. He needed an actual plan, one that excited him at least half as much as baseball once had. Still did, honestly. The grief over losing that career path was something he was still grappling with, and he didn't have the emotional bandwidth to go there today.

Heart Lake was going to give him a second chance. This entire summer was meant to give him the time and space to figure out who he wanted to be in this next phase of his life. But until then, he had seven or eight history books queued up on his audiobook playlist and a beautiful dock to sit on and listen to them, he could take naps whenever he wanted to, and would eat every possible carbohydrate he could find for the next two months without interruption.

Definitely without interruption from the girl next door.

Chapter Three

Amanda

I swear to God, his little teeth are going to rip my nipple clear off next time I stick it in his mouth," Amanda's best friend Rosie said as she picked up her glass of water with lemon and took a long gulp. "I'm so done breastfeeding. I cannot wait until he weans."

Amanda cringed, finding her arms automatically covering her chest in some sort of pseudoprotective move at the very thought of a teething baby going to town on his mom.

"Kate was like that too," Nola said from her side of the table at the restaurant that the three of them were dining at a few towns over from Heart Lake.

It could be hard to find great restaurants closer to home that they didn't always go to, so they made it a point to venture out a little farther every once in a while. Last month they'd gone back to Wish You Were Beer over in Grand Haven, but today, they were dining at Pastabilities right on the water in Pentwater. Amanda couldn't believe how hard it was to get the three of them together these days, so she really cherished their monthly dinners. But tonight had started with husband chats and now moved to motherhood—neither topic did Amanda have anything to contribute to.

"Kate was a biter?" Rosie replied as she twirled some spaghetti noodles around her fork and lifted it to her mouth. "How did you handle it?"

Amanda turned her attention to Nola, forcing a smile that she hoped would mask the growing emptiness inside her. As the conversation flowed around her, she couldn't shake the feeling of being an outsider looking in. This conversation wasn't exactly something she felt she could insert herself into, and most of the dinner had been going this way so far, and the void within her seemed to expand.

She understood how important her friends' marriages and children were, and she didn't blame them one bit for wanting to talk about them. However, she didn't have either of those things, and there was only so much complaining she could do about Clayton or a disgruntled client before her stories became repetitive. She was beginning to realize that she really needed to get out there somehow and make new stories.

"Constantly icing them, then heat, and lots of nipple cream," Nola continued. She lifted the bottle of red wine they'd bought to share from the center of the table and refilled her glass. "Breastfeeding is the actual worst. I can't believe people tell you it'll just come to you and it's the most natural thing ever. It's one step away from cannibalism once teething begins."

"I'll take some more," Amanda directed toward Nola, lifting her wineglass as well. "All this talk about babies and nipples is making me think we should probably order a second bottle."

Nola laughed but refilled Amanda's glass. "Sorry. I know it's boring when it's all mom talk."

"Yeah, that's my bad," Rosie agreed with a small chuckle. Not that Amanda blamed her one bit, since she was still deep in the throes of the postpartum era, and Amanda loved her newest godson James to pieces. "Being a wife and now having four children under one roof has completely consumed my brain. I really need to step out of that mode every once in a while, which is why I look forward to these dinners so much."

"Me, too. We need to make each other more of a priority, starting this summer," Nola added. "Amanda, tell us about what you've been up to. What's happening in the sexy, uncomplicated world of singlehood and freedom from children?"

She swallowed the sip of red wine she'd just held to her lips. "Uh…"

Oh no. Amanda could feel the welling of emotion building in her chest faster than she could put it down. Suddenly her face was hot and the dam of tears behind her eyes threatened to burst.

"Are you okay?" Rosie reached a hand out and placed it on Amanda's arm, and that was all she needed to lose complete control of the cascade flooding down her cheeks.

"I'm sorry," Amanda gasped in between stifled sobs as she shoved her cloth napkin into her eyeballs in an attempt to both hide her face and shove the tears right back in her eyes. *What the hell was happening right now?* She was not a crier—hell, she rarely showed emotion unless it was irrational or sarcastic. "I'm so ridiculous right now. I don't even know why I'm crying. This is so embarrassing, sorry. I must have had too much wine."

"Stop apologizing." Rosie comforted her, squeezing her arm gently and then rubbing her hand up and down her forearm. "You never have to apologize for tears around us."

"Yeah, seriously, Amanda," Nola confirmed, handing her an additional cloth napkin from the fourth table setting that they weren't using. "We've all seen each other cry more times than I can count."

"You better not be counting," Rosie teased Nola. "We have way too much dirt on each other at this point to start keeping score, and I'm pretty sure Amanda's the least likely crier of the three of us. I can't even remember the last time..."

Amanda hiccupped a small laugh as she tried to get her breathing under control and slow herself down. "I know. I'm not normally like this. I just...I don't even know where that came from."

Nola signaled to the waiter for another bottle of wine before turning back to Amanda. "My therapist says if we don't release emotions ourselves at a controlled time, they will do it for us whenever they see fit. You need to be vulnerable more often to let the pressure off."

"Nola, stop trying to convince everyone to go to therapy," Rosie quipped back, though her tone was lighthearted. "Not everyone wants to pour out their feelings for two hundred dollars an hour."

She put her hands up defensively. "I'm just saying

it was very helpful for me after losing Gigi, and then again after having Kate. I swear grief and postpartum depression aren't that dissimilar."

"At least you have something to be upset about," Amanda finally interjected, feeling like she'd been able to calm herself down enough to logically come up with what she wanted to say. "I just have been feeling so empty lately. Like…what do I have? Rosie, you have Evan and the kids, and the bookstore is thriving. Nola, you and Tanner are like a storybook romance, and you're the best stay-at-home mom who has ever existed in the history of the world with Kate. And then there's me. Just me."

The words spilled out of her so fast that she was processing them at the same time that her friends were hearing them. *Was she jealous?* Her monologue sounded jealous, but the word didn't seem to fit the feeling in her chest.

"Oh, Amanda." Rosie put her hand over her heart. "I'm so sorry that we both just sat here and rambled on about our families. That was so insensitive of us. I honestly had no idea that you were thinking any of that at all. I mean, the last time I thought maybe you wanted some of that was when Lizzie was here for the summer, but after everything that happened with her mom, I thought you'd closed that door."

Lizzie was Amanda's goddaughter who'd spent a full summer with her once when her mother—Amanda and Nola's cousin—had taken a job in Europe for the summer and couldn't bring her. Amanda loved Lizzie, but her cousin had ended up permanently moving to Europe and Lizzie had gone out there to be with her. She hadn't seen her in the years since, and at this point Lizzie was close to graduating high school and focused on college goals. It had been a nice experience to be a pseudomom for a summer, but it had only made it more clear to her that being an actual mom wasn't part of her future.

That didn't mean being a partner wasn't, though.

"I thought the same," Nola agreed with Rosie, but nodded emphatically toward Amanda. "I am really sorry, too. I guess I was under the impression that romance and family and all that wasn't of interest to you. I mean, don't get me wrong—you're an incredible aunt. But I always just thought you weren't interested in dating."

"I literally can't think of one time I've ever seen you on a date since high school," Rosie added. "And every time we try to set you up with someone, you want nothing to do with it."

"Maybe you should have tried to set her up with better people," Nola teased Rosie.

Rosie shrugged. "If I knew better people, I wouldn't have been single as long as I was."

"Guys!" Amanda laughed and put her hands up to indicate they should stop talking. She definitely had been on dates since high school, but she wasn't one to share that information easily. It wasn't even something she'd told her friends about. "I'm in no way interested in romance. At least, not like *that*."

Rosie wiggled her eyebrows. "*That* meaning hanky-panky in the bedroom? Or *that* meaning men in general?"

Amanda rolled her eyes. "For the millionth time, I'm not a lesbian."

Rosie put on a pretend pout. "Are you sure? Nola and

I would be so much cooler if we had a lesbian friend. We need the street credit. Becca literally told me the other day that I wasn't cool, which I guess is par for the course when you have a high schooler. God, I have high school–aged children."

Rosie's twins—Becca and Zander—were going into ninth grade at Heart Lake High this coming fall but already acting like they were king and queen of the block since their recent middle school graduation. Their older stepsister, Tess, had already been in high school for a year now, and she was not looking forward to them attending with her.

"Well, you have an uninteresting, nonlesbian friend," Amanda assured them. "But sometimes lately I've been thinking maybe it wouldn't be that awful to have someone in…in a partner way. Someone to do life with, to come home to, to spend time together."

The part she left out was that she was fine with leaving anything physical out of the arrangement. Her sex drive had been nonexistent her entire life, but that didn't mean she didn't want the companionship or to feel the warm butterflies of being in love. But from everything she knew about marriage and romance, sex was a pretty important part of the package deal. It seemed highly unlikely to her that anyone would be willing to compromise in that way, or that anyone would like her enough to make having a life together with minimal sex actually worth it.

She knew that was a shitty way to think, but the world was pretty shitty, and sex was a worldwide motivator. There was no denying that was the reality of the times. It just made her feel that much more isolated in her own experience.

"In a partner way? You mean like a husband?" Nola asked as she swiped another roll from the shared garlic bread basket. "Because I am so down for making you a dating profile right now and getting this whole show on the road."

"Being your matchmakers would be the highlight of our year," Rosie confirmed, then nodded her head toward the front of the restaurant. "Like, for starters, what about that hottie over at the host stand?"

Amanda turned way too quickly to look, only to find her gaze squarely slamming into Dominic Gage's. The air in her lungs seemed to freeze into a block of ice that made her want to melt down into her seat and slide under the table. There was a slightly confused expression on his face—concern, maybe? He looked like he was worried, or that something was wrong.

She suddenly realized her eyes were probably puffy and her cheeks still tear streaked from crying.

Could things get any worse right now?

"Oh my God, kill me now," Amanda muttered under her breath, but her friends caught it.

"Wait, isn't that your new neighbor?" Nola asked, blatantly staring at him along with Rosie. "What's he doing all the way out in Pentwater?"

"Look away from him right now," Amanda hissed loud enough for only them to hear. "Don't look at him!"

Rosie and Nola quickly snapped their gazes back to her as she crouched down as low as possible in an attempt to completely disappear.

"I know you said to look away, but he's coming over," Rosie informed her, her voice a strained whisper. "Should we keep ignoring him?"

Amanda could feel her insides literally spiraling. "Are you sure he's coming over? Maybe he's just going to the bathroom and we're in his path."

"I'm not going to the bathroom," Dominic confirmed, now standing behind Nola across the table from where Amanda was sitting. "I had a doctor appointment near here and wanted to grab some food before making the trek back. Surprised to see you here, and wanted to check if everything was okay."

Nola didn't turn to look at him, but just stared at Amanda with wide eyes as she grabbed another piece of garlic bread to shove in her mouth. No doubt she wanted an excuse not to be involved in this.

Rosie very much wanted to be involved, however. "So, you're the new neighbor? I hear you don't like sunflowers."

Dominic finally let his gaze leave Amanda and flickered over to Rosie. "I tend to be more partial to a navy blue, but I'm okay with some orange and white as well. Sunflowers . . . eh, not so much."

"Aren't those the Detroit Tigers colors?" Rosie's face scrunched up for a moment, then her eyes lifted back to him, and she slapped her hand against the table. "Oh my God, you played for them! Evan watches them all the time, and I remember your face from—holy shit, are you okay?"

If Rosie and Dominic were at the pitcher's mound, then Amanda was in the outfield because she had absolutely no idea what they were talking about.

"You played baseball?" Amanda asked, genuinely surprised by this new piece of intel about her neighbor. The realization that there was more to Dominic than she initially thought sparked a sense of curiosity within her, a welcome distraction from the isolation she had been feeling tonight.

"I did," he responded, then looked back at Rosie. "And to answer your question, yes. I am okay. But are *you* okay?"

His last question was posed back at Amanda.

She wiped at her cheeks and cleared her throat. "Peachy keen. I'm great. Fantastic, actually."

Dominic's expression clearly showed he didn't believe her, but she could tell he wasn't going to push the issue.

She appreciated that he had at least some boundaries in that way. Not in a mailbox-trampling way, but she had to pick her battles.

"Okay. Well, I'll see you around. I'm just picking up a to-go order." With that, he stepped away from their table and made his way back to the host stand where they now had his order ready to go in a large paper bag.

"Whoa. He's hot," Rosie said once he was far enough away to no longer hear them. "And he is clearly interested in you, Amanda."

She barked out a too-loud laugh. "Not even. He's weird...like super aloof and unpleasant, but also sort of nice? It really doesn't add up. Something is off about him."

"What's off about him is the ninety-five-mile-an-hour fastball he took to the face in the last season," Rosie continued. "Completely ended his career. I hope it didn't knock a few screws loose up there."

Amanda raised her brows in alarm. "Shit. That sounds rough. I seriously had no idea he used to play baseball, let alone professionally, until a minute ago."

Rosie nodded. "You know Evan's going to want to come over to your house now just to see if he can spot him through the window."

"Tanner, too," Nola added. "He's a die-hard Tigers fan. It's like it runs in the family or something."

Rosie grinned, given that Tanner was Nola's husband but also Rosie's brother. "We can't help ourselves. Either way, next meetup is at Amanda's house."

Nola grinned, then wiggled her brows conspiratorially. "Until then, let's brainstorm some dating profile ideas—knock it out of the park, get you to hit a home run."

"I don't know if I'm dating-profile ready. And I'm *really* not ready for those metaphors." Amanda grabbed her glass of wine again and took a long swig. "Could we start with baby steps?"

Nola shook her head. "No way. You've been baby stepping your whole life. And, as your friend, I cannot continue to stand by and watch you hide all the incredible parts of yourself from the world any longer."

"Same," Rosie agreed. "Because it's not just dating. Clayton? Your job? You've been living on scraps long enough. You deserve to have the best summer of your life—a summer of romance!"

"And moving up at work," Nola added. "A summer of you. Showcasing yourself, your talents, and the amazing person you are to the world."

"Guys..." Amanda could feel the blush heating her cheeks. Their kind words were making her night, but, admittedly, it wasn't as easy to digest and believe them as it was to hear them. "I don't know. The summer just started..."

"Perfect timing. Let Nola and me take care of it. You just need to clear your next few Friday nights, and we'll take care of the rest. We'll make sure you have a new blind date to meet every week. It'll be like *The Bachelor*, Heart Lake style."

"All summer?" Amanda balked. "Absolutely not. That's a lot of Fridays."

"Okay, just four then," Nola countered. "Four dates. Four men. That's not a lot. Anyone could do that."

Amanda hesitated, but that seemed a lot more doable than the first option. "Fine. Four. But that's it. And they have to be actual blind dates—not anyone we went to school with or already know. No one I'd run into on Main Street regularly and make things awkward with."

Nola and Rosie glanced at each other.

"Okay, deal," Nola finally agreed.

Rosie grimaced. "Though we can't promise you won't know them. I mean, this is a small area. But no one from our high school. We can promise that."

Amanda didn't feel so sure. "And absolutely not Blake."

"Definitely not Blake," Nola agreed. "You made your feelings very clear after he bailed on the Boat Parade. Plus the whole toilet thing."

"What toilet thing?" Rosie asked.

"Nothing," Amanda quipped. "Let's move on from that."

"Doesn't Marvel have a grandson around our age?" Rosie tapped her chin. "I feel like she talked about him once or twice."

"I don't think that was a literal grandson, but rather just some young guy she met when she was high and decided to adopt him metaphorically," Amanda said with a laugh, referring to the older hippie woman who was a staple around town. Everyone loved her and her cookie recipes, but her brain was clearly forever changed by the substances she partook in during the '70s. "So he's off-limits, too."

Rosie shrugged. "Well, we're going to knock this one out of the park, Amanda. You have our word."

"Ooh, ballpark!" Nola's eyes lit up. "I wonder if the new neighbor is single?"

"He's off-limits, too!" Amanda dropped her fork against the edge of her plate, and it made a loud clanging sound. "Completely off-limits. I am not blind-dating my neighbor. I didn't go to Carl's swinging parties, and I'm not dating the guy he sold his house to, either. Dominic Gage is absolutely off-limits when it comes to romance."

And yet, even as she said that and her friends reluctantly agreed, she wasn't sure she completely believed herself. There was something about the man that had wiggled its way under her skin, and she wasn't sure she hated it . . . but she knew she didn't like it.

Chapter Four

Dominic

Dominic had no doubt that he had stumbled upon Amanda crying at dinner with her friends, but he had no idea what it might have been about. Or why it bothered him so much. When he'd spotted her and seen the tearstained cheeks that she was dabbing at with a napkin, he'd forgotten all about his eyestrain, which intensified most evenings, and felt this surge of protectiveness go through him that he hadn't felt since . . . maybe ever.

It's not that he *wasn't* a protective person—he definitely was. If anyone tried to mess with his mother, they were asking for trouble. And he'd been that way with his ex, too, to some extent. But this still felt different. It felt like something had been activated in a part of himself that he'd forgotten he had access to. Or maybe he never knew it was there in the first place.

Dominic pushed his key into the front door of his new house and walked into the entryway. He kicked off his shoes to the side and made his way into the expansive kitchen that had been redone before selling, which now included a huge island countertop and a wall of glass windows to look out at the lake behind the house.

The house itself was still relatively small given that it was an older home, but the last owners had put on a pretty large addition in the back that allowed for a bigger common area.

He placed his cell phone and the bag of takeout from Pastabilities on the counter and began pulling out everything he'd ordered—chicken parmesan, of course, with a side of garlic bread and a starting order of a house salad with way too many croutons. They'd included paper plates and utensils, thankfully, since he was nowhere near unpacked yet and hadn't a clue which box the kitchen dishes were in.

Two bites into his dish, a notification popped up on his cell phone that caused him to pause—fork halfway to his mouth.

Us Weekly announces: Star Detroit Tigers hitter's soon-to-be-ex-wife steps out with new love interest.

"What the…"

His reaction was almost immediately cut off by the phone screen turning to an incoming call with Melinda Gage's name appearing on the screen.

The soon-to-be-ex-wife.

He swiped to answer. "Hello?"

"Hey. I wanted to give you a heads up about something," Melinda responded, and he tried not to pay attention to the sinking feeling in his chest at the sound of her voice.

If there was one thing Dominic knew, it was that he wasn't still in love with Melinda—that was absolutely certain. But she had been his college sweetheart, the woman he'd spent the last eighteen years of his life with. She was his family in many senses of the word, and even though they'd decided against having a family of their own, she was still a huge part of his story.

"I think I have a guess," he replied, though he wasn't sure he wanted more details after the headline he'd just seen.

"I'm dating someone," Melinda finished her thought anyway. "And I just wanted you to be the first to know."

Dominic tried not to scoff. "You mean before *Us Weekly*?"

"Oh." She was quiet for a moment on the other end of the phone. "You saw the article?"

"You're allowed to date, Melinda," he replied, shoving the bite of chicken parmesan into his mouth. "We're separated."

She cleared her throat. "Actually, um…we are divorced."

"The judge signed it?" He knew they'd been waiting on that, but he hadn't seen anything come through yet.

"Yeah," she replied. "I got the packet in the mail today. The judge actually signed it about three weeks ago, so I don't know why it took so long to get to us."

Dominic frowned, but he wasn't surprised at the court system at all. "I haven't gotten anything."

"Do they have your new address?" she asked.

"Shit." He hadn't thought about that part delaying it, even though he had set his mail to begin forwarding to Heart Lake as of a few days ago. "Maybe it's held up because of that."

Melinda sighed heavily into the phone, but it was sadder than it was passive aggressive. "Well, I can send you a copy if you don't get it, but yeah…it's done."

Dominic stayed quiet. He wasn't sure how to follow that up, or what he was supposed to say.

"It's fine, Dominic," Melinda finally answered for him. "We're going to be fine. We're going to stay friends, and it's all going to work out."

He wanted to say he was on the same page with her about that, but his hurt was still close to the surface. They'd been best friends for as long as he could remember, but as soon as he'd gone into a major depressive episode after his career ended, she'd decided that the spark was no longer there. And he understood where she was coming from. She was right. The spark was long gone, but it wasn't about her or them. It was him.

His spark was gone.

Everything he'd hoped to become, the life he'd hoped to lead had been just within his grasp and then it was suddenly ripped away from him. There was nothing else left. There was no backup plan or follow-up. It wasn't like he had a second career lined up or any sort of side passion. He didn't have children, and now he didn't have a wife. He had a few friends scattered across the country from college, but they only checked in on birthdays and holidays for the most part.

He didn't have anything except for baseball.

"Sure," he agreed with Melinda, even though he didn't believe it one bit. "You know where to find me."

"Yeah, I got your new address. Maybe I'll come visit later this summer?"

Dominic highly doubted she'd ever step foot in Heart Lake, but he wasn't about to burst her bubble just to be contrarian. "You're always welcome."

"Thanks," she said. "I...I'm sorry you saw the article before I could tell you. This new relationship is...I think it's special. I'd love for you to meet them one day."

"As long as they treat you well, that's all I care about," Dominic replied. "But listen, I have to go. I've got a lot of boxes to unpack. It's still kind of a mess up here."

"Oh, of course. I'll talk to you later, Dominic." Melinda said goodbye and then hung up the phone.

Dominic finished the remaining few bites of his dinner as he looked out the window over the kitchen sink at the lake behind his house. Thankfully, the sun was out a lot later in the summer, and he could still enjoy the beautiful view, but after that conversation, he was beginning to realize that a pretty view wasn't going to be enough.

He needed a plan.

Sure, he'd moved. He was in a new place, a new house, a new town. Great. But now what? His not-fully-thought-out plan for this summer had been to kick his feet up at the lake and read all the books he'd been wanting to catch up on, as well as binge-watch the list of Netflix shows he'd saved to his queue over the last year but hadn't had the motivation to watch yet.

Suddenly, however, this seemed wholly unsatisfying. His ex-wife was falling in love, and he was streaming every season of *Suits* and watching World War II documentaries. That was just pathetic.

Dominic sighed, then tossed his empty take-out container in the trash can.

A knock at his front door caught him off guard, but he walked through the living room to the entryway and pulled it open.

"Welcome to Heart Lake!" An older woman in a poncho with a long gray braid down her back twisted her hands around a small paper confetti cannon and suddenly Dominic was splattered in rainbow-colored glitter.

He jumped back in surprise. "What the hell?"

"My name is Marvel," the older woman said as she shoved the now-empty confetti cannon into some hidden pocket in her clothes. She then put her hand out toward him. "I'm the Heart Lake Welcoming Committee!"

Dominic began brushing the pieces of confetti off his sweater, then stepped forward to look around behind the older woman. Finally, he shook her hand. "Where's the rest of the committee?"

Marvel frowned, turning to look behind her as well. "Oh, no. It's just me. I'm it!"

"It's a one-person committee?" he asked, frowning now. "That's a little lackluster, don't you think?"

"When that one person is me, there's nothing lackluster about it." Marvel placed her hands on her hips and tilted her head to the side in a way that made her thoughts clear as to what she thought of him in that moment.

Dominic grinned, because he couldn't help but enjoy the way she pushed back at him without a single care. "Well, Marvel, thanks for the visit. I'm Dominic—"

"Dominic Gage, hitter for the Detroit Tigers until

you took a fastball to the face," Marvel finished the sentence for him. "Whoo-whee, that was a real sucker punch. Your nose doesn't look too crooked, so the doctors must have done a good job."

He reached up to touch his nose, suddenly feeling a tad self-conscious. "It didn't hit me in the nose."

"Oh, so you were just born like that?" Marvel walked past him into the house like she lived there, making her way to the kitchen.

"Come on in," he whispered under his breath sarcastically before closing the front door and following her into his own kitchen. He glanced in the mirror leaning up against the side wall that he was going to hang later, checking the shape of his nose. There was the smallest of bumps in it, but damn, now he was very aware of that bump.

She placed the basket of cookies she'd brought on the kitchen counter and began unpacking it. "Are you allergic to nuts? I put the ones with nuts in a separate container just in case. You can't be too careful, you know. I have a friend whose son can't even smell a whiff of peanut dust without his throat closing up."

"I don't have any allergies," he replied, taking a seat on one of the counter stools next to where Marvel was standing. "These smell amazing. My mom makes the best cookies, too."

"A mama's boy? That's a great sign. But her cookies aren't as good as mine. Everyone loves my cookies," Marvel clarified. "I'm going to have a stand at the parade if you want to come grab more once these run out. No charge for newbies."

He took a white-chocolate-macadamia cookie from the stack. "What parade?"

"Oh, here." She pulled a folded-up flyer out of a different hidden pocket in her poncho and handed it to him. "The Heart Lake Boat Parade. It's a newer event—only been running a couple years—but everyone loves it. Half the people in this town own some sort of boat, so we line them all up at the little marina and everyone decorates to the nines. I'm talking big. Last year, Felix turned his and his sister's boat into a literal black sheep because they own the Black Sheep Diner. It had a cotton puff tail over the rudder and everything."

"Wow." He couldn't imagine a boat-size sheep, but there were a lot of surprises this town seemed to be throwing his way. "That sounds like quite the event."

"Your next-door neighbor is running it," Marvel added, leaning forward with her elbows on the counter as she munched on one of the cookies she brought. "Have you met Amanda Riverswood yet? Such a sweetheart, that one."

"I did," he confirmed. "Does she have a boat in the parade, too?"

Marvel shook her head. "She sold hers last year, but she came in second place with her sunflower decorations."

He grinned, not at all surprised. *What was it with that woman and sunflowers?*

"You should ask her if she needs help if you have the time, since her partner dropped out of the planning this year. That kid was a dumbass anyway, so she's better off without him."

Dominic felt his stomach flip-flop. "She has a partner?"

"Partner in the parade committee, but Blake was just trying to get a date out of the whole thing." Marvel shook her head. "These boys out here always have nefarious agendas. You're not going to be a Casanova around town now, are you? Because I'm very protective of the ladies in Heart Lake, and I will whack you with a clay pot if you hurt one of them."

He let out a loud, barking laugh. "With a clay pot?"

She kept her expression deadpan. "I own Dirty Birds Clay studio off Main Street, so I have access to as many clay pots as I need. And I can easily hide the evidence. It's the perfect crime, really."

Dominic put his hand up like he was taking an oath. "I promise not to Casanova around town."

He'd never used that word as a verb before, but it made sense.

Marvel nodded, seemingly satisfied with that answer. "So are you single? There's a pale line on your ring finger. Looks like you were wearing a wedding ring not too long ago."

He glanced down at his hand, and sure enough, there was a slightly less-tan line on his finger where the wedding band had once been. "Uh, I'm divorced. Actually, I just found out a few minutes before you got here."

She looked concerned now and handed him another cookie. "You found out? You didn't know you were getting divorced? Dang, that's like that soap-star actress I follow in *Us Weekly*—her husband divorced her via text message, but now she's married to a rock star without a gender. So, buck up, kid. Things can still really turn around for you."

"No, I knew," he clarified with a small chuckle. "It wasn't a surprise divorce, and, thank God, it wasn't via text message. I just meant the judge signed off on everything finally."

Marvel grabbed another cookie for herself as well. "So she left you, huh? Was it the shiner to the face? Because she must have already known about the nose situation when she married you."

Dominic made a mental note to look at his nose again in the mirror later, because he'd never considered it to be crooked before, but Marvel was definitely giving him a complex now. "I don't know if I'd say it was because of the fastball, but more so the impact it had on our lives."

She grinned at that. "You mean the impact on your face? See? I was right."

"Clearly everyone in Heart Lake knows about my career ender." He tried not to groan, but it escaped his lips anyway. "I guess I wasn't expecting everyone up here to be so clued in to the rest of the world. I moved here to get away from all of that, though."

"That's the problem with running away from your troubles," Marvel said. "They just tag along with you to the new place. And we have internet here. And televisions. And the newspaper, and radios…"

"I get it," he said with a laugh. She had a point about running away, though. "I used to come here when I was a kid in the summers with my mother and grandfather."

He had no clue why he felt compelled to tell this

woman anything at all, but here he was ready to spill his guts to a whacky stranger. There was a friendliness and openness to her that he couldn't help feeling comfortable around. He'd heard people described as a "calming presence" before, but this was the first time he'd genuinely felt it.

"Heart Lake holds some good memories for me."

"I thought you looked familiar," Marvel replied, then suddenly her hand went to her mouth, and she belted out the loudest laugh he'd ever heard. "Oh my God...are you Carleton's grandson?"

Dominic paused, a cookie halfway to his mouth. "Uh...you knew my grandfather?"

"If you mean did I know him in the Biblical sense?" Marvel asked, then nodded with a wide grin. "Then, yes. I knew him many times over. Sometimes I knew him a few times a night. He was a stallion, kid. You've got some good genes in you. Man, I had some good genes of his in me back in the day."

"Oh, dear God." Dominic groaned and shook his head as he placed the cookie he was eating back in the basket. "Please, please tell me you're kidding."

"I would never joke about my lovers," Marvel continued, her face completely earnest. "If I remember correctly, he had some shrapnel in his ass cheek still from the war. He'd get all cagey if you tried to touch it—he really wasn't a fan of butt stuff."

Small miracles. "Okay, well, that is an image that no amount of therapy can erase for me. I think it's time to call it a night."

Marvel laughed and started walking toward the

front door as he followed her out. "I left my card in the basket with my cell phone number, so call any time you need anything. And make sure you come to the Boat Parade—I'll introduce you around to everyone."

He opened the front door and ushered her out onto the porch. "I appreciate the hospitality."

"That's my job," Marvel replied while reaching into her pocket and apparently scooping up some confetti that she then tossed in the air between them. "Welcome to Heart Lake!"

Dominic closed the door fast.

Chapter Five

Amanda

She should have stopped at that first bottle of wine. Amanda had always been a lightweight, but when she got around Rosie and Nola, things tended to spiral out of control a bit. Those moms could hold their wine— no joke.

Amanda, on the other hand, found herself waking up the next morning after their dinner out wishing that she could completely shut off the pounding jackhammer that had taken up residence in her skull. She blinked slowly, trying to adjust herself to the sunlight that was streaming onto the duvet through her bedroom windows.

One entire wall of her bedroom was just floor-to-ceiling windows and a set of French doors that led out onto her large back porch with a view of the lake. And yes, there were sunflowers in the backyard, as well as in the design on her matching sham-and-bedspread set. And in the vase on her nightstand. And a few framed paintings of them on the bedroom wall as well.

When she'd finally mustered up enough energy to roll over toward her nightstand, she grasped around the surface until her palm landed on her cell phone. She pulled it closer and glanced at the screen to see three text messages in her group text chain with Rosie and Nola, and four missed matches from Hinge—a dating app.

Oh my God, I downloaded a dating app.

Amanda shot up quickly in bed but immediately regretted the decision as her stomach threatened to return its contents to her mattress. This wasn't the moment to look through her dating options, or even acknowledge the fact that she'd made a commitment to put herself out there. Right now, she needed two things—ibuprofen and coffee.

She pushed herself up out of bed, sliding on her slippers—which she kept on the edge of the bed to avoid walking on the freezing cold wood floors—and fluffy robe from the bench at the end of her bed. It didn't matter that it was summer up here in Michigan— the inside of her house was never allowed to be over sixty-nine degrees and she'd fight anyone who dared to touch her thermostat. Her life motto was that she could always put on more clothes and layers but could only take off so many before she was shit out of luck.

Not that she'd had that much experience with taking anything off.

When she reached the kitchen, she immediately regretted her bougie taste in coffee because there wasn't a single instant coffee packet or coffee machine anywhere. Instead, she had a coffee bean grinder and a French press that she made the perfect cup of coffee with every morning—which, most days, was the best gift she could give herself.

But today, it just felt like torture.

She got to work on pouring the beans into the grinder and beginning the arduous process as she searched the nearby medicine cabinet for some painkillers. The ibuprofen was halfway down her throat, however, when she turned to look out on the lake behind her house and realized that her willow tree was no longer standing in its usual spot on the shared property line with her new neighbor.

It was completely down, and it had taken half her boat dock with it.

"What the hell?" She abandoned the coffee-making process to step outside, wrapping her robe a little tighter around her as she made her way to the tree in her slippers.

The closer she got, the worse the damage looked. The tree had completely split down the middle, leaving the stump in the ground but everything above it gone. Half the trunk had gone through the deck floor, and the railing was in splinters.

"Looks like last night's storm took out our tree," said a deep voice that broke her concentration from somewhere behind her.

Amanda jumped and turned around to see Dominic standing there—and, of course, he wasn't wearing a robe or slippers. He was in a tight black T-shirt with dark jeans and a pair of sneakers, with a goddamn mug of—Amanda assumed—coffee in one hand.

She balked. "You have coffee?"

Dominic looked down at his mug, then back up at her. "Uh...yeah? It's ten o'clock in the morning. I'm already on my second cup."

"My French press takes forever," she said with a groan, even though her focus was still on her fallen tree. "Can I get a cup of yours?"

"Uh…sure?" Nothing about him looked sure, but then he motioned to the downed willow tree. "But what do you want to do about the tree?"

Amanda's brain was blank. "Coffee, then tree."

Dominic grinned and motioned for her to follow him back to his house. "Come on. There's still a half-full pot. I hope you like dark roast."

She followed him dutifully. "The darker, the better. Just like my soul."

He laughed as he ascended the steps to his back porch and slid open the door to his kitchen. He motioned for her to go inside, and she stepped past him into Carl Murphy's kitchen.

She hadn't been in this kitchen for several years, and Carl had clearly done a remodel. The backsplash was brand-new, and the counters were absolutely gorgeous. *That absolute asshole.* They'd been neighbors for years, but clearly Carl had gone with someone else to redesign his kitchen. She didn't remember any of this design coming across Clayton's desk, either.

"That fucking bastard," she said out loud before she could catch herself.

Dominic paused on his way to the coffee maker sitting on the edge of his kitchen island. "Uh…what?"

"Carl." Amanda waved around his kitchen as she made a lap around the entire thing. "He remodeled the whole kitchen!"

"Okay?" Dominic seemed confused, but he pulled a

mug out of the kitchen cabinet and began pouring her a cup of coffee. "I mean, I think he wanted to up the price when he planned to sell it."

"Obviously," she agreed, taking the mug from him as he extended it to her. She took a deep whiff of the delicious brew and then took a fast gulp that absolutely burned her tongue. "But he didn't hire me to do it."

The poor man seemed more confused. "You work in construction?"

Amanda shook her head. "Design. And I would have done a stellar job on this place. Nothing is even in the right spot."

Dominic looked around the kitchen. "What do you mean? It seems fine to me."

"It's not." Amanda pointed to the fridge. "I bet when you open the fridge, it completely blocks that entryway. The handles are on the wrong side. The island is too wide for this space, so the walkway looks smaller than it could be. And do you see the grout on the backsplash?"

"Yeah," he replied.

"It doesn't even match the tile," she continued. "It stands out way too much—and not in a cool, edgy way, but just in a stupid way."

"Well, damn." Dominic offered a strained laugh. "Why don't you tell me what you really think about the place I just sunk seven hundred thousand dollars into?"

She grimaced, suddenly remembering that people didn't often enjoy unsolicited design opinions about their spaces. "Sorry. That's my bad. I should shut up and just drink my coffee now."

"No, please," Dominic continued. "I'm fine with the feedback. Sounds like I should invest in a remodel at some point and make sure to hire you."

Amanda felt a flutter in her stomach at the idea of working together. *What was happening?* She never felt that way. It must have been the excitement about a job all on her own. "That's not going to happen as long as I'm still working at Clayton's firm. He is in charge of all the designs, and I'm lucky to get a word in edgewise."

Dominic didn't respond immediately but nodded his head as if he understood. "Working under someone else always has its drawbacks. Like you get smashed in the face and they fire you."

She gulped down more coffee and then cleared her throat. "You were fired?"

He shrugged, sipping on his coffee as well. "I mean, not in so many words. I wasn't medically cleared to return, and it was strongly recommended I consider another path in life. Another injury could be the difference between my current situation and losing my sight entirely."

There was no mistaking the look of anguish and pain that passed over his expression, but Amanda wasn't about to point it out.

"And so, you moved to Heart Lake," Amanda added, a sarcastic lilt to her tone. "As all ex–major leaguers do."

He chuckled. "I have a lot of memories here."

"Oh God, don't tell me you're a summer tourist," she replied, trying to keep her tone light to avoid addressing the trauma he'd sprinkled into their conversation. "Because I know you never lived here. This is a small town, and everyone knows each other—except the flood of tourists we get every summer for water sports and Airbnbs."

"Guilty as charged." He finished his coffee and placed the mug back on the counter. "My mother and grandfather and I would spend two weeks every summer here. In fact, I learned last night that my grandfather might have spent more time here than I thought."

Amanda's eyes widened. "Oh, my God. You got a visit from the Heart Lake Welcoming Committee."

Dominic tossed his hands up in the air. "Okay, so am I the one losing it or is it this place? Or do you guys actually send a wild woman to every newcomer's door?"

"To be fair," Amanda started, "Marvel's cookies are delicious and one of the best things this town has to offer."

"They *are* delicious," he agreed. "But that's still a low bar. All cookies are delicious."

"You clearly haven't tried my cookies," she countered, still working toward finishing the rest of her mug of coffee. "If there's one thing I can't do, it's bake. Cooking—I got that down. My flavor profiles would knock you out of this world. Baking, though? That's science, and I was always a B student in science, at best. So believe me when I say—Marvel's cookies are the best. Hands down."

Dominic just shook his head, and a small grimace appeared on his face. "I'm pretty sure she had sex with my grandfather, so I don't think her cookies will ever taste the same to me now."

Amanda barked out a laugh. "Well, she *is* the welcoming committee, Dominic."

"Yes, and now I know why my grandfather always felt so *welcome* here," he groaned. He lifted his hand to the back of his neck and rubbed at his spine. "But enough about that mental image. Let's talk about your dock."

She glanced out the window at the fallen tree. "I'll call someone to cut up the tree and remove it sometime today. I'm sure Tanner will help if he's not on a job right now."

"Who's Tanner?" Dominic's voice went an octave deeper, and if she wasn't mistaken, he sounded irritated. "Is that your boyfriend?"

Amanda lifted one brow as she stared at him over the edge of her coffee mug. She didn't hurry up and finish her gulp, but rather took her time swallowing the hot liquid. "Would that be a problem?"

He stood up straighter and lifted his chin. "I didn't say that."

She let the tension sit for a moment longer, and she wasn't even sure why. Something about this moment, this connection, felt enticing and exciting and she didn't want to squash it.

But finally, she cleared her throat. "Tanner is the husband of my cousin and best friend, and my other best friend's brother."

Now it was Dominic's turn to raise one eyebrow.

"It's a small town," she added, her smile returning. "No blood relation between them, I promise. But Tanner runs a construction business, so I'm sure he could help."

"I can help, too," Dominic volunteered as both of them walked toward the back door and headed out onto the porch. "I can go grab some tools in town and rebuild the dock for you after the tree has been removed. Consider it my gift as your new neighbor."

That was unexpected. "They teach carpentry in the major leagues now?"

He seemed to puff out his chest as they reached the broken dock and stood over the wreckage. "I was an Eagle Scout growing up. It's like riding a bike."

"No, it's like building a dock," she replied. "And if it's not done correctly, it can be dangerous."

"You can have your friend inspect it when I'm done if you're worried about that, but I guarantee you he'll give a glowing report." Dominic smacked his hand against the horizontal trunk of the willow tree. "This sucker did some damage, but the framework is still there. It won't be hard to rebuild."

She wasn't so sure, but she also wasn't about to turn down free labor. "The Heart Lake Boat Parade is in a month, and the dock would need to be rebuilt by then. Would you be able to have it done by July third?"

He waved his hand like it was the easiest thing in the world. "Absolutely. I'll have it done by July first, actually. Maybe even sooner."

"Okay..." Amanda was still skeptical. He sounded way too confident and had way too few calluses to prove his construction skills. "I'll get the tree taken away today, and if you want to start on the rebuild tomorrow...I guess that will be okay. Thank you."

He grinned like he'd just won a prize. "Don't

mention it. It'll be good to have something to distract me. I can use the work."

Aside from the free labor part, she wasn't sure why she'd agreed to let him do it. He clearly hadn't done anything like this before, but there was something about him that seemed so eager to do it. It was like she didn't want to burst his bubble. Plus, it was kind of cute that he even wanted to do it.

Cute? Who even was she? She never thought like that in the past, but she couldn't help herself now.

"Well…" She pulled her robe closed a little tighter. "Thanks for the coffee. I've got to get to work to finish some staging on a house for sale off Lakewood Drive. I'm already an hour late."

"Alcohol will do that to you," he said with a grin.

She rolled her eyes. "I wasn't *that* drunk last night."

"That's not what I saw," he teased, then pulled his cell phone out of his pocket as it began to ring. "Sorry, this is my manager. I've got to take this."

Normally, she'd want to curl up in a ball and die at being caught in a position like that, but there wasn't anything shaming about the way he was saying it. Instead, she just said goodbye and flounced back to her cottage feeling like she was high on something she couldn't pinpoint.

What the heck was happening to her?

Chapter Six

Dominic

I've got an opportunity for you, and I'm going to tell you right now that you're not turning this down," Dominic's manager said through the phone the moment Dominic answered.

"Good morning to you, too, Eric," he replied with a healthy dose of sarcasm. "You do remember that you're my manager, not my boss, right?"

Eric Minton had first signed with him when he was being recruited to the minor leagues and had stuck by his side for the last fifteen years. It was Eric who'd gotten him on the Detroit Tigers' radar, and it was Eric who'd been the first person he'd seen when he'd woken up from surgery for a detached retina after his infamous hit. There was a brotherhood between them now that Dominic felt incredibly grateful for.

"I'm not your best man anymore, either, now that you're single as hell," Eric replied. "How's Melinda doing, by the way? I saw about her new romance."

"She called me yesterday and told me the news. I invited her up here later this summer to visit if she wanted," he answered. "Everything is fine between us."

Eric scoffed. "You're being much cooler about all of this than I would be. Does *'til death do us part* mean nothing to people anymore?"

"You literally have a new girlfriend with each season," Dominic reminded him.

"Exactly! There are no vows in dating." Eric laughed, and it was so high-pitched for a man who was generally very rugged in his appearance that it always made Dominic laugh, too.

"Nah, man," Dominic finally said, his laughter subsiding. "I'm fine. I promise. The last year since we separated has been shit, but I feel like moving here is a new start. My head feels like it's coming out of the clouds. I even have a new project to work on."

"What new project? I didn't vet anything," Eric said.

Dominic shook his head. "I'm rebuilding a dock."

"You're rebuilding your dick? Well, damn, I don't want to vet that. No wonder Melinda went the other direction."

"*Dock.* Like a wooden dock where boats tie up," he corrected his friend, though he could already feel his face getting hot. "There is nothing wrong in the other department. Trust me."

Not that the other department had seen much action lately either, though.

"Why don't you just hire someone to do it?" Eric asked. "I've never seen you even pick up a hammer before."

"I'm doing it," he repeated. "You can find instructions for anything on YouTube."

"You're going to teach yourself how to build a dock

off the internet?" Eric scoffed. "Okay, you are so lucky I called because I have something a thousand times better than that for you."

Dominic suddenly remembered Eric's opening line about an opportunity. "What do you have?"

"MLB Strike Zone is looking to fill a commentator position, and your name is in the hat."

He could practically hear Eric smiling through the phone. "You got me a commentator position with them?"

"I got you an interview for it," Eric clarified. "It's not a done deal. You're going to need to fly into Newark Airport and meet them at their offices in Secaucus next month. There are at least three other people that they are considering, but I think you could easily knock their socks off. There's no way you're not top pick."

"New Jersey? As in, I'd have to move there for it?" Dominic had never been there before, but it was one of the most well-known baseball channels out there. "When would the position start if I got it?"

"Yeah, it's an in-person position," Eric confirmed. "You'd need to live nearby at least four to five days a week, but there are some really nice places in New Jersey, and I know a few realtors out there who'd help you get set up."

"I just bought a house here," Dominic reminded his friend. "I literally moved a week ago."

"Yeah, and you're building a dock. A dock, Dominic. At least in New Jersey you'd have an actual job back in the sports world."

He had a point. The itch to get back into baseball any

way he could was hardwired in his veins, and, admittedly, he couldn't help but get excited at the possibility. He hadn't even thought something like this would come along at all, let alone so soon after getting out of the league. Even then, though, he felt his mind race to all the reasons why he wouldn't be able to do it…why he couldn't do it.

"What about, um…" He paused for a moment, cleared his throat, and then just decided to be transparent. "What about reading a teleprompter?"

"Already told them about your vision, D." Eric wasn't one to mince words, and he didn't treat him even the slightest bit different now that he was losing his vision. "They said that commentating is mostly you saying what you think to verbal prompts, so no teleprompter involved. If they need something specifically said, they'll have someone else do it, give it to you up front to memorize, or they can even give you an earpiece and tell you what to say."

"Really?" That all seemed very accommodating, and it made the pit in his stomach get a tiny bit smaller. It was hard to face the reality that his world was changing and would continue to change. The surgery to reattach his retina had not gone perfectly, and they hadn't expected the level of damage they found. It was suspected that the fastball had just magnified a former injury or issue, maybe even something he'd been born with. Either way, it was getting a little darker every day, and, according to the doctors, it was very possible that there would eventually never be light again.

He wasn't ready for that, and he felt this rush of

needing to live his life as much as possible before that day. Although he still held out a lot of hope that he could avoid that diagnosis entirely, and he had another appointment with his ophthalmologist soon to discuss next steps.

"All right," he finally agreed. "I'm in. Send me the details and I'll book a flight."

"Great," Eric said. "I'll meet you there. It's been too long since I've last seen you, brother."

"You, too," Dominic replied. "I'll see you in Secaucus."

He hung up the phone and slid it back into his pocket, then focused his attention on the fallen willow tree in front of him. He looked behind him, but Amanda was long gone inside her little yellow cottage.

A nagging feeling began to accompany the pit, and he considered what it would be like to leave Heart Lake at the end of the summer—what it would be like to leave Amanda. Something about the thought felt uncomfortable, and he wasn't sure why. He'd only just gotten here. But he didn't even know if he'd get the commentator position, and if he did, he could always keep the house here and come back during the off-season or on vacations. Hell, he could even do long weekends here once a month or something.

Apparently, he was more like his grandfather than he thought.

Dominic laughed to himself and headed back to his house to grab his car keys so he could take a trip to the hardware store. If he was really going to build this dock, he was going to need tools, and he currently only had a Swiss Army knife that had a flip-out screwdriver head.

And either way, he needed to get his neighbor out of his mind because he was in no position to be sneaking looks at her anytime she walked out onto her back porch.

Thirty-eight years old, and sometimes he still felt like a teenager.

Twenty minutes later, Dominic pulled his car into a parking space in front of Hammered and Screwed in the middle of Heart Lake's downtown. There was a large sign on the window that just said "Come get screwed!" so he wasn't entirely sure if this was a hardware store or something else, but this was where Google had led him.

"Good morning, sir!" An older man's voice reached him the moment he opened the front door to the store. "We're running a special on Phillips-heads this week! For every screwdriver you buy, you get a coupon for a free head of iceberg lettuce at Hobbes Grocery Store."

What the hell?

Dominic made his way up to the counter to find a man in his sixties or seventies sitting on a counter stool and working on the crossword puzzle in the paper with a ballpoint pen. Ballsy to use ink instead of a pencil.

"Did you say lettuce? Like the greenery?" Dominic asked.

The man lifted his head. "Yup! I'm Jack Hobbes. My brother owns Hobbes Grocery, so we like to do promotions together sometimes."

It really was a small town.

"Oh, well I don't think I need a screwdriver." Though he honestly wasn't entirely sure. "What kind of tools would you recommend for building a dock?"

Jack surveyed him skeptically. "*You* are building a dock?"

"Well, I'm rebuilding one. A tree fell on it," he clarified. "I just moved to town. I'm...it's a summer project of sorts."

Jack snapped his fingers. "You bought Murphy's place, right? We played canasta together before he moved down to the sunshine state. You ever play canasta? We have an open spot."

Dominic shook his head. "Just looking for dock tools."

"Suit yourself," Jack replied as he stepped out from behind the counter and motioned for Dominic to follow him down one of the aisles. He began pulling items off the shelves and tossing them to Dominic, who started stacking them under one arm before finally needing to take a trip back to the counter to set the pile down.

Ten minutes later, the counter was full of everything Jack said he needed, and he had an order for new wood being delivered to the house tomorrow.

"Thanks, Jack," he said as he handed over his black American Express card. "I appreciate all the help."

Jack took the card and swiped it over the machine, then handed him back both the card and a receipt. "If you need a hand to show you the ropes, let me know. I close the shop around two o'clock most afternoons and can come on down to help after that."

"I appreciate that," Dominic replied, though he had no plans to ask anyone for help. And honestly, he wasn't that keen on this now being the second person to doubt his ability to get this done. How hard could it possibly be to build a dock? "I'll definitely keep it in mind."

"It's really no problem," Jack continued. "I'm retired now, so I have the extra time and nothing good to do."

"You don't look retired," Dominic countered, gesturing around him to the store.

Jack laughed. "Believe me—this *is* me retired. Used to have the place open dusk to dawn and worked out on field project sites at least two days a week. Now I'm here after breakfast and leave after lunch. I'd leave the place entirely if I could find someone to buy it from me, but real estate isn't exactly flying off the shelves up here. Hell, Murphy's place was empty for six months before you bought it."

"Probably why I got such a good deal on it," he commented, pushing the receipt Jack had handed him into one of the bags of tools. "It was a steal, to be honest, but I wasn't very picky."

"You been up here to Heart Lake before? Your face does look familiar," Jack replied. "Let me guess—former tourist?"

"Caught me," Dominic confirmed. "I came up here in the summers with my mother and grandfather a few times. Apparently, my grandfather made his way up here more than I realized, though, and he had some sort of dalliance with a woman here in town."

Jack snapped his fingers. "That's who you look like! You're Carleton's kid!"

"Grandkid," he corrected. "But yeah. You met him, too?"

The old man nodded, his face taking on a nostalgic

lilt that seemed like he was far away for a moment. "Never once beat that son of a bitch in canasta when he was sober, but get one or two old-fashioneds into him, and you could wipe the floor with him. He's a good man. He coming around here to stay with you sometime?"

Dominic shook his head, feeling the familiar lump return to his throat. "No. Lost him a while back."

Jack let out a sigh, his hand rubbing the back of his neck then dropping heavily to his side. "Damn. He was one of the good ones."

"One of the best," Dominic echoed. "But hey... thanks for the help picking out the tools. If you are free tomorrow after work, you're welcome to come by and assist me get started. Happy to compensate you for your time, of course."

He wasn't sure why he was suddenly agreeing to this man's help, but something about the connection to his grandfather through Jack felt like he didn't want to let go.

And the way Jack's face lit up like he'd just heard the best news helped, too.

"I'll be there at two fifteen," he confirmed. "Get all the tools laid out before I get there, and we can just get right to it."

"Absolutely," Dominic agreed, though he wasn't entirely sure what the instructions meant outside of unpacking the bag of tools he'd just bought and taking them out of the plastic. But that was a problem to figure out tomorrow. "See you then."

He waved goodbye, made his way back outside, and

loaded the bag of goods into his trunk. As he was walking around to the driver's side of the car, however, a flash of black ran past his feet and took up residence under his car right next to his front tire.

Dominic frowned and bent down to look more closely, only to find the smallest black kitten he'd ever seen. This little thing could barely be old enough to be away from its mom, and it looked petrified. With tiny white spots over each of its eyes, it looked like it had eyebrows. But the moment he made eye contact with it, the kitten hissed at him. It sounded more like a tiny puff of air rather than a scary hiss, but he admired the little punk's bravery.

"Hey, buddy," he spoke softly, getting down on one knee and scooping the kitten up with one hand. It tried to get away for a moment, but he kept it secured in his palm as he stood back up and cradled it against his chest. "Can't have you underneath the car when it starts. Parking lots are way too dangerous for you. Let's look around for your mama."

Dominic walked a lap around the hardware store, checking any nooks and crannies he could find for a mother cat. There was a café next door and a small alleyway behind it, but despite spending several minutes looking around each box and dumpster, he didn't find any signs of another cat or sibling kittens.

Meanwhile, the kitten in his hands had rolled up into his shirt and was kneading at the fabric with his little paws.

"You settling in, buddy?" Dominic grinned down at the kitten as he made his way back to where he'd parked the car. "I don't know where you came from, but it looks like you don't have anyone."

The tiniest mewing sound came from the kitten as it looked up at him.

"I'll let you in on a secret," he said back in a whisper. "I don't really have anyone here, either. So maybe we can have each other for now until we find where you belong."

Something in his gut also wondered if he'd find where he belonged one day, but that feeling felt much further away.

He slid into the driver's seat and placed the kitten on the passenger seat, where it immediately slid down into the crook of the seat. Dominic grabbed his jacket off the back seat and made a little bed for the kitten, placing him on that instead.

"There you go," he said, pulling on his seat belt as he felt comfortable that the kitten wasn't going to slide around on the drive home. "You're safe now. Let's see what we can do about getting you some milk or something to eat."

Dominic remembered that Jack had pointed out his brother's grocery store down the street, and he figured that would be a good place to stop next to find some cat food and other supplies. Something he'd never thought he'd be doing his second week in a new town, but things were changing at a pace he couldn't keep up with.

Looks like he was a cat dad now, and, frankly, he didn't hate it.

Chapter Seven

Amanda

Amanda had not expected to line up this many dates so quickly. She'd posted her profile to a dating app three nights ago and already she had six matches. Plus, she had lined up four in-person dates from those six matches in an attempt to keep her promise to Nola. The summer of romance menu was shaping up to look like the following:

Gerry, 35: *Looking for that missing piece who makes my life whole.*

Stone, 29: *Chill guy looking for an even more chill girl to chill with.*

Maxwell, 34: *My Labrador needs a mom, and I'm looking for a MILF.*

Raad, 39: *If you love game nights, I'm down to play.*

She wasn't feeling entirely hopeful having read each of their bios, but honestly, this was the best of the batch. Plus, they were all decently attractive, even though she didn't find herself feeling any butterflies when she looked at their pictures. And none of them went to her high school or were super recognizable from around town, so that was the most important part.

Either way, Amanda was trying to be open-minded to the fact that she knew a simple dating profile wasn't going to be enough to actually get to know who someone really was, so she was willing to at least meet these four men and see if there was anything there.

Her cell phone lit up and her cousin Nola's name appeared across the screen with a text message notification. I'm so excited to hear how your first date goes!

Amanda slid the phone into the pocket of her messenger bag as she reached her other hand for the local bookstore's door handle. Rosie had opened Fact or Fiction years and years ago, and it was still one of her favorite places to hang out now that Rosie had expanded it to have a small café section with comfy couches, hot coffee, and premade sandwiches and pastries. Before the expansion, it had struggled for quite a few years there, and Rosie had been very worried she was going to lose it entirely, but she'd really turned it around after meeting Evan and getting some of her confidence back.

"Amanda!" Rosie called out to her and offered a hearty wave from where she was standing behind the counter, checking a customer out at the cash register.

Amanda waved back but didn't walk over to her—not wanting to interrupt her friend while she was working. Instead, she made her way to her favorite couch against the back wall and sank into the cushion as she placed her bag down next to her. She dug inside and pulled out a faux leather-bound journal that she'd gotten as a gift a few Christmases ago from her mother that she'd never actually used yet.

Her mother and Nola's mother were sisters, but that was mostly where their connection ended. For some reason she couldn't explain, she and Nola had stayed very close their entire lives, but their mothers had drifted apart and were now more like strangers. Nola's parents were travelers in their retirement, always off on a different cruise or adventure, so they were rarely back in Heart Lake for more than a few weeks at a time. Amanda's mother, however, had fallen on hard times after divorcing Amanda's father, and her mother's way of emotionally coping was to glue herself to her job instead.

Amanda was quite certain at this point that her mother had no plans to ever retire, and, given that she worked concierge at a local hotel, it was probably not very attainable. It meant that Amanda rarely saw her, either, unless she stopped by the hotel, which she sometimes did with the girls for high tea on Sunday afternoons.

Amanda pulled the plastic off the journal and shoved it into her bag, then found a pen in one of its pockets and flipped the journal open to the first page.

Tonight, I'm meeting Gerry, and I haven't been on a date in...

She paused what she was writing and tried to calculate back to the last time she'd gone out with someone. There'd been that one impromptu coffee with the tourist she'd met on the lake a few summers back, but that was barely a date, and she had never called him back. Before that, she'd had a long-distance relationship with a man she'd met online who lived on the West Coast and who she never actually met in person. People could judge all they wanted, but that had actually been perfect for her in a lot of ways. It had met her need for attention and validation and connection but kept the option of anything physical completely off the table. Eventually, though, he'd met someone in person that he'd developed a stronger connection with—meaning: could actually have sex with—and that relationship fizzled.

Let's just say, it's been a long time, she wrote.

She kept scribbling for a bit, trying her best to manifest what tonight might look like on her date. That was actually advice from Marvel—*manifest what you want from tonight and then it will happen*. Why she still listened to the elderly hippy, she didn't know. But that woman was the heart and soul of this town, and it was impossible not to acknowledge that her advice and wisdom was often right on the money, even if it was often a little—or a lot—odd.

As she was writing, her cell phone began ringing in her bag. She retrieved it quickly and noted that it was from an unknown phone number but decided to answer it anyway.

"Hello?"

"Is this Ms. Riverswood?" A female voice on the other end of the line sounded on the verge of panic. "Amanda, is that you?"

"Mrs. Crawford?" Amanda seemed to recognize the voice as one of Clayton's current clients, whom they were remodeling an entire master bedroom and bathroom for. "Is everything okay?"

"Nothing is okay!" the woman screeched, then let out a pained cry. "I'm sorry. I'm all out of sorts today. We went to Chicago for the weekend, and when we came home, we found that a pipe in the master bathroom had burst and completely flooded the downstairs hall bathroom and living room. We have to literally go stay in a hotel because the place is unlivable!"

Amanda gasped. "Oh my gosh, how horrible! Mrs. Crawford, I'm so sorry. Has the leak been fixed?"

"It has," she confirmed. "Everything is finally in working order from a plumbing standpoint, but not aesthetically. The drywall is all brown and melty looking, and the furniture is water stained and smelly. It will have to be entirely gutted and redone."

"I completely understand," she replied. "Clayton will be back in town in early July, and we can get started on that immediately for you. I'll make sure it's a top priority for the firm."

"That is forever from now!" Mrs. Crawford sounded back on the verge of a panic attack. "I can't wait that long. And you're the one who fixed the designs from our first job anyway. I don't need Clayton or his vision for this. I just want to work directly with you, Amanda."

She could feel her ego basking in the warmth of that compliment. "Mrs. Crawford, I am so appreciative of that, but I have strict instructions to wait on any new projects until my boss is back. I'm—"

"I'll pay double your hourly consulting fee," Mrs. Crawford cut her off. "And I won't say a thing to the firm if you don't want me to. Hell, if this goes well, open your own firm, and I'll fund the start-up. I only want to work with you, Amanda, and I'm willing to invest in you if that's what it takes."

Double her hourly fee and a potential future investor? Amanda was speechless. It felt like all of her dreams were being dangled in front of her. There was no way Mrs. Crawford actually meant any of this—Amanda recognized the pleas of a desperate woman as something not to hang her hope on.

"Amanda? Are you still there?" Mrs. Crawford's voice brought her out of her shock. "Is that a yes?"

"Uh…" Amanda swallowed hard as she tried to weigh the pros and the cons—the biggest con being that Clayton would be furious if he found out, and it would violate the noncompete contract she'd signed with him when she started. She was unsure if Clayton was the type who'd actually follow through on suing her over that contract because noncompetes were pretty hard to enforce. But legally, he could if he wanted to, and even if he didn't, she didn't want to create a lot of bad blood between them. He was the only other designer in town, and he could either be her biggest competitor or her biggest asset.

And she couldn't afford the former.

"Yes, I'm still here," she finally responded. "And I'd love to do it. I'll meet you at your house later this afternoon. Does three o'clock work?"

"Perfect," Mrs. Crawford confirmed. "Thank you so much, Amanda. You are an absolute answer from heaven."

"You're welcome," Amanda replied before saying goodbye and hanging up the phone.

She slid the phone back in her bag just as Rosie walked over and dropped down on the couch next to her.

"It's been back-to-back busy today with customers," Rosie voiced with a happy sigh. "Thank fricking God, because Becca wants to join Pentwater Pliés Ballet School, and the tuition is six hundred dollars a quarter—that's for two forty-five-minute classes each week. Children's extracurriculars are the world's most expensive racket, I swear to God."

Amanda offered her a wry grin. "Sorry to hear that, but you know Madame Hoar is the best in this area. If Becca wants to become a ballerina, Pentwater Pliés is the way to go."

"I know." Rosie let out a whine. "I'm going to let her do it, but I just have to come to terms with the price tag."

Amanda shrugged, fiddling with the pen in her hand as she reread her manifestation journal entry.

Rosie paused and surveyed Amanda for a moment. "What's wrong? What are you doing? Your face looks like you've got a secret."

"It's not a secret." Amanda found herself defensive immediately. "I'm just... I'm in flux."

Her friend frowned. "In flux? What does that mean?"

"I just got offered a design job," Amanda admitted. "And it's not with Clayton."

Rosie sat up on the couch, her elbows resting on her knees. "Does he know that? Because Clayton can be kind of strict, and you know that."

"I *do* know that," she confirmed. "But he's out of town, and she needs this done immediately—like today. She was panicking, and I couldn't say no! But he also told me very explicitly not to take any new jobs, and Mrs. Crawford said she didn't even want to do it with his firm. She wants to do it directly with me."

"Mrs. Amal Crawford?" Rosie questioned, her eyes widening. "She's literally the richest person in town. Also the most eccentric, if you don't count Marvel."

Amanda nodded. "Working on her house is literally a dream. She lets you take complete creative control. I can't pass up a project like that...especially when she's saying that if all goes well, she'd fund me starting my own design firm."

"What?!" Rosie nearly jumped up off the couch, but she'd always been an overly expressive person. "You've wanted your own firm for years!"

"I know!" Amanda's tone was hushed, and she looked around to make sure that no one was listening in on their conversation. "But I still have two more years on my contract with Clayton, and I signed a noncompete."

Rosie waved her hand like that was irrelevant. "Those are so easy to get out of these days. They are really just shitty to begin with. All noncompetes do is keep small businesses down and populate monopolies."

Amanda wasn't about to get into a political discussion with her because Rosie also worked at the newspaper part time and had a lot of strong opinions about the world. Which was great, but not helpful to her in the emotional paradox she was storming through right now.

"I told her I'd take it," Amanda added. "I'm meeting her today to get started."

Rosie grinned and snapped her fingers on both hands. "Look at you getting it, girl. You're out there doing your thing, and you're going to make a name for yourself. Do you want to remodel Fact or Fiction? We could probably use it sometime soon."

She shook her head and waved Rosie off. "Don't get so ahead of yourself. We have no idea how this is going to go—or how Clayton is going to react. Plus, I appreciate the pity job, but Fact or Fiction is pretty perfect as it is right now."

Her friend laughed and proudly looked around the room. "You're right. This place is like a library meets someone's grandparents' living room. Just the right amount of cozy."

Amanda couldn't think of a better description. "Hence why half the town spends their afternoons here."

"Still, I think you're going to kill that job," Rosie replied, her voice softer and supportive now. "Mrs. Crawford is absolutely going to want to get into business with you. Wait! Don't you have a date tonight?"

Amanda nodded. "Gerry, but that's not until six o'clock, so I should be able to do both."

"I mean, you *can*," Rosie agreed, but the tilt of her eyebrows looked skeptical. "But should you? You tend to get kind of messy on jobsites. First dates are about making an impression."

"I'm not going to get messy," Amanda assured her. "But even if I did, isn't dating supposed to be about getting to know me for who I am? I don't want to pretend to be something different and then get in a bind later."

"It's not pretending to put your best foot forward," Rosie countered. "It's just hedging your bets. Getting them not to overlook you before getting to know you."

"And you did that with Evan?" Amanda asked.

"Well, no," Rosie admitted. "He kind of saw me at my worst and we went from there. Okay, maybe that advice is actually hogwash. Just show up to the date unshowered and in a pair of overalls."

Amanda laughed and shook her head. "Overalls might be a step too far, even for me."

The friends chatted a little longer before Amanda looked at the clock and realized she had to head out if she wanted to make it to her new jobsite on time. She tried not to think about the fact that she was going to be meeting *Gerry, 35* a few hours after that.

After all, this was the summer of romance, and tonight was only a first pit stop on the way to forever. At least, that's what she was trying to convince herself of.

Chapter Eight

Dominic

What the hell is Amanda doing coming home at eleven o'clock at night? Dominic thought as he watched out the front window of his living room while her car came up their shared driveway then veered toward her house.

Sure enough, her car sidled to a stop in front of her garage and then turned off. A moment later, the driver's side door opened, and a woman's figure stepped out into the night. The motion-detector lights on the garage shot on, and Dominic saw that it was, in fact, Amanda.

He wasn't trying to be creepy or anything, but he decided it was probably time to check on the potted pine tree on his front porch to make sure that it had been watered recently. His newest roommate—the kitten he'd now named Tom—was adamant about going with him, so he just slipped him into the front pocket of his jacket.

"Dominic?" Amanda called out from her driveway as he not-so-inconspicuously poured a cup of water into the soil pot. "What are you doing out here so late?"

He looked up at her with as innocent of a face as he could muster—like he'd had no idea that she was there at all. "Amanda? What are *you* doing out so late?"

She crossed the small patch of grass and row of sunflowers between their houses and walked up the two steps to his front porch, leaning her arm against the railing. Her face was flushed, and she looked like she'd just been out exercising or something. Either way, she looked like she was on cloud nine.

"I just had the *best* day," she informed him, unsolicited.

Every nerve ending in his body seemed to come alive, and he felt a frustration bubbling up in his gut that shouldn't even be there. Why was he so upset at the idea of her having a good day? He wasn't, but maybe it was the way she'd said it that he couldn't help but think someone was the reason for her good day.

And it wasn't him.

"I got a new job," she continued. "And it could potentially lead to my own business."

He felt his nerves deflate a little. "A new job? Oh, I was thinking you were about to say you'd been on a great date or something."

Amanda laughed, then pointed at him. "Actually, I *was* just on a date. It was good. I don't know if I'd say *great*. But he was decent I guess."

The buzzing bees of jealousy in his gut began swarming again. "You were on a date?"

"Gerry," Amanda confirmed. "He's divorced with a young kid and works over in Grand Haven as a contractor for an engineering firm. The really buttoned up type—has every duck in a row."

"Good for Gerry," Dominic replied, though nothing about his tone agreed with his words.

"Yeah, it is," Amanda agreed. "But I don't know if

that's for me. I don't have ducks in any sort of row. I have squirrels, and they're chasing each other in circles in the attic and occasionally giving people rabies."

Dominic let out a laugh and shook his head. "Relatable."

Tom decided that that was the perfect moment to make his presence known and popped his head out of Dominic's pocket with a loud, high-pitched meow.

Amanda's eyes widened as she looked down and spotted the kitten. "I didn't know you had a cat!"

"I don't," Dominic replied. "I just found this guy today at the hardware store, and I'm taking care of him until I can figure out where he belongs."

Amanda cooed at the kitten and reached her hands out to him. "Oh my gosh, he's so cute. Look at the little white spots over his eyes."

"I named him Tom," Dominic told her as he scooped him up and handed the kitten to Amanda.

She immediately kissed Tom's head and rolled him over in her hands. "That's such a weird name for a female cat, but I love it."

"Tom's a girl?" Dominic had absolutely no idea. "How do you know that?"

Amanda laughed as she pointed to Tom's underside. "Usually, the complete lack of a penis is a dead giveaway."

He looked where she was pointing, but it still wasn't apparent to him. "I don't know what a cat penis looks like."

"I'd be concerned if you did," Amanda joked. "And to be honest, you don't want to. Male cats have like barbed wire penises so the female cat can't get away before they plant their seed."

Dominic's eyes widened. "Are you joking right now?"

"Nope." Amanda shook her head. "I'm being dead-ass serious. It's why if you hear cats mating, it sounds like someone is getting murdered."

"That's the worst science fact I've ever heard in my life," he informed her. "I literally could have gone my entire life without knowing that."

"The privilege of being uninformed and male." Amanda grinned at him, and he could tell that she was being lighthearted even though she probably meant exactly what she'd said.

Dominic struggled to find a way to respond to that. "Well, I can tell you for a fact that I am well-informed about the human penis, and it's nothing like that."

She lifted one brow. "You're well-informed about human penises? How progressive of you."

"I mean, not in a weird way." He tried to backtrack because he wasn't sure what the hell he'd been thinking when he said that. "Or a gay way. Not that I'm homophobic. I love gay men."

Amanda's brows lifted, and he could tell she was fighting a smile. "You love them, huh?"

"Shit. This is really not coming out right." Dominic could feel his face flushing and his cheeks heating. "What I meant was—"

Amanda lifted a hand as she cuddled Tom against her chest with the other hand. "Relax, Dominic. I understand what you mean. Straight men get so weird and uncomfortable when anyone mentions a penis."

He had no planned response to that. "Well, uh...I guess I need to rename Tom."

She shook her head. "Don't you dare. Tom is a great name for the little lady." A few quiet moments passed between them before she placed Tom down on the porch floor and kneeled next to her. She was the one to finally break the ice again. "This was my first date in years."

"Really?" He hadn't expected that. Not that he thought she was out there dating 24-7, but Amanda was drop-dead gorgeous and there was no way any breathing male in this town hadn't noticed that. "How was it?"

She shrugged her shoulders as she ran a finger down Tom's back in a gentle caress. "It was okay. Not my soulmate, you know? But I promised my friends I'd get out there and try this summer. I have three other dates with different people lined up."

He tried to squash the feeling of lava churning in his gut. "Three?"

Amanda nodded. "Yeah, just people I met off a dating app. And technically, I did tell Gerry tonight that I'd be open to seeing him again. Which I am. I wasn't lying. I just..."

She let her words trail off for the longest moment of his life, and Dominic found himself hoping she'd say how ugly or boring or stupid Gerry was and that she never wanted to see the slob again in her life.

Poor Gerry.

"I just think I don't know what I want," Amanda finally finished. "Or maybe I do know what I want, but I don't think it exists out there."

"What do you mean?" he asked. "It's a pretty big world. There's someone out there for everyone."

"Is there someone out there for you?" Amanda asked, gesturing toward the house. "You moved here alone, and I haven't seen any sign of a wife or girlfriend—or male partner, sorry—moving here with you."

Dominic laughed. "If I were dating, it would be with a woman. But actually, I'm divorced. Recently."

"Oh." Amanda looked down at her hands. "I'm sorry to hear that."

"Don't be," he assured her. "Melinda and I were college sweethearts, and we really grew apart the older we got. Or maybe we were never a good match to begin with, and time just made that more apparent. The more I got into sports, the more she got into anything but. Once my sports career ended, I thought, for a brief moment, that might reunite us, but I think it was too far gone at that point. We just wanted different things, and I was in such a bad place after the injury that I had no interest in putting in any effort with her."

Amanda nodded her head like she understood.

Dominic couldn't believe he'd shared all that. It was a wild amount of information to give someone who was still a relative stranger. Sure, they were neighbors for the last two weeks, but he'd just told her that he'd given up on his marriage and failed his wife. Not being the person she'd needed still left a pit in his gut, as he felt guilty for everything he put her through. She'd given him her entire youth, and he'd just kind of let her go along with everything else.

He couldn't help but also wonder about Amanda's

relationship history and if she'd ever been married before. After all, he hadn't seen any man at her cottage since he'd moved in, either.

"You're still friends?" Amanda asked.

He nodded. "I hope so. I'd like to think so. She's dating someone new now."

"Do you like him?"

Dominic wanted to say no immediately, but something inside him felt more open to the idea than he expected. "I honestly haven't met him and don't know anything about him. If Melinda likes him, though, he must be a good guy."

Amanda smiled, and he could tell he'd given the right answer, though he didn't know why.

"I can help, you know," Dominic continued, even though he immediately wanted to tell himself to stop talking. "With your next few dates, I mean."

She looked as utterly unconvinced as he felt. "How can *you* help with *my* dates?"

"Not *on* the dates," he tried to course correct. What the hell was he even talking about? "I mean, like after the dates. Like right now. I can debrief with you. Help you weigh the pros and cons and figure out what you want. You said you weren't sure, and I could be an impartial third party."

"Impartial, huh?" The unconvinced look was still clearly on her face.

Dominic looked away. "I'll prove it. Tell me about Gerry."

She paused for a moment, like she was weighing the decision. Finally, though, she started talking.

"He's originally from Minnesota," Amanda began, but now she was looking off into the dark night sky instead of at him. "Really close with his parents and older sister. A family man, for sure. He's ready to settle down and wants to have more children. Has a good job, owns his own house. All the things you'd want in a man."

"If that's the case, why do I get the feeling that that isn't all *you* want?" Dominic asked.

She cleared her throat and finally returned her gaze to him. "It's what I'm supposed to want."

"But what does *that* mean?" he pressed further. "Everyone wants something different."

"Maybe," she agreed half-heartedly. "But I'm thirty-three and a single woman. I was supposed to want a husband, children, and all of that two years ago. Now my ovaries probably just blow out dust."

He laughed at the mental image. "I mean, that's *one* version of what people want. It's not what everyone wants. For example, I don't want children."

"You don't?" She looked surprised, though he wasn't sure why that was particularly shocking news. "You don't want to be a father?"

Dominic felt himself getting defensive for a moment but tried to push those feelings away. "I mean, not really? Is that bad? I'm thirty-nine years old, and if I were to have a kid right now, I'd be sixty when they graduate high school. Nothing wrong with that, but I don't think I want to be playing catch with a kid at the same time I'm planning for retirement. Plus, these next twenty years are my time. Baseball was a huge responsibility, and, as much as I miss it, I didn't get to do a lot for myself during those years. If I had kids, I'd just be giving up the rest of my life to another responsibility, and I don't think I want that for myself, or for a kid."

There was also the matter of losing his sight in the future, but he wasn't about to bring up another traumatic topic like that right now. This conversation was about her, and he wanted to give her the space to explore her own needs instead of continually trauma dumping on her.

She nodded like that made complete sense. "Honestly, that's such a refreshing take. You don't hear that often these days. Everyone around me has kids already or is having kids. It just feels like this pressure I can't get away from."

"Well, you can get away from it here," he promised. "This house is a kid-free zone."

"But not a kitten-free zone," Amanda joked, pointing to Tom, who was now chewing on one of the leaves of a potted plant on Dominic's porch, smaller than the one he was still pretending to water.

"Baby felines don't count," he teased back. "Human babies, absolutely not."

"So you think I shouldn't see Gerry again, then?" Amanda asked after a quiet moment passed between them.

Dominic shrugged, because that wasn't really a question he could answer. He was happy to help her think about it, though, because even if there was a pit of jealousy in his chest, he'd never be the type to sabotage her—or anyone's—experiences. "Do you want children? Do you want to settle down? Do you want all the things he said he wants?"

"Not if I'm being honest," she admitted, though her voice was quieter now. It was the first time he'd ever heard a timidness to her tone. "I love being an aunt, and I think that might be enough for me. I also feel like . . . I already have settled down."

"What do you mean?" he asked.

Amanda pointed toward her cottage and then past it toward the lake. "The Sunflower Cottage was my life's dream. Still is. I'm living my dream. I don't want to leave here."

He stared in the direction she was looking, and even though it was dark, he could still see the stars and moon reflecting on the lake's surface. It lit up the entire area in a way the light pollution in Detroit never allowed for. He could understand her impulse to not want to leave a view like that.

"Then I guess it's about building the life you want here, in your home," he finally replied. "Maybe that's not with Gerry, but from the looks of the other night, you've already got a great family around you."

Amanda smiled in a warm, nostalgic way. "My chosen family is everything I could have ever dreamed of. You should meet them more formally sometime, honestly. Nola's husband's birthday barbecue is next weekend. You should come."

Dominic frowned. "You don't think they'd be confused as to why a complete stranger is showing up?"

"Absolutely not," she assured him. "You can be my

date! Evan will lose his ever-loving mind that I brought a former major leaguer. There will probably be plenty of people there I don't know, either. Tanner is pretty popular around this area, and people tend to come out in droves to anything he's at—much to his chagrin."

"He's not the social type?" Dominic asked.

Amanda shook her head. "Not really. Kind of like you, to be honest. I think you guys would get along pretty well. Both just a bit grumpy and sullen with a permanent knitted brow."

Dominic laughed out loud. "You think I'm grumpy?"

"Not *grumpy* grumpy, just like…unapproachable grumpy," she clarified.

"Oh, great. That's so much better." He shook his head again and scooped up Tom from the ground, petting him on the top of his head. "Glad to know I'm giving off those vibes."

"In case you haven't noticed, no one in Heart Lake pays attention to stuff like that, so this is kind of perfect for you," she teased, pushing back up onto her feet and walking down the porch steps. "Heart Lake has zero boundaries and will blow right past your walls, whether you like it or not."

"Something to look forward to," he replied sarcastically. "Send me the details for the barbecue. I guess I'll be your date."

"Then I can tell Nola I checked off my second date." She grinned at him. "Although I have an actual date beforehand—a lunch date. Not with Gerry. This is a guy named Stone. So we can debrief after at the party. It's perfect timing."

He felt his stomach sink in his gut. "Right. Sure. Yeah, perfect timing. Good luck with...Stone."

What the heck kind of name was that?

"Thanks!" She waved a hand and headed back in the direction of her house.

Dominic waited until she was inside and the door closed securely behind her before he and Tom returned inside as well. If he were being honest with himself, he was actually looking forward to the barbecue and spending more time around Amanda and the people she cared about.

But right after she'd gone on another date with another man? That part he could do without.

He still couldn't figure out why any of her dates bothered him so much, but there was no doubt that the feeling in his stomach was jealousy. And the more he admitted that to himself, the more he began to consider not going to that interview in New Jersey...

Chapter Nine

Amanda

My parents are geologists," Stone said from across the table at Crazy Cool Cow, the local ice cream shop where Amanda had decided to meet her next date. "So, that's my end goal, too. I'm working on my graduate degree now."

She'd planned the date for lunchtime because she had Tanner's birthday party after, and that was the perfect excuse to have a built-in end time. Out of the dates she'd agreed to, Stone had been Rosie's pick and not even close to top of the list for Amanda. But Rosie had insisted that she just give someone a bit younger a try—and the fact that he looked like he stepped out of *GQ* magazine probably helped, too.

"Oh, so that's why you're named Stone?" Amanda asked, scooping a spoonful of cookie-dough ice cream from her bowl into her mouth.

"What?" He looked puzzled by her question. "What do you mean?"

Amanda swallowed the icy-cold bite. "Oh, uh, never mind."

"What about you? What do you do?" he asked,

filling his spoon with the rocky road that was in his bowl. Then he snapped his fingers and pointed at her. "Wait, let me guess. I'm really good at this. I bet you're in healthcare. Nurse?"

She frowned. "Uh... good guess, but no."

It was not a good guess, and she had no idea why he'd even ask her that question when her dating profile clearly said she was an interior designer.

"Shit." He sat back and returned to eating his ice cream. "Okay, so what do you do?"

"I work in interior design. I'm actually working on a project right now—a hall bathroom and living room remodel." Amanda cleared her throat and smiled a little. Talking about work was exciting, and she couldn't help but feel really proud of the project she'd just taken on—even though she was still absolutely terrified of what Clayton would say when he found out. "I just delivered the design to the homeowner this morning, and she basically said yes without even looking it over."

"Wow," Stone commented. "She must trust your vision."

Amanda nodded. "It would seem so. I love what I do. Taking a space that is either damaged or struggling for some identity and bringing it to life feels really meaningful to me."

Stone smirked like she'd just said something funny. "You talk about it like it's some sort of spiritual experience, but we're talking about just adding, like, new furniture and paint, right?"

Okay, Stone was not getting a second date. "That's part of it—new furniture, sometimes a paint job, or a mural, or wallpaper. But it's not that simple. It's about creating an atmosphere, an environment that the home-owner feels themselves in. It is putting your stamp on something and creating a home for yourself or the client."

He just shrugged and scooped up the remaining bite of his ice cream. "I've lived in my town house for three years now and still haven't even bothered hanging up anything on the walls. It feels homey just fine to me. I never really understood paying for someone to do that kind of thing for you. Seems like a waste of money, you know? But I guess that's the whole point of the racket, right? Just rake in other people's cash for things they could easily do themselves."

"No, I *don't* know any of that." Amanda felt herself bristling. "Because design is literally my career. It said it on my dating profile, and you couldn't even be bothered to remember, and now you're insulting me about it. It's not a cash grab, and I am not some hustler out there just taking advantage of people. It's art, and some people actually really care about that in their lives and in their spaces."

Stone's eyes widened and he put his hands up defensively. "Jesus, calm down, lady. You're really overreacting. It's just my opinion. I'm allowed to have opinions."

"You're not allowed to just voice those opinions however you want without any regard to the people around you, asshole," Amanda replied, now standing and picking up her purse from where it was hung over the back of her chair. "And do *not* ever tell a woman to calm down."

With that, she turned on her heels away from him and walked over to the trash can to deposit her empty ice cream container. She could hear him sputtering and huffing from the table behind her but didn't bother to give him a second glance as she walked out the front door of Crazy Cool Cow.

"Hey, watch out!" a man said as she stormed out of the shop and directly into his chest. He reached out and grabbed her arms to steady her as she nearly fell over, and Amanda looked up to realize that it was Dominic.

She was near tears at this point, and for some reason, seeing him was bringing them right to the surface faster than she could stuff them down. "Dominic? What are you doing here?"

His expression was full of alarm. "I had to grab a few things from the hardware store. Jack's been helping me on the dock and is holding some extra wood for me."

"Oh." Amanda just nodded her head and looked away as she tried to still her racing thoughts. "Right. Of course. Thanks for still working on that."

"Amanda, you look really upset. Are you okay?" His voice was a little softer now, and he stepped in closer to her, leaning down to catch her gaze. "What happened?"

"I, uh, I just had my date." She pointed behind her to the ice cream parlor. "I really want to leave right now, though. I don't want to be here when he comes out."

"Come on." Dominic circled his arm around Amanda's waist and led her down the sidewalk quickly, and she felt a level of protectiveness that she hadn't known she'd like this much.

But there was something about this moment that felt like she was being held—not just physically, though she was, but emotionally. She spent so much of her life living like an island, and it wasn't often that she let people see her vulnerability unless it was Nola and Rosie. Letting Dominic see it, however, felt different.

And she found herself leaning into his side even more.

When they reached the hardware store, he motioned for her to sit on the bench out front and then took the seat next to her. She leaned against his shoulder, her head resting on him quietly for a few minutes, and neither of them spoke.

Finally, he broke the silence. "Amanda, did he hurt you?"

She heard an undertone of fear and horror in his voice, and her heart squeezed as she realized that he genuinely did care about her. She wasn't sure what that meant or how, but it still filled her with a rush of warm, cozy feelings. This was not how she expected things to go with her new neighbor, but something was definitely happening between them that she didn't want to push away from. And she was usually the queen of pushing away from emotions.

"No," she assured him, lifting her head up. "He was just...he was mean."

"He was mean?" Dominic lifted his brows. "What did he say? Want me to go talk to him? I'll set him straight right now."

Amanda let out a mostly deflated laugh. "No. Don't. I just want to pretend that he doesn't exist."

He shrugged. "Okay, but if you change your mind..."

"He made fun of my job," she replied, then felt the heat beginning to rush to her cheeks. "I know that sounds stupid. Petty, really. Like, okay, it's just a job. I don't know why it really triggered me. He just acted like design work is pointless and a waste of money."

"That's fucking rude," Dominic replied. "What an absolute asshole."

His validation made her feel an iota better. "It *is* rude, right? Like, who tells someone that about their job?"

"Someone who is clearly insecure about their own lack of direction. I bet he didn't even have a job." Dominic leaned back and let his hands rest on his knees. "You don't need his opinion about your life. Your design work is important, whether he understands it or not."

"If I told this story to Nola, she'd tell me to talk to a therapist about why he triggered me so much," she commented with a sigh. "She's always trying to push me into talking about my feelings more. This whole dating process is so much work. It seems like ninety percent of it is just opening yourself up to getting hurt."

If she were being honest, she was pretty sure the trigger that Stone had hit was around the concept of her feeling a lack of worth, not necessarily in what she did, but in who she was. It was a concept she struggled with a lot—the things she wanted out of life didn't follow the normal path of society or womanhood. Because of that, it often made her feel superfluous or...pointless. Like she wasn't as important to the world as the mothers and wives and people who were following the standard life path expected of them.

"I've been in therapy for a year now," Dominic said like it was no big deal.

"You have?" she asked, then laughed. "Well, damn. Nola would love you, then."

He shrugged. "It's hard work, and I see the guy virtually now once a week. But it helped a lot with all the changes I've been going through. It definitely has opened me up more—for better or worse. Hell, my theory is that either you go to therapy, or you're the reason someone else goes, and I was tired of being the reason other people went."

"That's actually pretty admirable," Amanda admitted. "I don't think I know another man who goes to therapy."

"I did couples therapy with Melinda for about a year before the injury," he admitted, rubbing his hand across the back of his neck. "But I definitely wasn't ready for it back then. I just kind of sat there, numb to everything. You have to go when you're ready."

"How did you know you're ready now?" She was genuinely curious because hearing he was in therapy only made him feel like a safer person in her eyes. Plus, she appreciated that he had tried to put in the work in his marriage before they'd split. "Aside from the injury, I mean."

"It was mandated at first by the coach," he replied. "Then when I was let go, I kept going. I don't know why it was the right time, but I was just suddenly more open to it than I had been before. Maybe because I had to be, you know?"

She nodded because that part, she definitely understood. Some of the times she recognized that she'd changed the most were moments where she'd had no other choice but to.

"My mother is actually going to school now to become a counselor," he continued. "But when I was growing up, therapy wasn't really spoken about. Mental health in general wasn't. She's really changed her tune since then, but I guess some of that is still hardwired in me. The stigma piece, you know?"

She nodded because the stigma around mental health was absolutely real, even in a world that claimed to be more progressive and supportive about it. "I get that. I think I feel some of that, too. Maybe why I haven't pulled the trigger on it yet."

He didn't respond, but his silence felt overwhelmingly nonjudgmental. They sat there for a few minutes longer as she regained her bearings emotionally.

"Since we're already together, do you want to just head to Tanner and Nola's now?" she asked him finally. "For the barbecue? I got Tanner a bottle of whiskey and put both our names on it for his birthday."

"Sure," he agreed. "Let me stop in the hardware store for a second and then I can drive us there."

She waited on the bench a few more minutes as he went inside and picked up his purchases, which Jack then came out and helped him load into the trunk of his car. She had walked from her cottage to Main Street for the date earlier, so it worked out that Dominic had his car and could drive them. Nola lived out a little farther on the lake in an old, beautifully restored house called the Castle that her paternal grandmother had once owned. She'd hired Amanda off the books for the design work—a fact she was never going to admit to Clayton—and Tanner had done most of the construction work himself.

When Dominic pulled his car into the driveway of the Castle twenty minutes later, he let out a low whistle. "Wow. This place is incredible."

"Right?" she agreed. "I could never live in a place this big, but it works for them. It was her grandmother's house on the other side of her family—Nola and I are cousins, but on our moms' side. I helped do some of the design for the restoration."

"I can't wait to see the inside, then," Dominic said as he stepped out of the driver's side of the car.

She swallowed hard, touched by the fact that he cared. "Thanks."

When she opened the front door to the Castle— because family never needs to knock—the boisterous noise of children and guests hit her immediately like a sound cloud. She ushered Dominic in farther until they got to the back room, which was an open living, dining, and kitchen space that had glass French doors leading to the back porch overlooking the lake. Tanner and Evan were out on the porch standing around the grill with several other men, putting spareribs on the fire, while Rosie and Nola were sitting at the kitchen island having a glass of wine together. Children were running around playing a game of tag or something equally raucous, and Amanda had to step around at least three tantrums before she got to her friends, who were clearly hiding out in the kitchen from the rest of the partygoers.

"Nola, Rosie, you remember my neighbor, Dominic?" Amanda introduced him to the two women. "Dominic, these are the girls."

They both shot Amanda a grin that clearly had some sort of undertone to it.

"Welcome, Dominic! The men are outside trying to figure the grill out if you want to join them. There's a cooler out there with beers in it, too. Help yourself," Nola said, reaching a hand out to him.

He shook her hand, then Rosie's. "Nice to see you ladies again. This house is absolutely gorgeous, Nola. The design work in this kitchen is impeccable, and I'm so impressed by this view."

"It's my favorite thing in the world," Nola agreed. "Amanda did amazing work in here, too. Come on. Let me take you out to meet Tanner and Evan. Thomas and Marvel will be here soon, and we're expecting a few other locals aside from the people already here. Most of the crowd in the living room are people from Tanner's job and their wives and kids, so I don't know all of their names but can try to introduce you."

Nola walked off with Dominic, and Amanda took her spot at the island next to Rosie.

"Soooooo," Rosie began in a singsong lilt and wiggled her brows at Amanda as she poured her a glass of wine. "Is this a date? You're really knocking these out of the park for your summer of romance, aren't you?"

Amanda took the glass but shook her head. "No, this is actually the after-party from a date."

"What?" Rosie seemed confused.

"I went out with one of the guys on the app—the guy *you* picked, actually—and he was such an asshole. I swear to God, I might never date again after that experience."

Rosie cringed. "I'm sorry. I should have read the profile a bit closer. I think I got distracted by the abs."

Amanda laughed and then took a sip of her wine. "Well, I didn't see the abs. But he did show his ass."

"Screw him, then." Rosie waved her hand. "We knew going into this that there might be a few turds in the bucket. Stone was a turd. Who's the next date with?"

Amanda pulled her phone out of her bag and clicked on the app, scrolling until she found the person she'd planned her next first date with for next Friday. "A guy named Maxwell. My hopes aren't very high with him either, though."

"There is always another option, you know," Rosie said, tipping her chin toward where Dominic was standing outside with Nola, shaking Tanner's hand as she introduced them to one another. "You could just date your neighbor."

"Absolutely not," she replied instantly, even though the words felt like sawdust on her tongue. She cleared her throat. "I mean, that would be a terrible idea. We are *neighbors*. If things go badly, I still have to live next to him. And I'd have to look at him."

"What do you mean *look at him*?" Rosie eyed her over the rim of her wineglass before taking a large gulp. "You make it sound like a chore. He's hot as hell."

"Exactly," Amanda confirmed. "It would never work."

Rosie put her glass down on the countertop. "Amanda, you are gorgeous. Don't sit here and tell me that you don't know that because I will not stand for my best friend thinking that she is anything less than absolute perfection. He would be lucky to even be considered remotely in or near your league."

Amanda laughed, and she could feel the heat in her cheeks again. It wasn't that she didn't think she was attractive. She knew she had good physical qualities to her. She was the girl-next-door, low-key type of vibe, and the feedback she'd gotten was that it was definitely physically appealing to men, even if she wasn't being picked for prom queen like Nola had been or dating rock stars like Rosie had.

"I'm not saying that," she tried to clarify, though her words were getting a bit jumbled, even inside her own head. "I'm just saying, it's probably not a match. A guy like that? He probably just wants to have sex all day every day."

Rosie laughed. "And that's a problem because . . ."

"Someone like that wouldn't be happy with some-one like me," she finally said, her voice a little quieter now. She took a larger gulp of her wine now and looked away, unable to make eye contact right then and there. This wasn't a part of herself that she'd been very open with her friends about, and they had never really pried into why she wasn't a very sexual being.

One conversation about therapy with Dominic and she was somehow already being more vulnerable than she'd ever been with her best friend.

"What are you talking about?" Rosie leaned forward

and put a hand on Amanda's knee. "Amanda, any guy would be damn lucky to be with you exactly as you are. No strings attached."

She sighed heavily, feeling the weight of her shame on her shoulders again. "What if that string is a complete lack of interest in the bedroom?"

"What if it is?" Rosie shrugged her shoulders. "After giving birth to James, I wanted nothing to do with sex for what felt like forever. Poor Evan, but he never complained once. He just took care of himself, and I'd send him the occasional sexy picture every once in a while, when I felt guilty about it. With breastfeeding and hormones and all that shit, my sex drive was nonexistent."

"Okay, but you had a baby," Amanda countered. "That's normal and understandable. Nothing you should feel guilty about. What excuse do I have?"

"You don't need an excuse, Amanda," Rosie replied and then huffed. "Man, I'm so fucking tired of society telling women that we have to be these specific sexual beings. Sometimes we're just not. Sometimes we're just tired. Or not interested. Or don't feel sexy. And that doesn't mean you can't have a healthy, normal relationship."

Amanda wanted to believe Rosie, but everything she'd ever seen among her friends or in the media was that sex sells. Sex was a strong motivator, and a relationship without sex, or with minimal sex, meant it was a dead relationship.

"I can tell by your expression that you are discounting what I'm saying right now," Rosie continued. "But really think about it for a second. If sex was the end-all-be-all for relationships, then anyone with a disability, or an injury, or lack of time or opportunity, or little kids running around, or a million other reasons would be doomed to a life without love. And that's just not the case. People find love in all kinds of ways, and as long as those two people are on board with things being the way they are, that's all that matters."

"But that's the problem—finding someone who would be on board with who I am." Amanda finished the last gulp of her wine and placed it down on the counter. "Jesus, this is such a depressing topic for a birthday party."

"Seriously. We need to break out the sheet cake now," Rosie agreed. "But I refuse to believe that there isn't someone out there who is capable of loving you for you, Amanda. There's no one more deserving of that than you. Maybe it's not Dominic or Stone or whoever the next guy is, but he's out there somewhere. Or her. I'm still rooting to have a lesbian friend."

Amanda laughed and shook her head, but she did feel the smallest bit of hope bubbling up in her chest at the possibility of someone being out there for her. She looked out to where Dominic was now standing over the grill, helping the other men.

Nola made her way back in toward them as Rosie opened up the next bottle of wine.

"They hit it off like wildfire," Nola said as she pulled up a chair and joined them at the counter. "Evan already asked for Dominic's signature and wants you to bring him a marker, Rosie. He says Dominic can sign his arm."

Rosie rolled her eyes but didn't say anything.

Nola frowned, glancing between the two women. "Why do you guys look so weird? What did I miss?"

"Amanda's having an existential crisis," Rosie replied, topping off Amanda's glass with a second pour of wine from the bottle she'd just opened. "And I'm telling her she's crazy and deserves the world."

"Amen," Nola agreed, lifting her glass to them both. "Cheers to that."

The three women laughed and clinked glasses, and Amanda did her best to try not to just spend the rest of the party watching Dominic interact with her friends and imagine what it would be like if he was a part of their group more often.

Chapter Ten

Dominic

It's coming together really nicely," Jack admitted as he stood next to Dominic on the shore and they both looked out at the dock. "I think it'll be ready by the Boat Parade for sure."

Admittedly, Dominic hadn't actually believed he could pull this thing off, and without Jack's help, that would absolutely have been the case. He chuckled remembering the time Jack accidentally fell into the lake when they were repairing the posts and how they both laughed until their sides hurt. And just a few days ago, when they sat on the partially completed dock in companionable bro silence, drinking a cold beer as the sun set, admiring their hard work. Yeah, spending the last few weeks working on it together with him had actually been a really great experience and reminded him a lot of when he'd done joint projects with his grandfather.

He hadn't realized how much he'd missed it.

"Thanks for all your help, Jack. I'm excited to show Amanda the progress." Dominic crossed his arms over his chest and made a mental list of the few remaining things he needed to do to the dock before the parade. "She's going to love it."

"You two are getting pretty close. I've seen you guys around town together here and there," Jack commented, giving him a sly grin and side-eye. "She's a pretty great girl, you know. Everyone in town will be pretty sour if you do anything less than what she deserves."

Dominic let out a wry chuckle. "Nothing like that is going on, Jack. I promise. She's dating other people, and I just got divorced."

"Divorced means you're single, though," Jack countered. "You still hung up on the ex or something?"

"No," Dominic assured him. "Nothing like that. I just don't know what's next for me right now. I wouldn't want to jump into something with anyone if I can't give them certainty."

"Well, that's dumb." Jack gave him a friendly smack on his back. "No one can guarantee anything in life— especially not in relationships. You could get hit by a bus tomorrow. Or a baseball."

"Gee, thanks," Dominic replied, not missing the reference.

"I'm just saying, all you can do is follow your heart and spend your time with and around people who make you feel happy, who make you feel like you belong. That's all there is to life in the long run, you know?"

Baseball had been the place he'd felt like he belonged, however, and this upcoming interview was likely his way of getting back into that setting. But that meant moving away, something he wasn't ready to tell anyone about yet, in case it didn't work out.

"That's a nice way of looking at it," Dominic told him. "Are you married, Jack?"

"Nah." Jack shook his head. "My sweetheart and I don't believe in all that paperwork crap. We just choose to be together every day because we love each other. Been together almost thirty years now. Met in the Navy and then he moved back here to be with me after we both got out."

Dominic hadn't been expecting that, but it warmed his heart to hear the man's story.

"It wasn't like we could get married for the longest time anyway, and thirty years ago, everyone just thought we were roommates. I'd guess a lot of people still do," Jack mused. "Which is fine. The world is changing, but not fast enough, you know?"

"Yeah," Dominic agreed. "There was a guy on my team who was gay. We all knew it, but no one ever talked about it, and he never said anything. The media can be brutal about that kind of stuff in sports. To be honest, I kind of feel like an asshole that we weren't more openly welcoming about it."

Jack shrugged. "Don't beat yourself up, kid. That's just the world we live in. All any of us can do is just keep trying to do better in the future."

"Yeah," he agreed, then glanced down at his smartwatch as a notification beeped. "I have to get going. I've got a doctor appointment."

"Your eyes?" Jack asked.

"Uh, yeah." He wasn't sure how Jack knew that, or how he guessed. "My vision hasn't been the same since the accident. Still hoping that there is more we can do."

"I could tell while we were working on the dock," Jack confirmed. "It's hard to do manual labor if your vision isn't right. If you need anything or just want to vent, let me know. That kind of shit can be hard to cope with. I would know, believe me. I'm losing my hearing, and these hearing aids are the only reason we're talking right now."

"Thanks, Jack," he replied, unsure of how he felt about the current conversation. All he did know, though, was he wanted to leave. He didn't want to sit here and talk about what might be coming down the pike or that he might lose his vision entirely. There were a lot of things that he'd learned to become more vulnerable about thanks to therapy—like his marriage history and his injury—but the future was still a terrifying prospect that he preferred to just avoid entirely.

Plus, his vision was another reason why he couldn't imagine dating or being with anyone right now, or maybe ever. It would be so much work for a partner one day to be with someone who couldn't see easily, or at all. He wasn't about to put someone else through that just because he felt lonely sometimes. And he had Tom now, so he shouldn't be lonely anymore.

He was a cat dad, after all.

Dominic's ophthalmologist was a little north of Detroit, so it would be a several-hour drive to get there, which was why he was leaving early in the morning when normally he'd have spent a few more hours working on the dock that day. Instead, he said goodbye to Tom, made sure that she had enough food for the day, and placed her cat bed in front of the back window so she could watch the birds.

An hour into the drive down, his cell phone rang, and he answered it with his car's Bluetooth.

"Hello?" He gripped the steering wheel, a bit of a headache creeping in from his eyestrain.

"So looks like the interview is getting moved up," Eric said through the speakers. He had never been the type for pleasantries or niceties, but always just got right to the point. It was one of the things Dominic loved about Eric, because he never had to guess where his head was at. "And one of the other interviewees just took a different contract, so he's out."

That was an interesting development. "That means it's down to me and one other person?"

"Theoretically, yes," Eric explained. "I mean, they could always find someone last minute, but the odds are looking better and better. You might be a New Jersey resident soon."

"You'd love that," Dominic kidded.

"Hell, yeah, I'd love that, man. You could take the train into New York City anytime and we'd be able to actually see each other more than two or three times a year," Eric confirmed. "But listen, I don't want to pressure you. I know last time we spoke you had some reservations about the whole thing. I think if you get this position, it could be amazing, but I'm always going to advocate for you to do what's best for you—whatever that looks like."

"Even if that means full retirement?" Dominic asked, slightly joking but also…he wasn't. The possibility was very real, and there was, somewhere deep down, an insecurity that he might lose this friendship too if their professional relationship ended.

Eric's response seemed unfazed, though. "I'll be the first one at your retirement party, D."

He smiled as he merged into a faster lane on the highway. "Thanks, Eric."

"Send me a text later about what the doctor says. Sending good vibes your way," Eric said before hanging up the phone without saying goodbye.

He was only about half a mile farther down the road when his phone rang again. This time, his mother's picture appeared on the screen. He clicked the answer button on his steering wheel to connect to the Bluetooth again.

"Hey, Mom," he greeted her. "I'm another hour out still."

"That's fine, baby," she replied. "I'm leaving the house now and will be there probably a little before you. You know how I like to make sure I can always find parking."

Ellen was perpetually forty-five minutes early to everything just in case she couldn't find it, or there wasn't close parking, or who knew what other anxious reason her brain convinced her of.

"I appreciate you going with me," Dominic continued. "I'm sure you had plenty of better things to do today."

His mother clucked her tongue into the phone. "Don't be silly, Dominic. No one should have to go to these types of appointments alone. It's always good to have support at things like that."

He'd been to appointments like today before, but there was the tiniest of chances that today he might actually get good news. At least, that's what he was hoping. There was a surgery that he was potentially eligible for as long as no further deterioration had occurred since his last tests. Today would determine if that was the case or not, and he refused to get his hopes up.

But even if he was telling himself not to hope, he could still feel the hint of a future with vision stealing its way into the back of his brain as a possibility.

"I mean, don't get your hopes up or anything. We have no idea what the doctor is going to say," he reminded her. "It very well could be bad news."

"And if it is, we'll deal with that when it comes."

He thanked her and they said their goodbyes as he finished the last leg of his journey. When he pulled up to the familiar office, his mother's car was idling out front. He pulled into the empty space next to her and they both got out of their cars. After a quick embrace and hello, they headed into his doctor's office and he checked in at the receptionist's desk.

"Want me to come in with you?" his mother asked him before gesturing to the waiting room. "Or stay out here until you're done?"

"You can stay here," he confirmed as one of the nurses called him back. He gave her an awkward wave goodbye, then followed the nurse into the back offices.

"How are you doing, doc?" he greeted the man he'd been working with for the past year and a half after his traumatic retinal detachment. Dr. Jerry Ahn was probably only in his late forties, but he was already one of the best in the field in this area, and Dominic trusted that he was giving him the best treatment he'd find out there.

Dominic's doctor did the usual tests for eye pressure, including numbing drops in both of Dominic's eyes, the slit lamp pushing against his cornea, and a retinoscopy to check his current prescription status. All of it was awkward and uncomfortable, and he found himself just sitting quietly through each exam in complete silence like he was waiting for someone to say something he didn't want to hear.

"Well, it's not the news we'd hoped for," Dr. Ahn finally stated as he returned to the exam room after leaving Dominic there for about twenty minutes to sweat it out. He sat on a small swivel stool and placed a laptop on the counter next to him that had Dominic's medical chart pulled up. "The good news, however, is that the deterioration is minimal. It's not moving at the pace we had worried about, so I'm hoping that means you have your vision a lot longer than expected."

Dominic appreciated the encouragement, but he could read the subtext to what Dr. Ahn was saying. "That means it *is* still deteriorating, though."

"It is," the doctor confirmed. "We could try the surgery—either laser or cryopexy—but I'm not going to lie to you. The chances of either being successful are minimal. And what would be considered successful in this scenario would only be an insignificant improvement for a period of time. It would potentially slow things down even more, but it's not an outright cure. We wouldn't be able to return your vision to the way it was before the injury was sustained. And honestly, you're at a pretty big risk of it detaching again with any sort of even small injury."

"I'm out of the game now, so no worries about getting injured again," he replied, since that was the whole reason the league had let him go. The risk had just been too high. "But slowing things down sounds like a positive step, right? Can we do that?"

Dr. Ahn nodded, but he didn't seem completely convinced himself. "That's one outcome. The best outcome. There is also the possibility of things progressing faster or losing vision entirely from the surgery itself. There was nothing standard about your detachment, and the scar tissue is so thick."

He'd known that the odds weren't stellar, but he hadn't expected that the surgery could make things worse. "It could get worse?"

The doctor confirmed. "It's a possibility."

"What are the chances it works well and just slows the deterioration down?" Dominic asked after a quiet moment of contemplation. "What are my odds if I do it?"

"About a thirty percent chance it works and buys you another five years with your current vision level, assuming there's no further aggravation to the eye." Dr. Ahn didn't look directly at him when he delivered this news, but rather stared at the computer screen as if he couldn't bear to see Dominic's reaction.

But Dominic refused to react. He shut down any emotion he might have been feeling leading up to that moment and chose numbness instead. "Okay. Thanks, doc."

Dr. Ahn looked up at him now, a little surprised.

"Maybe take a few days to think about it? Then let my office know if you want to schedule it or not."

"Will do." His voice was flat now.

"Do you have a ride home?" Dr. Ahn asked. "The numbing drops in your eyes have probably worn off by now, but it's best not to operate heavy machinery for the rest of the day out of an abundance of caution."

"My mother is driving me," he confirmed, barely even noting the feeling of appreciation for her taking a day off to do that. "Thanks, doctor. I'll think about it and get back to you."

With that, he stood up and walked out of the exam room, not even waiting for Dr. Ahn to dismiss him. When he entered the waiting room where his mother was sitting and scrolling through her phone, she took one look at him before jumping up and shoving her phone in her pocket.

"Come here, baby." She put her hands out and wrapped them around him before he could even object.

He stayed still and stiff, letting her hug him but unable to let in any more than that.

"Jenny just picked up my car from me," his mother informed him as she ushered him toward the office door, talking about her roommate who had agreed to the favor. Jenny was also going to come up to Heart Lake to pick up his mother tomorrow, which he appreciated. He was glad he'd had the forethought to give his mother her own room at his house. "Do you have your car keys?"

Dominic reached into his pocket in what felt like a robotic move, scooped the keys out, and handed them to her.

She took them from him, then wrapped her arm around his and guided him out to the car. "Let's go home, Dominic. If you want to talk about it, let me know. But we also don't have to right now."

He said nothing as he let her lead him out to the car and even open the passenger side door for him. She waited until he climbed in, then closed the door behind him and circled the car to the driver's seat. He pulled on his seat belt and buckled it, then just stared out the windshield as she reversed out of the parking spot.

He wanted to tell her, but what was he going to say? He didn't know what he wanted to do. He'd already had multiple surgeries on his eyes, and none of them had been easy. They were really difficult experiences, and going through that again for—potentially—no good outcome felt like insanity. But then again, if it did mean he kept his sight longer... shouldn't he try?

He didn't know the answer, and he was afraid to admit that maybe the answer was... he didn't want to try.

Chapter Eleven

Amanda

Maxwell was absolutely a bust. Her third date had been more of a babysitting experience than anything else. They'd met at the local dog park with his Labrador to chat and get to know him and his dog in a low-stakes environment, and it became anything but. Amanda loved dogs—truly, she did—but this man's dog would not stop trying to hump her leg. And instead of stopping his dog or acting like a normal person, Maxwell thought it was hilarious and would just stand, laugh, and point instead.

Literally the worst way to get humped on a date.

The moment she'd untangled the dog from her leg, she'd made an excuse about checking to see if she'd accidentally left the lights on in her car...and then just left. And did not come back.

She didn't feel even remotely sorry about it, because she did not owe someone like that her courteousness.

Pulling her car up her driveway, she turned down the path toward her cottage and came to a stop in front of her garden of sunflowers, which were getting really tall at this time of year. They were perfectly in bloom, and she couldn't help but smile every time she saw them.

She found her eyes swinging over to Dominic's house like they usually did. There was also an older woman Amanda didn't recognize sitting on his front porch in one of the two wooden rocking chairs that she'd refurbished and given him last week. The woman had what looked like a giant textbook sitting open in her lap and was clearly reading studiously.

Amanda sat in her car for a minute and tried to decide—did she ignore it and go home? Or go say hi? That seemed like the neighborly thing to do. She didn't always have to be neighborly. She and Dominic had also been spending a good amount of time together and clearly were friends. So if she didn't go say hi, would that be rude? Social norms were really annoying.

She pushed open the car door and her feet took her in the direction of Dominic's front porch before she'd come to a firm decision.

"Good afternoon!" she announced herself as she rounded to the steps at the bottom of the porch.

The older woman lifted her head, seeming to notice her for the first time. "Oh, hello!"

"I'm Amanda. I live next door. Just thought I'd say hi, as your neighbor." She gave a small, awkward wave, even though she knew full well this woman didn't live here.

"I love that. This place is such a small-town stereotype, and I just want to eat it up." She put her textbook down on the table next to her and Amanda read *Abnormal Psychology* on the spine. The woman stood and offered her hand to Amanda. "I'm Ellen Gage. I don't live here, but my son does."

"You're Dominic's mom?" Amanda asked, shaking her hand. She could see the resemblance now, and it was actually pretty endearing how much they did look alike.

Ellen gestured for her to come join her in the other rocking chair next to her. "For nearly four decades now, yup."

Amanda sat and gave herself a little push to begin swaying back and forth. "What are you reading?"

"Believe it or not, I decided my early sixties would be the perfect time to go back and get a graduate degree in counseling." Ellen lifted the textbook and showed her the cover. "I'm calling it my final-chapter career."

Amanda smiled at the morbid humor. "Wow. That's really impressive."

"I'd like to think so," she replied, putting the book back down. "You do a lot of things when you're a parent—and having Dominic meant that a whole phase of my life was about someone else instead of myself. Ironic that I'm choosing counseling now for myself, when that's all about helping other people."

"Well, do you enjoy it?" Amanda replied. "Because that's really what matters."

Ellen leaned back in her chair and pushed herself to rock back and forth. "So far. I get nervous about how much I can really help, especially on days like today."

"Today?" Amanda frowned, unsure what Ellen was referencing.

"Dominic just had a really hard day today at the

doctor, and I worry he'll give up on a second chance or another future that isn't just baseball. Tell me to stop if this is too much information. I don't know if you know that much about him, or if I'm just trauma dumping on a stranger."

Amanda laughed lightly and shook her head. "Actually, I can see where Dominic gets it. You're both very emotionally open right off the bat. It's . . . it's refreshing, honestly. I don't experience that in people too often."

"That's good to hear," Ellen admitted. "Maybe I did something right with him."

"You definitely did," Amanda agreed. "He and I are a new friendship, but he's been great to live next to so far. He's rebuilding my dock after a tree fell on it."

"He's what?" Ellen's head leaned forward and turned to her, then she let out a loud barking laugh. "Please have a safety inspector or someone approve it when he's done before you use it."

"I will," Amanda said with a chuckle. "But he is doing things up here, I promise. He's not just been holed up in this house."

Ellen sighed. "I really needed to hear this tonight. Thanks, Amanda. You've given me a real gift today. On the drive home from Detroit today, he didn't speak at all. He gets like that after the doctor now."

She swallowed hard at hearing this piece of Dominic's life. It felt like a glimpse behind the curtain she'd been wondering about but hadn't gotten to see yet. Amanda had a hundred questions she wanted to ask as a follow-up, but she'd already intruded on this woman's study hour, and it felt like too much to then snoop about her son. Even if she wanted to know all of it. Instead, she decided to leave it simple and validate the feeling. "I'm sorry. That must be really hard for you as a mother."

"It is." Ellen breathed in slowly, then released it. The air between them seemed to lift, and Amanda found herself envious of this older woman's ability to regulate herself so seamlessly. She was clearly in tune with her body to be able to allow just a deep breath to calm her so easily. Amanda had tried mindfulness and meditation but had never been able to actually figure it out.

Ellen turned to look at her again. "But enough about us. Tell me about you, Amanda. I asked Dominic when I pulled up about the yellow house. It's just so cheery! I love the sunflowers. It must have taken some time to grow them all that tall."

"Thanks," Amanda replied. "I love my house. It's the cheery vibes I always imagined for myself but never had. My mother tries hard, but she is always working. Beautifying our space or our home growing up was the last thing on her mind. Not that I blame her, but I definitely told myself when I had my own place, it would feel every bit of beauty and warmth I could muster."

"Well, you certainly completed that task," Ellen commented. "It's incredible."

Amanda nodded, letting a moment of quiet pass between them. "I actually just got back from a date."

"Ooh." Ellen's interest was definitely piqued, and she sat forward. "God, I can't even remember what dating is like. Tell me all about it. What do the kids call it these days? The tea? Spill the tea."

"Oh, it was terrible. You're missing out on no tea—I

promise." Amanda laughed as she glanced down at her jeans that still had a small crusty stain on the shin where her date's dog had been humping her. *Ew.* "We met at a dog park with his Labrador."

"Man with a dog…always a good sign," Ellen commented. "Love Labradors."

"You wouldn't love this one. This one was *too* loving, if you know what I mean," Amanda countered, gesturing to her jeans. "I couldn't peel it off of my leg, which my date found to be the most hilarious thing ever."

Ellen grunted. "Sounds like a middle school boy."

"Right?" Amanda agreed. "I booked it out of there so fast. Didn't even say goodbye."

Ellen laughed and then gave a long, reflective sigh. "That's what I love about this new generation of women like you. Back in my dating days, I'd probably have stuck it out until the end out of some sense of duty to his feelings. The fear of hurting his ego far outweighing my discomfort. Women aren't putting up with that shit anymore, and I could not be happier about that."

"I hadn't thought of it that way," Amanda admitted. "I was trying not to think about it like some kind of asshole move."

"It was an asshole move in some ways, self-preservation in others," Ellen replied. "But men have been doing that shit for all of history, and no one blames them. It's always about whatever the woman did to push him away. Your husband cheats on you? Why weren't you satisfying him enough? What did you not give him as a wife? It's all patriarchal bullshit and generations of lack of male accountability."

Amanda wasn't sure how to respond to that, but she respected the hell out of Ellen for saying it.

"Oh, sorry," Ellen followed up. "I can get on my soapbox sometimes after doing this studying. The things we learn in graduate school...man, I wish someone had taught me about all of this when I was younger. Body autonomy, self-advocacy...it shouldn't be a foreign concept to me, but it really was."

"Those are big concepts to everyone, I think," Amanda countered, trying to soften the stance. "I think every generation struggles with figuring those things out in their own ways."

"That's true," Ellen agreed. "I definitely have a tendency of sometimes seeing things in all black or all white—especially when it comes to looking back on my own time line and wishing things were different."

Ellen was so easy to talk to that Amanda couldn't help but continue. Clearly whatever that trait was would lend very well to her being a therapist in the future. "I mean, don't we all look back with regrets on our life? That seems like the human condition. Always wanting what we didn't or couldn't have."

Ellen shrugged, but her gaze was off in the distance as she contemplated. "I think I'm beginning to see it doesn't have to be that way, though. That there is a way to sit with both the emotions and reality of loving who you are and where you are, while also holding space for the parts of you that were hurt or neglected or never fulfilled in the way you'd hoped."

That certainly hit home with Amanda. "Shit, maybe Dominic is right, and I should go to therapy."

His mother laughed. "He told you that?"

She nodded. "He might not be wrong."

"I was twenty-two years old when I met Dominic's father. I was twenty-three when I got pregnant, and yet, he still left me for a nineteen-year-old. I never heard from him after I told him I was pregnant, and over the years, it just became pointless to try and track him down," Ellen explained. "My parents stepped in a lot to help me raise him, and I am forever grateful for that. I do think their influence on him—especially my father—was a saving grace."

"I'm so sorry Dominic's father acted like that," Amanda replied. "I am sort of familiar with dads doing that. Mine got remarried and started a new family that I just wasn't invited to be part of."

Ellen raised her brows and gestured out in front of her. "See? Everyone has a story like that. You should hear some of the stories of my friends back then, too. We let men get away with the world. I mean, we didn't *let* them. But we accommodated them. We made arrangements with one another, we had back-up plans, and we left when we had to. But that was the extent of the consequences to them. The men lost us. That was their only consequence."

"I mean, losing you would be a huge loss," Amanda tried to counter. Not even knowing this woman well, she could already tell that Ellen was not someone to mess with. She was very clearly *not* a woman anyone would want to lose.

"Thanks, hon," Ellen replied but then shook her head. "But I'd be a lot happier if I also had his castrated balls on a necklace."

Amanda burst out laughing. "Oh my God!"

Ellen grinned. "I'm not saying it needs to be graphic. They were already very small. Like two dainty little stones."

She gestured to her neck, pretending she was wearing a necklace.

Amanda only laughed harder.

"What the hell is going on out here?" Dominic stepped through the front door and bellowed at the two of them. When his gaze landed on Amanda, he looked just as surprised to see her as she was to see him.

"Oh!" Amanda jumped up from her chair and suddenly couldn't figure out where to put her hands. "I was just talking to your mother."

"Dominic, sweetie," Ellen interjected, not missing a beat. "Why don't you go grab a bottle of red for me and your neighbor here? Pour us both a glass."

"Mom, I think—"

"You think the white in the fridge is better? You know, I agree. Switch that order to the sauvignon blanc instead." Ellen cut off her son like it was the easiest thing she'd ever done.

Amanda grinned at Dominic sheepishly and slowly sat back down. "I *do* like white wine…"

Dominic all but growled at her, but the flicker of amusement in his eyes was enough to give her permission to stay. "Fine. But I'm having a glass, too."

Ellen put a hand to her chest. "Only if you come out here and chat with us."

He paused in the doorway, seeming to survey them both for a moment. "Fine."

After he went inside, Ellen giggled in the way a young girl might and Amanda couldn't help but join in the laughter.

"Oh, he's *not* happy with me," Ellen joked. "He thinks that every time I drink, I whip out the childhood pictures of him. But I'm actually going to pull some up right now before I even start to drink, so he can't complain."

Ellen pulled her cell phone out of her pants pocket and began swiping across the screen.

"Wait, really? You have baby photos of Dominic?" Amanda asked, her curiosity on full display. "Is he frowning in all those photos, too?"

Ellen laughed. "He *is* quite the grump, isn't he? He always has been. Long before the ball-to-the-face thing. Grumpy is just his baseline. It's actually gotten a lot better in the last year, if you can believe it."

"I believe that. He's not very grumpy with me," Amanda admitted. "And honestly, it seems more showy or defensive than real."

"It is. Complete defensive mechanism." Ellen lifted her phone screen to Amanda to show a photograph of a younger version of Ellen sitting on a floral couch with a young toddler in her lap. Sure enough, the grim look on the toddler's face matched Dominic's usual resting dick face. "But look how cute he was. Such a little love-bug as a kiddo. Always wanted to be in my lap. Always wanted a cuddle. We bedshared 'til he was almost seven years old. Some of the best years of my life."

Amanda smiled at the thought but felt a familiar churning of nervousness in her own gut. Physical affection was so important to Dominic—it was to all men. Would she ever be able to measure up in that way?

"Two glasses of sauvignon blanc," Dominic announced as he walked back out onto the porch holding two full wineglasses. He handed one to each woman and then pulled a bottle of beer out of his pants pocket. "And a lager for me."

"A beer man?" Amanda asked, lifting her glass to him as if to toast.

He was too far away to clink his beer to her wineglass, but he held it up in solidarity anyway. "It was that or risk dropping one of the three wineglasses on the way out here."

Ellen laughed, then took a big swig of her wine. "Typical man. Could have made two trips but never will."

"This lager is better than a second trip," Dominic countered. "What are you two even talking about out here? All I heard was cackling from inside."

Ellen rolled her eyes and gave Amanda a meaningful grin. "Girl talk, kid. You wouldn't know about that."

"Am I the subject of girl talk?" he countered. "Because I happen to be an expert on the topic of me."

"Everything isn't always about you, Dominic," Amanda said, suddenly feeling a renewed sense of bravery she had probably gleaned from Ellen. "Your mother is a very interesting woman. I could talk to her for ages."

Dominic eyed his mother with one raised brow like he didn't believe a word she was saying. "She's a real wealth of information," he agreed. "But feel free to check any facts about me with the actual source."

Ellen grinned at her and wiggled her brows. "Ooh, someone is feeling a little territorial it sounds, Dom. You haven't shown so much interest in my renditions of your life before."

"You weren't talking to my neighbor before," he countered, but his defense felt off somehow. "She has to live next to me. More importantly, I have to live next to her."

Ellen waved her hand. "Nonsense. You two clearly already have a friendship going here. I completely approve. Amanda seems like a real gem."

"Thanks, Ellen." She tipped her wineglass toward them both. "I happen to agree. I really *am* a gem."

Dominic laughed and shook his head. "Jesus Christ, I'm never inviting you back up here, Mom."

"Oh, hush," Ellen countered. "I have my own bedroom. Also, I want Amanda to decorate it. You put stock photos on the wall. I want sunflowers."

Dominic paused the beer bottle as it was about to reach his mouth. "Absolutely no sunflowers in my house. Not happening."

Amanda laughed, and the warmth filling up inside of her in that moment felt like it could sustain her for years. Maybe this was what it could be like...family, closeness, depth of conversation. If this was what could come out of putting herself out there emotionally, then maybe she wanted to do it more often.

Chapter Twelve

Dominic

Dominic had said good night to his mother at least an hour ago now, but he still found himself pacing back and forth in his kitchen, unable to sleep. It was too late at night to go anywhere in this small town, but he needed to burn the energy he was feeling somehow. It wasn't even bad energy, it was…excitement. Or fear? He wasn't entirely sure what label to put on it, but all he knew was that he'd had the best evening in a long time laughing with Amanda and his mother. They'd all done dinner together and finished off a bottle of wine and cracked open another.

It had felt seamless and happy, and after the way his morning had gone, that felt like whiplash. One minute, he'd been numbly staring at a possible future of blindness and the next he was laughing with his mother and his neighbor about childhood stories of that one time he'd put VapoRub all over his hair as a toddler and had smelled like menthol for a month.

Dominic paused his pacing and glanced out the back window at Amanda's dock. With the right lighting, he might be able to get some more work done on it. That would definitely help get some of his anxious energy out. It wasn't the safest idea—carpentry at midnight—but he needed to expel his frustration somehow.

He headed for his garage and gathered up the toolbox that Jack had slowly helped him build to full capacity. Jack had also given him a floodlight that was battery operated. They'd meant to use it for working in the fog that sometimes came over the lake in the early mornings, but working in the pitch-black night seemed as good a use as any.

It took about ten minutes to haul everything out to the dock and figure out how to set up the light, but once he had, the area was decently lit, and he could pick up where he and Jack had left off earlier. Admittedly, his lessened vision made things a bit more of a gamble, and he found himself going back to the house twice for a second, then a third flashlight.

But as awkward as it was working in the middle of the night, it was successful in distracting him from everything he was feeling. He had to focus intensely to be able to see what he was doing, and there was absolutely no room for emotional ruminations at the same time.

"It's literally twelve thirty at night," a voice came from behind him as he was hammering a railing into the base of the deck.

Startled by the sudden sound, he slammed the hammer down squarely on his thumb with all his force.

"Ouch!" Dominic shouted and jumped up so fast that he lost his balance. He swung his arms fiercely to try to recenter his gravity, but it was of no use. Seconds later, Dominic was plunging into the cold, dark water of Heart Lake with a sore thumb and an even sorer ego.

"Oh my God! Dominic!" the voice shouted, and he recognized it as Amanda now.

Thankfully, the water at the shore was still shallow enough that falling in only dropped him in to his shoulders. He splashed and pushed himself closer to the shore, climbing his way out next to the dock onto the grassy slope of Amanda's backyard.

"I'm fine! I'm fine," he repeated as he climbed out. But he was definitely not fine. He was shivering. Like, full-body shivers where he had no doubt Amanda could hear the chatter in his voice.

"You're freezing!" she countered, rushing down to the shore, grabbing him by his wet shoulders, and pushing him toward her back porch. "Come inside, quick. Let me help you get warm!"

He wanted to argue and protest more, but honestly, he was shaking so hard he could barely take a full breath. It was almost summer, but for some reason, the water was still like ice. Maybe because it was the middle of the night; he wasn't sure. What he was sure of, however, was that he wasn't going swimming in Heart Lake anytime soon.

"Thanks," he tried to voice between chattering teeth.

Amanda ushered him into her house, leaving him standing in the back entryway for only a moment as she grabbed several throw blankets off her couch and wrapped them around his shoulders.

He held them tight around him, but it didn't make the chattering stop.

"Maybe you should take off the wet clothes?" she offered. "I can put them in the dryer."

"I don't have any other clothes," he replied between frigid breaths and shakes.

She shrugged. "I won't look. I promise."

With that, she turned her back to him and opened a nearby small closet, procuring several towels from it.

"Strip everything off, and then I'll give you these towels," she continued. "It'll be a lot better than staying in wet clothes."

With her standing only three feet in front of him, he did what she commanded. Quickly and carefully, he peeled off each layer of soaking wet clothes and dropped them onto the tile floor beneath him.

"Okay, towels, please," he said, his hands cupped over his groin in an attempt at privacy, even though she wasn't facing him.

Amanda handed him the towels while keeping her eyes forward, meaning she missed him at first and he had to find her hands to get the towels. But once he did, he took both towels quickly and wrapped one securely around his waist and the other like a shawl around his shoulders for more warmth.

"All good?" she asked, still turned away.

"Yeah," he said, his voice smoothing out as his shivering began to calm. "I'm covered up."

She turned to face him, and he saw her try to keep her eyes on his, but they faltered briefly and glanced down the length of him.

He wanted to pretend her gaze didn't affect him, but it did. She was incredibly beautiful, and the way her lashes hung heavily over her brown eyes was hard not to find mesmerizing. He swallowed, trying to push the thoughts away. "I…uh…well, thanks. That was very cold."

"The fireplace is going," Amanda continued, now looking away. "Come on. Join me in the living room. You need to get a lot warmer than just those towels."

He followed her to the couches that surrounded her fireplace and instantly felt warmer from both that and the extra blankets she piled on top of him. She put his wet clothes in the dryer before returning to check on him.

"This is perfect," he admitted but looked at his bruised thumb, which was already beginning to turn different colors. "Ironic, but would you happen to have an ice pack for my thumb?"

She laughed and nodded, heading for the kitchen. She returned a moment later with a small blue gel pad, handing it to him.

He held the cold, soft surface against his finger and sat there quietly, gazing at the fireplace. There was something about staring at flickering flames that could make a person get lost.

Amanda sat in the love seat perpendicular to him, tucking her feet beneath her on the couch. He could still see the slight stain of the red wine they'd switched to earlier on her lips, and he tried not to think about what it would be like to kiss them.

"What the hell were you doing working on the dock in the middle of the night?" she said. "That's crazy-person behavior, you know."

He could feel his cheeks flushing but didn't make eye contact with her. "I needed the distraction."

"Why?" she pushed, and, God, he didn't want her to. And yet, he also did. "You know why."

She wasn't taking his bait as easily. "Me? What would I know about your craziness?"

"You. My mother. All of tonight," he replied, wrapping the towel tighter around his shoulders. "You're not innocent here."

She frowned, her head tilting to the side. "Sorry. Was getting to know your mother overstepping neighbor boundaries or something? She's really nice, and we have been becoming friends lately. Haven't we?"

"Of course we have," he replied, now finally shifting his gaze to hers. "It was actually really nice to see how well the two of you got along."

Amanda nodded, but he could see a hint of worry etched in her furrowed brow. "If my mother ever comes over, you're welcome to meet her. She just tends to work a lot, and we're not as close as it seems you and your mom might be."

Dominic let out a sigh as he dropped his head back against the couch and stared up at the ceiling. "We're meeting the parents now."

She laughed lightly. "I didn't mean it like that."

"Maybe I wish you did though," he countered, rolling his head to the side and finding her eyes again. He swallowed the lump forming in his throat. "I think I'd actually like that a lot because I'm wanting to get to know you better, and maybe it will reveal a thing or two."

Amanda's gaze skittered away from him, and she stared into the fireplace. "The Boat Parade is this weekend. Are you going to be there? You could always bring your mom."

He hadn't expected the sudden change in conversation but went with it anyway. "Yeah. I know how much work you've put into it. I don't think my mother will still be in town then, though. I'll be there."

He wanted her to address what he'd just said, how he'd just put himself out there and basically told her he wanted to be dating. He wanted to be meeting the parents and doing all the things that people who date do. He shouldn't want that. He knew he shouldn't. Who would even want to date a recent divorcé in his position? It wasn't practical for her, and it wasn't practical for him.

But he still couldn't help what he was feeling in that moment.

Amanda nodded, still not looking at him. "The parade is fun. We've done it a couple years now, and it's just a contest basically of who has the best-decorated boat. Nola and Tanner will have a boat in it, and I'll drive one for my boss. You're welcome to join us if you want."

"I can't," he replied. "I promised Jack I'd be on his. We're doing a Halloween theme."

"Oh, that's cool. Jack almost won last year. He's hoping for a comeback," Amanda said. "I, uh...I have another date before it. My last date of the four."

If that was her way of dropping the hint that she wasn't feeling the same thing he was feeling, he was beginning to pick up on it. Clearly, he'd put himself out on an emotional limb alone, and she was trying to nicely let him off the hook.

"Nothing serious," she continued. "I thought it would be less pressure to have it before the parade so I had an out time locked in, you know? So maybe we can debrief about him like we've been doing at the parade. I'll want to know what you think."

He already knew what he thought, and it was that he didn't want her going on a date at all. But he kept that thought to himself and instead just nodded. "Sure. Happy to help. Four dates in a month, huh? You really knocked out your goal."

She pulled her lips tight. "I am never one to not follow through on what I promise."

"That's good," Dominic said, feeling like he was just throwing out words and none of it even made sense anymore. His thumb was still throbbing, and now his ego was bruised on top of it all. "Good for you."

"It's complicated, Dominic," Amanda finally added after a few moments of silence fell between them. Her voice was quieter now, barely above a whisper. "I... I'm not sure who I am right now. I'm still trying to figure it out."

He could relate to that. "I feel you on that one."

"Did you ever have plans for a post-baseball career? Before the injury, I mean? Like, had you ever thought about it?" She stood up to stoke the fire a bit, and then, instead of going back to sit on the love seat, she sat on the same couch he was on. The opposite end of it, but still... she was moving closer. He could smell the lavender in her shampoo and the hint of wine from earlier on her breath. He tried not to let his body react to the proximity, keeping his focus on the fire instead.

She leaned back into the couch. "Are you warm enough?"

"I am," he replied, keeping his gaze on the flickering flames. "And to answer your question, I think I just assumed I'd be in the game long enough to build up a good financial base, run some investments, and just be set for life. Not have to work, you know?"

She tucked her bare toes under the edge of one of the blankets that was on top of him. "But now you *do* have to work?"

"Well, technically no," he clarified, definitely not focusing on her feet being less than an inch from his bare thigh. There was only a towel between them under the blanket, and he wasn't about to make a move on her after she'd just rejected him. "I don't have to work. I am pretty blessed from the length of time I was in the game and the contracts I had. If I make smart choices, I'll be fine for the rest of my life."

"That must be nice," Amanda said with a teasing laugh. "I never understood how athletes made such large paychecks like that."

He shrugged sheepishly. "It can be exorbitant. There's no doubt about that. But also, it's taking a lot more from you than a nine-to-five job. There are no off-hours. There is no individuation of yourself outside of baseball—you're just a player and that's it. That's your identity. It's the only identity you have the time to foster. You give up any privacy or right to making your own choices without the rest of the world weighing in on them. That money didn't just pay me a salary—I sold my entire life and self to that team."

She didn't respond right away but then reached forward and placed her hand on his forearm. "That's a really beautiful—and also painful—way of describing it. I'd never thought about it like that, to be honest."

"Being here in Heart Lake is the first time in fifteen years that I've really gotten to ask myself...who am I? Who do I want to be?" Dominic continued. "But I'm not sure I know the answer to that question without baseball being somehow involved."

He thought about the upcoming interview and briefly considered telling her about it right then and there. But that wasn't a door he wanted to open right now.

"I feel that way about design sometimes." Amanda's hand continued to rest on his forearm, and he felt his skin burning in the best way beneath it. "Like a home or a room is a canvas, and every time I put my designs on it, it's like art I'm breathing into the world. It feels like part of me...not just something I'm producing. Little bits and pieces of me left in everything I create."

He nodded, understanding that feeling more than he wanted to admit. "I think there's a piece of me left behind in that stadium..."

She moved closer on the couch now, her shoulder pushing up against his. She leaned her head against his shoulder and sighed again. Both of them just stared forward and watched the flames flicker in the fireplace, and at some point, sleep must have begun to pull at him.

It was strange to feel so lost in a moment where he also felt so found.

Chapter Thirteen

Amanda

It had been a long time since Amanda had woken up to a naked man. And yet, when she'd opened her eyes this morning, she'd found herself staring at a cold, died-out fireplace with her head on Dominic's naked shoulder, attached to his naked body, that was sleeping naked under her blanket next to her on the couch.

Naked. So very naked.

She'd gotten him his dry clothes as quickly as she could, they'd awkwardly said good morning, and he'd apologized for falling asleep. No part of her needed or wanted him to apologize for it—it had actually been one of the nicest nights of sleep she'd had in a while. That felt really weird to admit to herself, but as she found herself standing in her client's hall bathroom later that afternoon, she couldn't think of anything else.

It had been really nice to sleep cuddled up to someone, to just hear someone else breathing softly, feel his warm skin against hers. Honestly, it wasn't something she'd realized she'd enjoy so much. It wasn't like she hadn't slept with guys before—she certainly had in college and a few times after. But those had always felt a little more like impositions. The guy was in her space, usually snoring or twitchy or somehow invading her personal sleep zone.

And Amanda really valued her sleep. Her bed, her space—that was personal, and she wasn't one to share. Hell, she had a king-size bed in her house and no one— not even a dog—to share it with. She liked it that way.

But curled up awkwardly on a small couch next to Dominic hadn't been awful...in fact, it had actually been really nice. It had just felt warm and cozy, and intimate in a way she hadn't experienced. Kind of a continuation of the coziness and intimacy the entire evening had been with him and getting to know his mother more—who she was sure probably had lots of opinions about finding Dominic sneaking back into the house this morning.

"Amanda, I don't know how I feel about this gray grout." Mrs. Amal Crawford was standing in the hall bathroom with her, pointing down at the floor. "What do you think about it with the concrete tiles?"

"I actually love it with this pattern," Amanda countered, gesturing toward the floor as well. "Do you see how it contrasts against the crown molding and the wallpaper? It's really striking, actually. Any guest of yours who comes in here is going to be dazzled—I promise. In fact, I'd be willing to bet there will be some Instagram selfies taken right here in this mirror."

"Instagram selfies?" Amal looked confused. "What's that?"

"Here." Amanda gestured for Amal to step over in front of the sink with her, and she pulled out her cell phone. "Pose in the mirror, and I'll take a photo of us."

Amal immediately pulled out the duck lips and popped one hip out. "Cheese!"

Amanda tried not to laugh but smiled for the camera as she held up the cell phone with one hand and threw up a peace sign with her other hand. She clicked on the camera icon until they had a few poses to choose from, then showed them to Amal. "Look at how the wallpaper pops in the back of the photo. Anyone who sees this online is going to be like, 'Where is this place? I want to go!'"

"Really? You think so?" Amal looked over her shoulder at the screen of her phone. "Like the younger generation? What about people my age?"

"You said the entire point of this remodel was to make your house a place your kids and grandkids would want to come to," Amanda reminded her. "How many of your grandkids are on social media?"

"All of them," she replied. "I don't understand stuff like that, but I know my daughter is always talking about the tweens being on the TikTok and stuff."

"Perfect, so watch this." Amanda clicked onto her Instagram and posted the selfie of her and Amal onto her personal Instagram with only the fire emoji as a caption. Within seconds, her notifications were going, and she clicked over to the photo to show Amal. "Look at the feedback."

The older woman held the phone and began scrolling through the comments already quickly lining up beneath their photo. "Oh...oh, wow! Someone said I'm a grand-MILF. What's that mean? Is it like milk? I'm lactose intolerant."

Amanda laughed and shook her head. "No, that means they think you're hot."

Amal's face turned slightly darker in her cheeks, a blush beginning to form. "Oh. And there's three people commenting about the wallpaper already. What's this icon mean?"

She glanced at what Amal was pointing at. "That's the mind-blown emoji. It means they are in love with it and shocked at the same time. You're a trendsetter."

"I *am* a trendsetter," Amal agreed, now handing back Amanda's phone. She was suddenly standing taller, seemingly a bit more confident, and holding the air of a peacock strutting their feathers. "This is what was missing in the last redesign that Clayton did. I know you tried to make some more modern changes to it, but it was still too traditional. My grandkids were absolutely uninterested."

"Your grandkids will be lining up to take a selfie in your bathroom now," Amanda replied, chuckling at what she was even saying. It was true, but good Lord, what a weird time she lived in. A big part of her job these days was exactly that, though, and as much as it felt strange to design for the internet, she also understood it. It was a way of displaying art to a wider platform, and, admittedly, she felt really proud every time she saw one of her designs in the background of a selfie or any other photograph. If she could create an environment in which someone would feel good about themselves, that was all she could ask of a career.

"Now I just need to figure out how to sell the price tag to Mr. Crawford," she joked. "But don't worry, he'll sign any check I put in front of him."

Must be nice, Amanda thought.

"In fact, I'd actually like to talk to you about more work," she continued. "I know we were focusing on the remodel after the water damage, but I think I want to completely redo the guest cottage out back to be grand-kid friendly. I was thinking every room could be a fun, cool theme and really make it a vacation spot. And I have more work for you after that, if you're interested."

Amanda smiled, feeling honored at the compliment. "I'll definitely tell Clayton and get a quote together for you."

Amal shook her head. "No. I told you; I don't want Clayton involved. Don't get me wrong. He's a lovely person, but he doesn't understand my design needs the way you do. Have you thought further about what I offered? Opening your own firm and letting me back you as an investor?"

She'd known this question was going to come around at some point, but she'd been struggling with how to answer it. "Uh, I have thought about it, Amal. It is so flattering that you'd even make me an offer like that. It honestly sounds incredible."

Amal clapped her hands. "Perfect. So you'll do it?"

"I didn't say that," Amanda interrupted, even though she saw Amal visibly deflate at that response. "It's just…it's not that simple. I have a noncompete with Clayton, and I do care about him. He's been a great friend and mentor, and he gave me my start. It would feel really underhanded to steal business from him."

"Amanda, darling," Amal began, "you're not steal-ing my business from him. After the last remodel, I wasn't going to go with him again. He did a good job—beautiful, truly. But it wasn't the feeling I was going for. It was stark and clean and beautiful, but it wasn't... I don't know, it wasn't what I wanted. You seemed to understand what I wanted without me even knowing it."

"What you wanted was something your family would love, something that would build connection," Amanda replied because that was her entire goal of design. There were plenty of designers, like Clayton, who focused on aesthetics and beauty, but Amanda focused on connection. There was space for both of those in the industry, but it was a very different demographic that she hadn't been able to crack into with Clayton's clients. Amanda wanted to accentuate spaces that created atmosphere and relationships, and that sometimes meant going beyond aesthetics and into feelings.

"Exactly," Amal replied. "See? You get what I'm saying. It's one thing to have a beautiful home—nothing wrong with that. I spent my whole life wanting to find that and have that."

She went quiet for a moment, and Amanda didn't say anything, wanting to give her space to finish her thought.

"I think now that I'm older and my priorities are different, I see this space as less of an homage to what I've accomplished and more as a potential gathering ground for everyone I love." Amal sighed and walked out of the hall bathroom toward the living room.

Amanda followed her, taking a seat on the couch across from her after she sat down. "Home is a gathering ground—that makes sense to me."

"Does it make sense to Clayton in the same way?"

Amal asked pointedly, her eyes now focused on Amanda in a manner that told her she had to be honest. "Truly—does it?"

She could feel the internal struggle bubbling up in her, but she knew she had to, at some point, choose herself. "Clayton is brilliant," she began. "But he is childless by choice. His aesthetic does reflect that. I'm childless, too, but I also think I never fully grew up."

Amal smiled at her in an all-knowing way, like she'd finally broken through Amanda's barriers. "Clayton is great at what he does, but you're great at understanding me, Amanda. That's what I need in a designer, and I'm happy to have my husband's lawyers look at the non-compete. I can talk to him. Generally, they're pretty unenforceable. If you want this to happen, I guarantee you that I can make this happen for you."

Amanda tried to calm the fluttering nervousness in her chest, but it literally felt like someone was offering her everything she had ever wanted. It was so close ... so tangible. Could she just turn it all away?

"Clayton is back in town after the Boat Parade," Amanda finally managed to muster out. He'd originally planned to be in the parade with his boat, *Drag 'N' Anchor*, but Adam's surprise vacation had changed his plans. "Let me talk to him first and see where his head is at. I want to move forward—I promise you; I do. I'm not uncommitted. I just don't want to burn bridges along the way."

"One of the things I admire about you so much," Amal replied, and Amanda remembered that they had a small yacht at Heart Lake Harbor. "I'll be at the Boat

Parade, too. We registered *Pura Vida* to be entered. So if you need me to talk to him, I will. I can smooth all this out easily, I promise."

"I'll keep that in mind," Amanda agreed, even though there was a 0 percent chance she was going to have Amal intervene for her. "I'll be fine, though, I promise."

Amal and her husband were Clayton's most wealthy clients—the richest couple in all of Heart Lake. Scooping them for her own new firm was not going to go over well. She hoped that he'd be understanding and supportive . . . but she'd also worked for him for enough years to know his competitiveness was strong.

Amanda said her goodbyes and finished her assessment of the remodeling work that had been done on the place before finally heading out to her car. The moment she sat in the front seat and placed the key in the ignition, her cell phone beeped with a notification.

She waited to move the car out of park and pressed the new text message notification only to see a message from Dominic popping up.

The dock will be done by Saturday.

She stared at the message, as if expecting a second text to come through, but none did. He had promised her that the work on her dock would be completed before the Boat Parade, and that was now only two days away. She typed out a reply, deleted it, then tried again.

Just in time for the parade—thanks!

Her response felt boring, but it was...something. Three dots in a bubble appeared on his side of the text screen, indicating that he was writing back. She found herself holding her breath as she waited to see what he was going to say.

Finally, the next message came through. Anything for you, Amanda.

She swallowed hard and clicked out of the messages, putting her phone in the middle console as she focused on backing her car out of the Crawfords' long driveway. She couldn't focus on the fact that his words held a stronger meaning—they had last night, too. She'd known when he was on her couch that he'd been talking about more than just their friendship or being neighbors. He had been blatantly telling her that he was emotionally invested, and she'd pretended to not understand.

And he had let her pretend that. He hadn't pushed, even though she'd seen the flash of pain across his face when she'd dodged his emotional bid. She couldn't make sense of what she was feeling—did she actually feel attraction and romance with Dominic?

That was so unfamiliar to her in general. She naturally wasn't someone who found herself *attracted* to anyone. Whatever that even meant. But there was a pull to Dominic, and she didn't know how to categorize that. She didn't know how to make sense of it in her head and in her body—and if she was ever truly honest with him about what she felt...would he actually want her?

Not to stereotype, but there was no doubt that he

was probably the typical athlete who wanted sex and romance and all the things that felt foreign and uninteresting to her. If she told him that a future with her didn't heavily involve those things, he wasn't going to continue to be interested. Period. That was a foregone conclusion.

So, the question now was…how did she let someone down who she also kind of liked without jeopardizing their friendship? Lately, Dominic had become an important part of her life, a true confidant. The last thing she wanted was to lose that.

Chapter Fourteen

Dominic

I told you the dock would be finished before the parade," Dominic said as he walked Amanda out onto her finished boat dock on Friday night before the Heart Lake Boat Parade the next day. His thumb was still wrapped in a large bandage and occasionally throbbed, but he ignored it.

Amanda walked to the end and twirled before turning back to him with a big smile. "I don't know how to thank you. You and Jack did so much work on this."

"I mean, Jack was an advisor at best," Dominic clarified with a joking laugh. "He's nearing his seventies, you know. I did all the manual labor."

She pretended to give him a fake bow. "Oh, I'm soooo sorry. Let me just bask in your manly, masculine carpentry abilities."

The banter between them had always been easy, and he was glad that they could at least fall back into that after everything that had happened the other night. He'd been worried that their night together on the couch would make things awkward, but it seemed like she was game to just pretend none of it had happened.

He couldn't really argue with that approach, either. He wasn't going to push it between them anymore. Instead, he was going to write it off as some emotional exploration he had to figure out on his own post-divorce. An attempt at a rebound, maybe. An awkward play at dating again after years of being off the market. Because that's probably all it was.

He laughed. "I'm getting a lot better, I swear. I helped Jack with his boat for tomorrow. It's going to blow the other boats away. We're definitely going to win."

"The first year, Tanner's boat won," Amanda said, reminiscing on the event. She actually did love it, even if it was a lot of work. Next year, she'd definitely be bringing on other people to help, though. "He did a whole lovebirds theme with Nola, and it was so grotesquely romantic that everyone voted for it. Honestly, the entire thing was a ploy for their self-esteem as a couple. More for Instagram than anything else, in my opinion."

Dominic tried not to laugh, but he was immediately unsuccessful. "Wait, so who won last year?"

Amanda's face turned to a scowl. "Blake."

"Who's that?" he asked, despite seeing the aversion in her expression.

"I actually started the Heart Lake Boat Parade with Blake," Amanda clarified as they walked out to the edge of the dock and looked out onto the lake. "And he did it with me for a couple years, but this year, he quit."

"Shit." Dominic frowned. "Does that mean you're on your own planning it?"

"Yep," she replied. "It also means that he's a fucking asshole."

Dominic lifted his brows as he took that in. "Why's he an asshole? It sounds like a big undertaking. Was he not up to the task?"

She shook her head. "It's not that it's a big undertaking— I mean, don't get me wrong, it is. It's a *huge* undertaking, and the fact that I've done it completely free three times in a row seems like crazy talk. But it's that I said I wasn't going to date him—that's why he quit. I really hurt his feelings, apparently."

"I mean, okay, his feelings got hurt...but is that on you? He said he wasn't going to continue sponsoring an event with you just because you weren't going to date him. That sounds like a him problem, and frankly, kind of an asshole move." Dominic kicked his foot against one of the railings on the dock, testing out the structure. It held up well, and he was proud of how he and Jack had put it together. "Definitely doesn't sound like it's your fault."

"I wish more people thought that way," she replied. "I told him there wasn't a future between us several times, but I guess he thought he could just wait out my no until it was a yes."

"That's shitty." Dominic was no stranger to the message men got that persistence was key to romance, but that was an old-school thought he wasn't about. If a woman said no, he was going to believe she meant it. Period.

Amanda sighed. "Blake is not a bad guy, I swear. I'm just pissed about the timing. I wish I'd gotten more notice on the parade so I could have brought more help in."

Dominic had no interest in letting this Blake guy off the hook that easily, the heat already turning up higher in his gut. "Tomorrow's Boat Parade is 100 percent going to be because of all the work and planning you put into it, and that's something to be proud of. Screw him. Tomorrow is about you."

"And a bunch of boats," she joked, clearly trying to lighten the mood or change the topic of conversation. That seemed to be her standard for any conversation that began to touch on something real.

"Sure," he agreed. "But if you need me to have a conversation with Blake, just say the word. I'll put him in his place."

"I don't need you to protect me, Dom," Amanda said, her voice a little quieter suddenly. Her stance physically softened in front of him, but there was something in her expression that made him feel antsy. "I don't need anyone, least of all some handsome neighbor who just randomly moved into my life and turned everything upside down."

The anxiety itching across his skin was only spreading at the way she was looking at him right now. He wasn't expecting any of this conversation from her, and he didn't want to say anything to ruin it. A stillness fell between them as he digested what she'd said. She didn't move, and he didn't, either. Until he felt like he couldn't stay still a moment longer.

Dominic walked closer to her, reaching out to touch her forearm with his uninjured hand. He traced his fingers down her arm toward her wrist but stopped before holding her actual hand. "Amanda, there *is* something here between us."

He wanted her to acknowledge it, to walk out onto the ledge with him and be willing to bare her soul.

She swallowed hard and shook her head, and in the process, she pushed him physically off of her and took several steps to the side. "I am not someone you would date, Dominic."

"What?" He frowned, a little confused at the abruptness of her sentence. And frankly, also a little offended, though he wasn't exactly sure what she meant. "Why would you say that?"

"I'm not someone *you* would date," she repeated.

Dominic was so honestly taken aback by the entire line of thinking that he didn't know what to say. "Okay."

That wasn't the right thing to say, but that was all he said.

The flash of hurt across her face and the extra step she took away from him told him that everything about his response had been wrong...but how else was he supposed to respond? What was the answer to that? She was making things clear, and he didn't know what he wanted from her, but *I won't date you* felt pretty damn clear.

At least, he thought it felt clear. Is that what she'd said?

But the next moment, Amanda completely changed course and stepped closer to him on the dock until she was directly pressed against him. Chest to chest, he felt his entire body freeze. He didn't know whether to put his arms around her and hug her to him—like he wanted to—or to stay perfectly still and not even breathe.

"Amanda?" he whispered her name like a question because he had no idea what the answer was.

Except he knew that he wanted her closer.

She was so, so close already, but he wanted more. That felt like the wrong answer, too. He didn't know which way was up right now, his heart felt like it was pounding in his chest, and there was that smell of lavender again from the other night. Everything about this woman was floral, and he didn't want to move away.

"Dominic," she replied in a breathy manner that felt like an answer but only created more questions for him.

Her chest was already against his, but she pushed up on her tiptoes until her mouth was also at the same level as his.

He could feel the anxiety taking over in his chest and his previously fast-beating heart was now exploding through his rib cage. It was quite likely she could hear it at this point.

"Amanda, I don't know if this is a good idea..." His words were barely a whisper, and he wasn't even sure she could hear him over the racing of his heart.

But her lips pressed against his anyway, and it was everything he hadn't known he'd wanted. Except he did want it, and he did know it.

Amanda's lips were soft and slow, and when she had first held them against his, he'd been hesitant to respond, but when he did finally kick into gear, they became voracious. She kissed him like she hadn't been kissed before, and his arms wrapped around her waist and pulled her against him like he hadn't held anyone this close before.

There was something hesitant and explorative and intentional about her all at the same time. Dominic didn't know how to navigate it and felt it better to stay on the safe side and let her lead. When her hand slid up the back of his neck and pulled him closer to her, he was hungry for more and pressed his lips against hers harder.

She gasped slightly at the merger, and when his hand wrapped around the small of her back, she shuddered gently—but he still felt it, and it set him on fire.

"Dominic," she breathed in the smallest of gasps as he held her close. "This is...this is amazing."

She sounded almost...surprised?

His confidence surged at her words, and he saw an entire future mapping out between them. Screw the job in Secaucus. Screw his eyesight and possible eventual blindness. Screw everything that told him he wasn't dateable or someone who couldn't be desired after a divorce and a game-ending injury. Here was a woman he felt nothing but deep adoration and affection for telling him that he was worth it...he was lovable. He wanted to believe her. He wanted to believe her kiss.

But then she kept talking. "But we need to stop."

He pulled away, an abrupt stop that felt like his heart ripping in half. "What?"

"We need to stop," she repeated, this time stepping back from him on the dock. She pushed her hand against his chest to separate them, but her breath was fast and heaving as she did so.

He didn't want to say she'd been the one to start

everything, and he was just along for what felt like a tortuous ride. But…it felt exactly like that.

And the ending of the ride? Even more tortuous.

"Amanda…" he tried to find the words, but nothing came.

"I have a date tomorrow," she reminded him, now turning around and beginning to pace back and forth. "Raad is expecting me before the parade. I have to see that through."

"But then why did you kiss me? And why is that relevant right now? You've never even met this Raad guy before."

"I just…I can't do this," Amanda continued, and it felt like she was on some sort of spiral because everything she was saying felt more for her sake than for his. She was still pacing back and forth, and he wanted to grab her and keep her still for half a second. But his brain was running on a hamster wheel just the same.

"I can't, Dominic," she continued.

"But hang on a second, I didn't…" He tried to make sense of what he was thinking, but he honestly mostly felt frustration and a little bit of betrayal. "I didn't ask you for anything. This feels like total whiplash. I didn't mean…"

She visibly swallowed, and there was nothing about her expression that was letting him off the hook. Her face said he'd been involved in every step of things, and he knew that was true.

"Amanda…" He tried to intervene, but she was already heading toward the shore like the flight risk he'd begun to realize she was.

"It's a beautiful dock, Dominic," she said, not hearing him at all. "You and Jack did an amazing job. I'll see you tomorrow at the Heart Lake Boat Parade."

He nodded his head. "I'll be on the *Jack-O'-Lantern*."

"I'll see you there," she said, her back already turned to him as she literally ran away from whatever could have been between them.

Chapter Fifteen

Amanda

The way a woman's body moves is intoxicating," Raad said from the other side of the lunch table at the Black Sheep Diner where Amanda had agreed to meet for a first date. "Your curves get me going, you know? I just... wow, I can't stop looking at them. I didn't expect all this from your pictures on the app."

He waved toward her when he spoke about *all this*.

Amanda wished, with every fiber of her being, that Raad would stop looking at her completely. "Uh... it's... I don't know how to respond to that."

"Most women would say thank you," he replied as he lifted the top off of the Reuben sandwich he had ordered. "I'm female affirming. Basically a full-fledged feminist because I think you should be in charge. I'd love to be in a world completely run by women. In fact, I'd let you run the entire show tonight if you want."

"I don't think saying you can't stop looking at my curves makes you a feminist," Amanda countered, though she felt unsure even of her own answer given how confidently he'd said his. "Actually, I don't think anything you just said qualifies as feminism."

He furrowed his brows at that. "Most women I go out with are less difficult. Are you going to be difficult, Amanda?"

She swallowed hard at that and picked up her glass of lemonade, taking a long sip. She couldn't believe she'd agreed to come on this date, and this was how it was going. Especially after that kiss she'd shared with Dominic—what had she even been thinking?

She didn't go around kissing guys. That wasn't who she was. It never had been. But there was something about him in that moment that made her just feel the desire to . . . claim. With her lips. And it had felt incredible in a heart-aching, soul-stirring type of way.

And now she was here. With Raad. Talking about the absolute opposite definition of feminism.

It would be easy to tell him off and get into an argument about politics and feminism and how he was an absolute douchebag, but she genuinely didn't want to expend her energy on him a minute longer. She looked around the diner, as if an out would be easily provided. One of the girls she'd gone to high school with, Mattie, was standing behind the counter cutting up a pie into slices.

Maybe Mattie could be her out?

Amanda lifted her free hand and waved at Mattie. "Mattie, I'm coming!"

Raad turned around and looked in the direction she was calling. "Who?"

"That's my friend Mattie. She works here," Amanda replied, coming up with any excuse she could think of on the fly. "She was just calling me over. Sometimes I help cover shifts when it gets too busy in here, so she probably needs me to work."

Raad looked around the diner, which was about 60 percent full and clearly had plenty of open tables. "You didn't tell me you're a waitress."

"So what if I am?" Amanda asked as she pushed herself up to standing, her tone confrontative. She had been trying to give him an easy out—or give herself an easy out—but if he wanted to go down fighting, she would absolutely walk the plank with him and toss him overboard. "What's wrong with being a server?"

He looked uncomfortable, clearly shifting in his seat. "Uh...I guess I'll just take the check, then. I don't date waitresses."

"What a blessing for them," Amanda said as she flounced off toward the end of the counter where there was a break in it to walk behind.

Mattie looked up at her with a confused look as she stepped behind the counter, but Amanda gave her *the look*.

Mattie didn't question a thing, pointing to the extra aprons dangling from a hook on the far wall. "You're late, Amanda. Hurry up and get drinks for table twelve."

"On it," Amanda replied, grabbing an available apron with the Black Sheep logo on it and tying it around her waist. "Thanks."

"Stop being late, or I'll have to write you up," Mattie called out behind her, loud enough that Raad definitely heard her. "Hey, lover boy. Get out."

Raad stood up and looked confused. "I haven't paid."

Mattie shrugged and pointed toward the door. "Your money isn't good here. Get out."

Flustered and clearly confused, he left, and Amanda made every effort to not look him in the eye as he did so. Instead, she walked over to table twelve and took their drink order—two cokes and a water—and relayed those back to Mattie.

"Thanks for covering for me." Amanda placed her apron back on the hook on the wall, and then gave Mattie a quick hug. "I'm absolutely done dating. This shit is for the birds."

Mattie seemed to freeze and shake the hug off, like she hadn't expected it. She was one of the younger staff members at the diner, but Amanda had heard rumblings that her life hadn't been very easy the last few years, so she appreciated the way she'd stepped up for her just then.

"Yeah, I know a little something about that. Don't worry about it," Mattie said, heading to another table. "Give it five minutes before you walk out—just to make sure he's left."

"Good idea." Amanda waited a few minutes longer, then glanced into the parking lot to make sure no one was lingering around. She scurried quickly to her car and set herself in drive, making the decision to head early to the parade route and begin getting set up.

Heart Lake Harbor was already fully decorated with signs for the event and balloons on every post. She'd done most of that last night, but there had, thankfully, been a few volunteers this year who'd agreed to be here earlier this morning to make sure things were in place.

All Amanda had to do at this point was check the roster of boats, make sure everyone was here, check in on the judges of the contest, and then tally up their scores after the boats finished the route.

"Add a few extra points to my score, Amanda," Tanner said, his tone joking, as he walked up to her on the end of the pier. *Nola Nation* was tied up to the right of where she was standing—Tanner's pride and joy that he'd named after his wife and Amanda's best friend. "I put a lot of extra work into her this year. Can you tell the theme?"

Amanda turned to take in the full sailboat for a moment. One end had a yellow goalpost attached to it, and there was fake AstroTurf across the entire deck with game lines painted onto it. Tanner was wearing a Detroit Lions football jersey and had black marker streaks on both of his cheeks. "Uh . . . volleyball?"

Tanner's jaw dropped slightly, and he let out a huff. "Seriously? Football, Amanda. We're the Detroit Lions stadium. Look!"

He gestured back toward the boat, and Amanda laughed because of course, it was obvious, but damn it was fun pretending it wasn't.

She kept up the ruse and nodded her head stoically. "Oh, I see it now. Yeah, the football game."

Tanner tossed his hands up in the air as Nola stepped off the boat and headed in their direction. "Nola, do none of your friends know anything about sports?"

"I mean, Evan coaches Zander's Little League team," Nola replied. "So Rosie might know about baseball?"

"Amanda didn't notice the theme," he replied.

"Yes, she did," Nola said, rolling her eyes at Amanda and smacking her lightly on the arm. "She's just giving you a hard time."

Amanda grinned and let out a laugh. "I mean, it's pretty obvious, Tanner."

He was definitely grumpy now and muttered something as he stalked off and left the two of them alone.

"How was your date?" Nola immediately asked— typical best friend who doesn't forget a thing.

Amanda shook her head and grimaced. "Awful. I hated him. I mean, he was actually very attractive, but his personality belonged in the dumpster."

Nola shook her head. "Damn. That's four for four."

"I know," Amanda agreed. "I told you I'd go on at least four dates, and I did. And I'm literally never ever doing that again."

"I'm very impressed that you gave it a try, though," Nola assured her with a smile. "But I was hoping one would pan out into at least a second or third date. It seems like they all just sucked."

Suddenly, Nola paused and lifted one brow as she looked past Amanda and then back at her. "Unless... unless there's a reason these dates all sucked?"

Amanda frowned. "Uh, yeah. The reason is he was an asshole."

"That's not what I mean," Nola continued, her voice dropping to a whisper. "I mean, maybe he is the reason."

Just as she said it, someone walked up next to them, and Nola's eyes were glued to him.

"Hey," Dominic greeted them as he came to a stop next to Amanda. "It looks like a pretty great turnout. Is this what it was like last year, too?"

Amanda hadn't seen Dominic arriving, but her skin felt hot at his sudden proximity. She cleared her throat and looked around, like she was assessing his question. "Uh, actually . . . it looks a bit busier than last year."

The harbor was alive with a vibrant array of colors and themes and over two dozen decorated boats gently bobbing in the water. One small sailboat had been transformed into an "Under the Sea" paradise, right down to the shimmering streamers in shades of blue and green, inflatable sea creatures, and a crew dressed as playful mermaids—shell bras to boot.

Nearby, a motorboat sporting a "disco days" theme caught Amanda's eye, adorned with people in groovy polyester and a disco ball. For those with a sweet tooth, the Candy Land pontoon boat was straight from a dream, featuring giant lollipops, gingerbread cutouts, and folks dressed as characters from the classic board game.

As Amanda took in all the creative, fun displays, she noticed people milling about, putting the finishing touches on their decorations and preparations. The parade was still at least an hour from starting, but the area was already alive with activity. The air buzzed with laughter, chatter, and a palpable sense of Heart Lake pride.

"Pretty great turnout," Dominic replied. "Are you on a specific boat this year?"

"I'm on *Nola Nation*," Nola answered him, even

though it seemed quite likely that he was aiming his question at Amanda. "Tanner's boat, of course. He's very proud about it. I don't get it, but whatever. Gotta let him have his thing, you know?"

Dominic nodded with a smile. "Fair. Detroit Lions theme?"

Nola nodded her head then pointed her gaze at Amanda. "See? He got it right away."

"I'm not on a boat," Amanda informed him while rolling her eyes at Nola. "I'm helping with the judging."

"You're a judge?" Dominic asked, his brows raised. "So you're going to help the *Jack-O'-Lantern* win, right?"

Amanda laughed and shook her head. "Jack's boat is on its own. I have no say in the judging. I just tally the scores and announce the winner."

"Well, get ready to announce the *Jack-O'-Lantern* as the winner because I spent all last night helping him turn it into a haunted house," Dominic informed her as they stepped away from Nola and he pointed her toward Jack's boat. "You've never seen anything spookier."

"It's July, Dominic," she teased, following him and giving Nola a quick wave goodbye. "Don't you think it's a little early for Halloween?"

"We can't choose when the ghosts of our past haunt us, Amanda," he replied, and she could hear the joking in his words but felt a shiver of seriousness all the same. "Embrace the haunting."

"Oh, God," she joked back. "Is this your way of telling me that your house is going to be all decorated for Halloween in gore and guts?"

Dominic waved a hand dismissively. "Gore is cheap. Anyone can buy red food dye and cornstarch. For Halloween, I do it up for suspense and thrill. I can promise to have you shaking by the end of the night."

She swallowed as she looked up at him, and he seemed to register what he was saying as he said it.

He quickly course corrected. "I mean, if you want. Like a good shaking. Fun shaking."

Amanda tried not to snort out a laugh, but she couldn't stop it entirely. "A fun shaking. Wow, what a promise. I've never had a guy give me a guarantee like that."

Dominic's cheeks were tinging pink. "Wow, I really painted myself into a corner here, didn't I?"

She placed a hand on his forearm. "I'll let you off the hook."

"Thanks," he replied, his eyes boring a hole into her hand on his arm. "Uh...how was...how was your date? You had a date today, right?"

Amanda let her hand drop, but wished she hadn't. She wanted to keep touching him, even if it just meant her hand on him. After the way things had gone the other day, though, she knew it wasn't fair to him. It wasn't fair to her, either, frankly.

"I wouldn't call it a date," she said. "I left halfway through."

A concerned gaze cropped onto Dominic's face. "Are you okay?"

She looked away, shrugging her shoulders noncommittally. "I'm fine. I'm not *not* fine. He was just an asshole. A really good reminder why I don't date. Why I shouldn't date."

She whispered the last half of that sentence, and she didn't miss the fact that Dominic stiffened slightly at those words. Her mind flashed back to the moment she'd told him he'd never date someone like her, and the look of hurt on his face after she'd kissed him and then verbally taken it back like that. A pang of pain took up residence in her chest and she looked away from him in an attempt to shake it off.

"I'm sorry," Dominic replied quietly, and the gentleness in his voice was like a soft blanket wrapping around her shoulders. "You shouldn't have experienced anything less than perfect on that date."

She tried to muster up a wry grin. "That's not how dating works in this day and age, you know."

"I guess I don't know," he admitted. "It's been a long time since I've dated. This postdivorce dating world is completely foreign to me."

Amanda looked up at him, and she wanted to say something. She wanted to apologize for kissing him. She wanted to ask to kiss him again, which was a wildly new feeling she still couldn't wrap her head around. She wanted to throw her arms around his neck and just hug her body to his, but it felt like there was a valley between them.

"I should . . . I should probably get back to the judges' table," Amanda finally said. She placed a hand against his chest and tried not to let it linger, but she failed almost immediately.

Shit, she really had to stop touching him.

Dominic placed his hand over hers, holding her palm against him. "Okay."

They stood like that for a moment, not moving. Amanda could feel her ribs expanding with every breath she took, and it felt like she'd forgotten how to exhale. She was going to float away on this cloud until he finally dropped his hand and let her go.

She swallowed hard at the break. "I, uh…, I hope *Jack-O'-Lantern* does well."

"Thanks," he replied. He stepped back, closer to the boat. "I'll see you around."

Amanda wanted to ask him to stay, but she didn't dare. She just nodded instead and gave a half-hearted smile that she didn't mean at all. "Good luck, Dominic."

Chapter Sixteen

Dominic

The fact that *Balls Deep*, the golf-themed pontoon boat, won the Boat Parade was beyond ridiculous, but Dominic was trying to be understanding that he was new to this town and didn't understand the dynamics of Heart Lake yet. Clearly, people loved their golf games and sexual innuendos here. Though he hadn't once seen a golf course when driving through town, so he couldn't exactly make sense of that.

"You'll get it next year," Dominic said to Jack, giving him a reassuring pat on the back. "This was the spookiest, most suspenseful boat I've ever seen. Hell, you should sell tickets to come on board around Halloween time. You'd make a fortune."

Jack laughed and shook his head. "That sounds like a young man's game, but if you're volunteering to run it, I'll be happy to collect the profits."

"I didn't say that," he countered with a laugh, even though he wasn't entirely opposed to the idea. "But we can talk about it."

If he was still here around Halloween. That was the part he didn't say out loud, but his interview was coming up fast, and every conversation he'd had with Eric about it made it all feel more and more promising and probable.

"I'll see you Monday?" Jack asked as he dropped his jacket over his shoulders and pulled his car keys out of his pocket. He fumbled with them, and his hands shook as he shuffled through the ring to find the car key.

Dominic wasn't sure he should still be driving, but he didn't say anything. "Yeah, I'll see you at eight."

"Good man," Jack said, giving him that fatherly nod of approval he remembered from his grandfather many years ago. "You're not going to regret it."

That part Dominic wasn't so sure about. Taking on a temporary part-time job in retail and sales at a hardware store three days a week so that Jack could take some time off seemed like an easy thing to commit to. Now that they weren't working on the dock together anymore, he wanted to be able to keep Jack in his life still. Helping at the store seemed like a way to do that. That didn't mean he knew a damn thing about tools or hardware to help any customers who came in, but Jack assured him that everyone in town already knew more than him anyway, and it would be fine.

"You guys should have won." A man that Dominic didn't recognize walked up to him just as Jack was stepping off the dock and heading to the parking lot. "Your boat is absolutely sick. That goblin looks realistic as hell."

"Thanks, man," Dominic replied, feeling a bit proud because the silicone goblin attached to the ship's wheel—posed like it was the captain—had been his idea, and he'd painstakingly hand painted it with fake blood and a semisevered head. "We were ahead of our time."

The man laughed. "Yeah, by like three months. Come October, this is going to be the place to be."

"I was just telling the owner that," Dominic agreed. He put his hand out toward the man. "I'm Dominic Gage."

"Oh! The baseball player, right?" The man looked surprised but took his hand and gave it a shake. "I heard you'd moved to somewhere around here. Didn't think I'd run into you so soon. Big fan, man."

"Thanks." Dominic shook his hand. "And you are?"

"Blake," the man replied. "I was on *Nola Nation*. I work for Tanner at his business, but I told him also that *Jack-O'-Lantern* was much better than his football stadium."

This was Blake? Dominic tried to keep his expression still, not wanting to give off the impression that he had already heard of him.

"I actually used to help run this event," Blake continued, and Dominic felt his entire body freezing as he tried to keep his opinions to himself. "Founded it, really. Once I got it up off the ground and running, I decided to let other people take it over. I'd already done all the hard work, you know? All they have to do is maintain it now."

They. Dominic knew he was referring to Amanda despite the fact that he was fronting like he knew shit about what was going on in the parade.

"I'd imagine maintaining an event this big would still require a lot of work," he found himself saying defensively in reply. "Hell, maybe even more than that if they are down a man, now."

Blake gave him a weird look, his brows slightly furrowed. "I mean, yeah. I guess."

Dominic pressed a hand firmly against Blake's upper arm. "I gotta go, man. It was great to meet you, though."

The hell it was.

"You, too," Blake agreed, smiling widely like he'd just been patted on the head and given a gold star.

Dominic walked away from him with no other words. He had one thing on his mind—find Amanda. And try not to punch Blake in the face.

Amanda wasn't hard to pin down after a quick lap around the harbor, though. She was standing at the judges' table being yelled at by the owner of the boat with the flower theme. Dominic assumed it must have been owned by a local florist, but from what he heard walking up to them, the owner was thoroughly upset that her begonias hadn't been properly recognized in the parade.

"Ma'am, I'm so sorry. I'd love to buy a whole bouquet from you. I mean, they're beautiful," Amanda was saying as he came to a stop by her side. "You do incredible work. We absolutely value Pansies and Peonies and their contribution to not only this parade, but to all of Heart Lake. There's nowhere else I would go for flowers. You and your team are it."

The woman who'd been upset seemed to stand taller at that and wiggled her shoulders with the tiniest bit of pride. "Well, of course. We are *the* venue for flowers for every Heart Lake wedding. Every Heart Lake event, actually."

Dominic stepped a bit closer and put on his most charming voice. "Wait, are you the owner of Pansies and Peonies?"

She preened at the recognition, seemingly forgetting her complaints for Amanda at that moment. "I am. And you are?"

"I'm looking for a florist for my upcoming party," Dominic continued, completely making that up out of nowhere. "I've heard nothing but incredible things about your store. I would love to talk to you on Monday about a quote for my event."

The woman produced a business card out of her pocket immediately. "We'd love to talk with you and help with any events you're having."

"Thanks," he replied. "I actually heard about you first through Amanda here. She was telling me that she hoped your boat would win—the floral display was incredible."

"It *was*, wasn't it?" the woman agreed. She finally offered Amanda a smile. "I knew you'd understand that. Thanks for recognizing, even if the vote went to the golf boat."

"Can you believe it?" Dominic feigned his most shocked tone. "*Balls Deep*? What a ploy to use a salacious name for vote grabbing."

He didn't actually believe that. It was a fucking great name, even if he still didn't think it deserved to win, but he wasn't about to say that out loud while this woman was just beginning to defuse.

She threw up her hands and gave them both an exasperated look. "Right? What an absolute con. No one even got to recognize my begonias."

"Despicable," Dominic agreed as she finally felt validated enough to walk away and leave him and Amanda alone.

Amanda waited until the florist was at least out of hearing distance. "Thanks for that," she whispered. "I felt like a deer in the headlights."

"I could tell," he teased. "Not that you weren't handling that beautifully."

"I mean, I can hold my own," Amanda said with a wry smile. "But I don't know how the golf boat won, either. Who even plays golf?"

Dominic shrugged. "I've got plenty of free time now. I guess I could get started."

"Don't you dare," Amanda joked, pointing her index finger at him. "You're going to be pretty busy with the event you're throwing."

"What event?" he replied, taking a moment to remember the fake event he'd just told the florist about. "Oh, ha. That was made up."

"I know," Amanda said with a smile. "But people in Heart Lake don't forget. You have to throw an event now. You promised her."

He blinked slowly. "Wait, are you serious?"

"Yes!" Amanda laughed and shook her head. "Mrs. Goldfarb does not play. You told her you had an event for Pansies and Peonies. She's going to follow up on that."

"Shit. Well, what kind of event would I even throw?"

Dominic wasn't entirely opposed to the idea, but it's not like he had any plans coming up that seemed florist worthy. "I mean . . . my birthday *is* later this month."

He wasn't exactly the type of person to celebrate birthdays, but it was all he could think up on the spot.

"Your birthday?" Amanda's entire face lit up and she bounced up onto the tips of her toes. "Oh my gosh, we have to celebrate. We do birthdays big here."

Dominic rubbed a hand across the back of his neck. "I don't know . . . I'm turning thirty-nine. It's my last year in my thirties, and I'm also retired. It feels like the end of an era."

"All the more reason to celebrate!" Amanda said.

"Is it, though?" he countered with a sarcastic lilt to his tone. "Or is it just sad?"

Amanda looked downright offended at that. "It is definitely *not* sad. It's incredible. We can do a combined thing—half birthday party, half retirement party. Oh, and half housewarming party!"

He grinned. "That math doesn't math."

But Amanda wasn't listening, already planning out the entire thing in her mind. "Actually, Marvel would absolutely love this. We could put her in charge of catering, and Mrs. Goldfarb could do a baseball bouquet— shape the flowers to look like a baseball. We could invite your whole family and your team, plus everyone in town for you to meet. It could be like your Heart Lake coming out party!"

"Do I need a coming out party, though?" he countered. "Thirty-nine isn't a milestone year. That sounds like more something for when I turn forty."

Amanda waved her hand. "We can do it all again next year."

"Uh…" He wasn't about to say that the first thought on his mind was that he wasn't sure he'd still be here next year. "This sounds like a lot of parties."

"Actually, speaking of events…I have a proposal for you?" Amanda phrased it like a question, but it seemed more like a statement.

He really needed to work on saying no more at some point, but he wasn't sure he'd ever be able to say no to Amanda. He lifted one brow as he looked at her. "What's the proposal?"

"Evan needs an assistant coach for Zander's baseball team. It's Little League, which I know is not exactly in your stratus…"

"Little League is very important," Dominic countered, putting his index finger up like he was about to give a lecture. "That's where I first developed my passion. Little League introduced me to teamwork and support and…family, really. It teaches discipline and sportsmanship. It can be a very foundational developmental path for a lot of young kids."

"Really?" Amanda looked surprised, though he wasn't sure why. "Sounds like it was formative for you. I never heard you describe baseball as family before."

He shrugged, suddenly feeling slightly bashful. "I mean, the guys on the team were really there for me after my injury. They still check in on me even though I'm not part of the team anymore. Honestly, it's…it's like an extended family that I know I can call up anytime. Coming from a smaller immediate family like I did, that really meant a lot to me growing up and in adulthood. Sports became a surrogate for the family I didn't have."

"I've actually heard Evan talk that way about some of the kids on the team," Amanda admitted. "Not all of them, but there are a few who come from homes where they don't necessarily get the attention they need. Evan describes coaching as like being a surrogate father to an entire group of kids every Saturday morning."

Dominic nodded. "Yeah, I can see that. Good on him for being involved in that. I would be happy to help out a bit."

For some reason, she looked surprised. "You'd coach Little League?"

"I mean, yeah? Why not?" He shrugged like it wasn't a big deal. Because it wasn't. But why was he feeling so challenged right now? It was like he felt the need to defend himself against a claim that she hadn't even made. Something about her tone had brought out a defensiveness in him he hadn't known was there. "I like kids."

"Oh. I mean, of course." Amanda began to back-pedal what she was saying. "I didn't mean that you don't like kids. I just mean it's a big commitment. It can be kind of long. A whole season at minimum, but most coaches stay on and keep going. I wasn't sure if that was something you'd be interested in, being so new here and all that."

"I could, well, I'm sure I could..." he stuttered out the words at the same time as his brain was digesting the scope of what she was saying. That he wasn't even sure he would be here long-term if the interview went well next week. And he'd just spoken this big game, like of course he'd coach Little League, and backing out now would probably seem like he'd been full of shit from the beginning. "Well, like anything, I'd have to look at the contract and stipulations. I'd need to check the hours against my schedule and stuff."

Jesus, even he didn't believe himself right now.

"Oh, of course." Amanda nodded like they were suddenly having an uber serious business conversation. "I'll have Rosie and Evan send you the contract. It's probably written on scratch paper in the back of a high school kid's notebook, so as long as you're fine with that."

He grinned and tried to stifle his laugh—unsuccessfully. "Give Evan my number. I'd be happy to help, at least temporarily. Maybe I can fill in until he finds someone with a longer commitment."

Amanda's face fell at that response, but she wiped it away so quickly that he almost missed it. She turned around and grabbed a stack of papers off the judges' table and acted like she was straightening it out. "Yeah. I'll do that."

"Great," he said. "I'll…I'll look for his call. It should be fun."

"Well, I have a lot of stuff I have to do to close up the parade," Amanda said, now on her second stack of papers that supposedly needed straightening. "I'll see you later."

He wanted to tell her that he wasn't done talking, that they hadn't even discussed what happened between them the other night when they had kissed. When she had said it had been amazing and then pulled away like it had never happened in the first place. He wanted to ask her more about her date today and if she was going on any more dates with that guy or anyone else. He wanted to ask her to come over to his house tonight and let him cook her dinner and have a glass of wine together on the couch and just talk until it was tomorrow.

But none of that came out of his mouth.

Instead, he nodded and shoved his hands in the pockets of his jeans. "All right. I'll see you."

She didn't even look at him when he walked away, and he felt like he'd just experienced emotional whiplash, which seemed to be becoming a pattern with her.

Chapter Seventeen

Amanda

I'm completely screwing everything up," Amanda said as she sat down on one of the open couches in Rosie's bookstore and café, Fact or Fiction.

Marvel was seated in an armchair next to the couch with an open book in her lap titled *Yoga for Witches*. "Aren't we all?"

"I'm not," Rosie countered, plopping down on the couch next to Amanda and crossing one knee over the other. "I'm killing it at life in every way possible. What are you two talking about?"

Amanda laughed lightly at Rosie's sarcasm, leaning farther back into the couch and letting out a sigh.

"Lies." Marvel shrugged her shoulders and turned to the next page in her book. "If I wasn't screwing something up, life would be pretty boring."

"I'd like my life to be a little more boring," Amanda admitted. "Clayton gets back into town tomorrow, and I have to tell him about the project I've been doing on the side for Mrs. Crawford. In fact, I think I might quit entirely. Oh, and I kissed Dominic, and I don't know why. And then I told him I'd basically plan his birthday party."

Marvel just let out a laugh, but Rosie looked like her eyes were going to pop out of her head.

"Well, damn," Marvel said as her laughter died down to a chuckle. "You weren't lying, were you?"

"Amanda!" Rosie finally said. "I...I don't even know where to begin with all of that."

"I'd say we begin at the kiss," Marvel replied. "How was it? Does he have soft lips? I bet the scruff on his face tickles, doesn't it?"

Amanda grinned at Marvel, and she could feel her cheeks heating at the memory. "I'm not a touchy-feely type, but it was...it was actually really nice. It felt... serene. If that makes any sense. Like there was something homey and peaceful about being joined together like that. I haven't felt that way with another person before."

Marvel hummed lightly and nodded her head like she understood completely. "Just like his grandaddy."

"Oh, good Lord," Rosie said with a groan. "That's a mental image I do not need, Marvel. Amanda, I thought you said you didn't want anything with Dominic."

"I don't," she replied, putting her hands up defensively. Her tone was clearly too high-pitched to be truthful, so she lowered it an octave. "I think. I mean, I don't know. It just felt really nice. I told you and Nola at dinner a while back that I've been feeling lonely. It feels isolated to be the only single one, to not have a family of my own. Kissing Dominic...it felt like having someone. He felt like family."

"You really shouldn't make out with family," Marvel added, licking the tips of her fingers before turning the page in her book again.

"Wise advice." Rosie turned back to Amanda. "And you're planning his birthday party?"

She nodded. "It's in a few weeks. I figured we could do it in our combined backyards on the water and invite his former team members and friends and family. Well, his mom is his only family right now. And his ex-wife."

"You're going to invite his ex-wife?" Rosie's voice had not returned to a normal tone once yet in this conversation. "Oh, I have to come to this. Please, please let me watch this all go down. I need to be at this party."

"First, I have to quit my job, or Clayton is going to fire me."

"Maybe we should invite Clayton and Adam to the birthday party, too," Rosie teased. "Bring Mrs. Crawford and her husband, too. Let's make it a whole town affair."

"You're enjoying this way too much," Amanda replied, but couldn't help letting out a laugh.

Rosie leaned back against the couch and let her body relax a bit. "I'm actually so happy about all of this. You're finally quitting a job that's just been holding you back. You've found a guy that you feel at home with. You're going to get out there and do things for you. This is literally all I've wanted for you since we met."

Amanda put her hand on her chest. "Aw. Rosie, that's really sweet. I mean, it sounds wonderful when you phrase it that way, but it's honestly just not that simple."

"Why can't it be?" Rosie asked. "I mean, yeah, Clayton might be mad. But he's a businessman first and foremost, and he's not going to want to burn bridges with you. He knows your talent level, and you'd be an asset to have in his network. He will see that eventually. I don't know how he wouldn't. I've also never gotten the vibe that he's that cutthroat like you say he is. I mean, I'm sure you know him better than me, but at last year's Christmas party, he and Adam really seemed to adore you."

"That's very true," Marvel added in. "He and his husband are like little chihuahuas in fancy sweaters—lots of bark, very little bite, and will definitely hump your leg. That boy definitely has a good business head on his shoulders, too. He might talk shit about you privately behind your back for a little while if he's hurt, but he knows better than to turn a feud public."

"I don't want a feud at all!" Amanda countered. "I want to just be on my own and do my own work. And I want him to let me out of my noncompete."

Marvel waved her hand. "Those things are barely enforceable. And if he did try to enforce it, everyone in town would think he's an asshole. Believe me, he won't."

Amanda knew that Marvel was probably right, and Rosie was firmly nodding her head in agreement. But it was still a scary step to consider. She wasn't one to naturally love conflict, and at the very least, there was going to be some initial conflict when she told Clayton. She wanted to be able to give him the benefit of the doubt like Rosie and Marvel were, but she couldn't imagine anyone would be happy hearing that they'd lost their biggest client and an employee at the same time.

"Things aren't that simple with Dominic, either,"

she added. "I'm not sure there's anything there for the two of us going forward."

"Why not?" Rosie asked. "You like him. You kissed him. He definitely likes you. Sounds like he kissed you back, too."

"Absolutely," Marvel agreed. "Everyone can see that he looks at you like a lovesick puppy. It's kind of sad, actually."

"Marvel!" Rosie scolded. "It's not. It's cute."

"Not if Amanda's going to rip his heart out," Marvel countered. "You saw what she did to Blake."

"Blake is an asshole," Rosie countered.

Marvel nodded her head. "We really need to start recruiting better men to this town. I'll bring that up at the next meeting of the welcoming committee."

Amanda waved her hands between the two of them. "It's not that. It's...I don't think he wants any sort of commitment, and if he did, it isn't going to be with me. He just got divorced from one of the most gorgeous women I've ever seen in a magazine, and he's a famous athlete. Those types of people have needs and interests that I'm just not equipped for."

"Needs and interests?" Marvel scrunched up her face. "You make it sound like a business transaction."

"Seriously," Rosie agreed. "Have you asked him what his needs are? And what kind of needs are we even talking about?"

"I think she's talking about sex," Marvel answered for her.

Now Amanda was sure her face was probably bright red. "I mean, that's *one* of them. But he's also newly out of a very serious commitment—they were married for basically forever. He doesn't know what he wants to do next, either. There's a lot that would make jumping into a relationship feel impossible right now—for both of us."

She also was concerned about how his future medical and vision journey might impact him and anyone he chose to be with, but that wasn't information she was going to share with anyone without his permission. Not that she cared at all about being with someone with no or little vision—she had no problem with it—but she could tell it was a deeply emotional and vulnerable topic for him, and she didn't know how to talk to him about it. Or if he wanted to talk about it at all.

"Well, maybe you should ask him about that before deciding it for the both of you," Rosie countered. "You don't even know how he's feeling yet."

She knew that was true. He'd tried to broach the topic with her at the Boat Parade, but she'd shut it down fast. She just hadn't been ready to figure any of that out, and she wasn't sure that she'd ever be ready. But she might just have to bite the bullet and have the conversation.

"But, uh…" Rosie added, suddenly sitting up on the couch. "Looks like you might need to have another conversation before the one with Dominic."

Amanda followed Rosie's gaze to the front door of the bookstore to see Clayton walking in with Mrs. Crawford. She gasped, her stomach dropping hard. "Shit."

They didn't seem to see her at first and were actively

chatting and laughing together as they headed into the café half of the store and went up to the counter to place a food order.

"Gotta go," Rosie said, hopping up and heading behind the counter to take their orders.

Amanda wanted to be absorbed into the couch, but there was nowhere to hide.

Clayton turned around just then, and his eyes fell on Amanda, his face lighting up with a huge smile. "Amanda! Look who I'm having lunch with."

Mrs. Crawford turned to look her way as well. "Amanda, darling! You have to come join us."

Amanda stood slowly, and walked over to them like there were bricks in her shoes. "Heeeeey, guys. How are things? Clayton, I thought you were out of town until tomorrow."

"I was, but Mrs. Crawford called me up for a meeting, and I can't say no to my favorite client," Clayton said, placing a hand against Mrs. Crawford's back affectionately.

A knot began to form in her stomach. "Oh, awesome. That's great."

It was absolutely not great at all. She didn't know why Mrs. Crawford had called this meeting, but she had very clearly told her that she didn't want her intervening with Clayton for her. She hoped to God that that wasn't what was about to happen.

Mrs. Crawford finished placing an order, and Amanda heard her add an extra sandwich for her before turning back to look at them both. "I actually think it's kismet you're here. Let's all three sit down, because I wanted to discuss projects going forward."

Shit. Shit. Shit.

Clayton ushered them toward a small round café table with three chairs, and they all took a seat as Rosie worked on prepping their food and drinks behind the counter.

"So, Clayton," Mrs. Crawford began, "I want to have Amanda take on a more senior role in my design projects going forward, and I've told her that I really think she should be out on her own. She has such an incredible eye—very different than yours, which is also incredible—and it doesn't make sense to me to keep that hidden away."

"Hidden away?" Clayton put a hand on his chest and looked over at Amanda with a confused furrow in his brow. "I would never want to hide away talent. Amanda is such a valuable part of our firm. Her design eye is incredible. In fact, that's why I have her look over all your designs, specifically. I only want you to have the best."

Uh, what? Amanda had not once gotten that type of open compliment from Clayton. She tried to wipe any look of shock from her face, but frankly, she wasn't sure she'd heard him right.

"I love to hear that," Mrs. Crawford continued. "So I'd like Amanda to take over my home projects on her own, outside of your firm. My husband wants to keep using your firm for business-related design needs— your style is perfect for the vision he has for his company. But, for my personal needs going forward, in both our house in Heart Lake and our vacation homes, I'd like to use Amanda exclusively."

"Use Amanda in my firm?" Clayton asked. "Like as the lead designer on your jobs?"

"No," Mrs. Crawford replied, and Amanda considered what it would be like to just stand up right then and there and run out of the store as fast as she could. "I think Amanda needs to be on her own. It seems to be what she wants. Right, Amanda?"

"It's, uh, it's . . ." Amanda cleared her throat, looking anywhere but directly at Clayton. "I had been mentioning to Mrs. Crawford that I did want to be in business for myself one day."

"Oh." Clayton looked surprised but then wiped that expression from his face and nodded slowly. "That makes complete sense. You certainly have the talent to do that. I hadn't known that was something you were considering so soon."

Rosie arrived right then, carrying three plates of premade sandwiches in one hand. She doled them out to each person at the table carefully. "I'll be right back with your drinks."

Amanda cast Rosie a rescue-me look, but Rosie just gave her an apologetic frown and skittered away.

"I'm guessing that Amanda's contract with you has a noncompete," Mrs. Crawford continued. "So I'm hoping you'll be able to waive that, since I don't want to deal with any red tape around transferring my business to her going forward."

Clayton waved his hand like it was no big deal at all, but now he was the one avoiding looking at Amanda directly. She could feel the pit in her stomach only getting bigger.

"Absolutely," he agreed. "Consider it gone. I want this to be a seamless transition for you, Amal. You and your husband have been some of my best clients over the years, and I'd definitely want to keep that relationship strong."

"Wonderful." Mrs. Crawford beamed as she picked up her sandwich and took a bite. "I think this could be the start of something amazing for both of you. I know it's none of my business, and I'm just clodhopping my way in here with my big feet telling you what to do, but I just care about you both so much. I had to say something."

"Of course," Clayton agreed, taking a bite of his sandwich now. "You've always been a loving friend. I'm glad Amanda has someone like you vouching for her."

"Yes. Thank you, Amal." Amanda gingerly grabbed at her sandwich and shoved it in her mouth so she didn't say that this was exactly the opposite of what she'd asked from Mrs. Crawford. She was both horrified and pissed off and literally couldn't think of what to say next.

So sandwich it was.

Clayton put his sandwich back down and turned to look at Amanda finally. "I'll make sure to send over some exit paperwork, and I can send you the previous measurements and designs for Mrs. Crawford's houses. If you need any help, I'd be happy to step in anytime with advice or whatever you need."

"Thank you," Amanda could hear her voice responding, but felt like she was not even inside her body right now.

Clayton put his hand on her upper arm and gave her a deep look. Something about his expression felt genuine but also deeply pained. "I want you to feel fully supported going out on your own, Amanda. Running your own business is very hard, and I know I would have appreciated having a mentor in my first year doing that. I want to make sure you have that through me and my firm as you're getting your feet wet out there."

"Oh, wow," Amanda said, swallowing the bite of sandwich that she was sure she'd choke on. "That's... that's really kind, Clayton."

He removed his hand from her arm and gave her a wide smile that didn't fully reach his eyes. Instead, his eyes just seemed sad. "Of course. We have to stick together in this industry, you know? It's always better to be out in the open and not go behind each other's backs."

Shit. She knew exactly what he was insinuating with that. She'd literally gone behind his back.

"Yes," she tried to find words to respond. "That's never ideal."

"No, it really isn't," he replied, his gaze firmly on hers. Finally, he turned back to look at Mrs. Crawford, who was already almost done with her sandwich. "We're going to help make this seamless for you, Mrs. Crawford. And I'm honored you brought this to me to talk about. It's really so inspiring how you invest in small businesses and people. You really see the diamonds in the rough and want to help them shine."

The older woman preened at the compliment. "I do do that, don't I?" she agreed. "It's really my mission in life. I love finding talent and helping foster it—kind of like how I did with you."

Rosie dropped off their coffees but then ran away from the table just as fast.

Mrs. Crawford picked up her paper cup after finishing the last bite of her sandwich. "I hate to dine and dash, but I have a facial at one. You two finish up, and I'll be in touch on Monday with you both."

Amanda wanted to beg her to stay and not leave her alone with Clayton, but instead she nodded and smiled and wished her the best of luck at her facial. Mrs. Crawford departed in a flurry of overpriced scarves and a designer handbag, and then Amanda was left seated alone next to Clayton.

A quiet moment passed between them before she decided to try to break the ice.

"Clayton, I..." She wasn't even sure how to finish that sentence, or of what she wanted to say. This entire exchange had been the absolute last way she'd seen this admission going. "I am so sorry that this is how you found out. I asked her to let me be the one to talk to you. And I was going to tell you tomorrow."

"You were going to tell me tomorrow that you poached my largest client and you're breaking your contract with me?" Clayton asked, his tone leveled and quiet. He wrapped up his partially eaten sandwich like he wasn't able to finish it. "Well, no need to worry about that. I think I got the gist after this lunch."

Amanda swallowed, because this was worse than if he'd just started yelling at her. He wasn't even mad. He was hurt. "You were out of town when she needed something done, and I was just trying to help. I didn't know it was going to go this direction when I stepped in, but she approached me with the idea, and it's just... I mean, how can I turn it down?"

"You can't," he agreed. "It's an amazing opportunity, Amanda. And she's not wrong. You're going to be great at it."

She sat there quietly for a few moments. "Clayton, I'm really sorry."

"Don't be, Amanda," he said, dabbing at the corners of his mouth with a napkin. "You deserve this opportunity, and I'm just sorry you felt like I was holding you back. I wish we could have talked about that more openly and figured out ways to help you feel more empowered at our firm. I guess I was under the impression that we were closer than that—friends, you know? But I'm sorry that clearly wasn't how you felt. Either way, I meant what I said—I'm happy to help support you as you build up your own business. Just let me know what you need."

She felt like the world's biggest asshole. Christ, she literally was the biggest asshole on the planet right now. "Thank you, Clayton. I'll, uh, I'll let you know."

"In the meantime, I'll send over the exit paperwork via email, and you can clear out your desk this week," Clayton said, placing the used napkin down on his plate next to the wrapped sandwich and pushing his chair back. He stood and offered her a weak smile. "I'll see you around, Amanda."

"You, too," she replied, though there was a tremor in her voice she was trying to get control over. "And again, Clayton...I'm really sorry."

He just lightly shrugged, not responding verbally, and then headed for the bookstore exit after dropping his plate into the trash can.

When he was gone, Rosie reappeared and slid into

the chair that Mrs. Crawford had been sitting in. "That was the most uncomfortable experience of my life."

"Of *your* life?" Amanda balked. "You weren't the one sitting at this table."

"I knew he'd be professional and cordial about the whole thing," Rosie continued, propping her elbow on the table surface and resting her chin in her hand. "But I hadn't expected how sad he'd be. I swear to God, I thought he was going to start crying."

Amanda could feel the lump forming in her own throat. "I mean, I *did* poach his biggest client."

Rosie shook her head. "That doesn't seem to be what he was sad about. He seemed sad about losing you. I told you that he and Adam like you. I think you really hurt his feelings, Amanda."

She looked toward the café exit, even though Clayton was long gone. She couldn't help but wonder if Rosie was right, and she'd misread the situation with Clayton entirely. She'd just been going on and on about how lonely she'd been feeling lately, but when push came to shove, she also had to admit that she didn't naturally allow people in. Maybe Clayton had actually thought of her as more than just an employee. Maybe he'd thought of her as a friend.

Shoot. She should have just talked to her boss. It would have cleared up so much. There had been nothing to be afraid of in opening up.

And maybe she shouldn't make the same mistake with Dominic by not letting him in, either.

Chapter Eighteen

Dominic

The front door of his house was cracked open when Dominic walked up the steps of his porch after getting home from his first shift at the hardware store. It had been a slow day—only two customers, both of whom knew what they wanted and needed nothing from him except to cash them out. He slowed as he approached and cautiously pushed open the door a little wider.

"Hello?" he called out into the foyer, though he didn't see anyone yet. He did, however, smell something burning and immediately felt himself bristling with alarm.

"Oh, crap," someone muttered from the back of the house. Finally, they called out. "I'm not ready yet!"

"Ready for what? To rob me?" Dominic called back as he walked farther into the house, searching around for what the burning smell might be. "Sorry to disturb your trespassing."

Amanda stepped into the hallway from the kitchen doorway like she was trying to block the kitchen from his view with her body. "Trespassing? The door was unlocked."

"That's still trespassing," he replied. "Were you going to burn the place down, too? What's going on in there?"

She huffed, her expression annoyed as she turned around and headed into the kitchen, motioning for him to follow her. "It's not trespassing if the door is unlocked."

"Literally still the legal definition of trespassing," he said, following her into the kitchen to see two baking trays of burned mounds of . . . something on the kitchen counter. "Seriously, though, is there a fire in here somewhere?"

"That's just the oven," Amanda replied sheepishly. "When's the last time you cleaned it out? I think stuff was spilled in there, and that's why it burned everything."

"It's a brand-new oven delivered last week that I haven't used yet," he replied, walking over to it and opening it up. A billow of dark smoke escaped from the inside, and he grabbed a rag to quickly begin fanning it out. "Go open the porch door. We need to get some air in here."

Amanda followed his instructions and opened the back door as well as two windows, helping fan the smoke out with another hand towel. "I swear, I don't know how this even happened."

They worked together for a few more minutes to clear the air as much as possible before he finally put the rag down and leaned against the counter, examining the trays that he now realized had at one point been cookies before they became bricks.

"What were you even trying to do?" he asked,

chuckling lightly. "And you absolutely owe me new baking trays."

Amanda tried to wedge a spatula under one of the cookie bricks, but it didn't budge. She sighed heavily and shook her head. "I told you when we met that I was not a baker."

"Okay," he replied. "So why are you baking? And why are you baking in my kitchen?"

"I was trying to surprise you with your grandfather's cookies. I got the recipe from Ellen, and I didn't think it would be that hard to follow, but clearly, it was." Amanda gestured toward the burned cookies. "I was just trying to do something nice for you and completely screwed it up instead."

She looked near tears, and he felt a pang in his chest that he'd probably made her feel more guilty with his line of questions.

"Hey," he said softly, reaching a hand out to her and circling his fingers around her wrist. He pulled her a bit closer to him, though not quite against him yet. "You were making my grandfather's cookies?"

She nodded but didn't look up at him. She sniffed slightly as she stared down at her feet. "I'm sorry. I'll get you new baking trays."

"Amanda, I don't care about the trays," he assured her. "That was... that was really nice. I've never had anyone try to do something like that for me before."

Hell, he'd told Melinda about his grandfather's recipe dozens of times, but she'd never taken initiative to make them. He'd made them for her a few times, but he'd never been able to get them quite right, either.

To be fair, when he'd made them, they had at least been edible.

"My grandfather would joke that this recipe was the only thing my grandmother ever let him come into the kitchen for," he continued. "And I don't even remember the last time I made them. It means a lot to me that you'd try and do something like this."

"Really?" Amanda looked up at him now, and the bottom rim of her lashes had the hint of tears beginning to form. She quickly batted them away and cleared her throat. "I wanted to do something special. I wanted to show you that I'm listening to who you are and what you want."

He lifted her hand slightly, this time interweaving his fingers with hers. "And what is it that I want?"

Amanda leaned one hip against the kitchen counter, moving her body ever closer to his. God, he couldn't help but notice how beautiful she looked right now in the skinny jeans and white T-shirt that she was wearing— even if she was covered in what looked like smeared chocolate chips and flour.

"Well, I'm hoping," she began to reply, but her voice trailed off slightly. She paused and glanced up at him. "I'm hoping that it's me."

Dominic had not been expecting that response, and he opened his mouth to say something, but nothing came out. He squeezed her hand tighter in his, letting his thumb rub gently against the back of her hand.

"Dominic, I know you wanted to talk about the kiss the other day, and I wasn't receptive. But you're right. We *need* to talk about the kiss," Amanda continued. "And I really want to now."

"Okay." He nodded his head. "Let's talk about it, then."

She had a deer-in-the-headlights look to her, as if she hadn't planned the conversation out beyond what she'd already said. She stood straighter. "I made a promise to Nola and Rosie that I'd go on at least four dates this summer—and I did. None of them were for me, and honestly some were just awful. But I did it. I put myself out there, and I tried to see if that was something I could do."

Dominic was following her so far but couldn't picture where she was going with this. "I mean, that's more than I can say for myself. I haven't been out on a first date since before I got married. So that's great that you were able to push yourself that way. I'm proud of you."

He really did mean that, even if he didn't love the idea of her going out on dates at all. At least, not with anyone else.

"I'm beginning to realize that I'm just repeating a pattern I've had for a while," Amanda continued. "I don't think I let people close to me. I keep stuff inside, all to myself, for better or worse. I don't think I believe that they would even want to be close to me if I allowed people to see . . . the real me."

"But the real you is amazing." Dominic frowned. "Amanda, people want to be close to you. I've seen you around your friends and in town. Everyone gravitates to you."

Her eyes stopped on his for a moment, as if debating what he was telling her. "Thank you. That means a lot that you see that. I think I need to see it more often in myself as well. I think I get hung up on the parts of myself that don't measure up to what I think a woman is supposed to be, or how I'm supposed to be—whatever that even means. I'm trying to embrace the idea that maybe I'm lovable the way that I am."

He was baffled that she'd think something like that to begin with. He was determined in that moment that whatever happened between them, he was going to make sure he never left her feeling that way. "You absolutely are. We all are."

"We've spent almost every day together over the last month since you've moved in, and I really consider you a friend. But I'm not sure I've made that clear to you. I'm not sure I've opened up to you about how much getting to know you has meant to me. I don't want to make that mistake with you. I don't want to hold anything back," Amanda continued, this time stepping closer to Dominic and closing the gap between them. She placed her free hand on his forearm and lifted her gaze back up to his face. "And I don't want to just be friends, either. I want to…I want to go out on a date with you, Dominic."

He could feel his heart beating faster in his chest, and he lifted one brow, a small smirk on one corner of his lips. "You're asking me out?"

Amanda dropped her gaze to his chest, biting at the edge of her bottom lip "Are you saying yes?"

Dominic slipped his arm around her waist, pulling her body firmly against his. "I'd love to go on a date with you, Amanda."

"Oh." Again, she sounded surprised, but then she seemed to melt forward into him in a way that felt like she'd belonged there the entire time. "Well, that's that then."

He laughed and shook his head. "That's that?"

"I didn't know if you'd say yes," she admitted, a nervousness in her expression as she let her arms lift until they were wrapped around the back of his neck. "I really hoped you would."

"There was never a doubt," he replied, dipping his head lower until the tip of his nose brushed against the tip of her nose. "I'll warn you, though—I might be a little rusty."

She pushed up on the tips of her toes and pressed her lips against his. It was hesitant and slow, and he didn't push them forward. Instead, he just let her lead the way and explore their kiss in whatever way she felt the safest. He exhaled softly against her, every muscle in his body feeling like the tension was melting away.

It just felt cozy. She felt comfortable in the most peaceful and homey way. Like he wanted to wrap himself around her or wrap her around himself. He wasn't sure which sounded better because both options sounded like luxury.

Finally, she pulled away, and they both just took a moment to breathe, their foreheads pressed together.

"I made a dinner reservation for us tonight at Naan Sense," Amanda admitted quietly. "Not to make an assumption of how you'd answer or anything, but just wanted to be prepared if you did say yes."

"Let's go," he replied. "That sounds perfect."

She stepped away from him and grabbed the trays of cookies, dumping them both into the trash can. She was smiling widely now and damn near skipping around the kitchen as she began cleaning up the mess she'd made. "The reservation is at five, so if we leave in the next hour, we'll make it there with plenty of time to spare."

She looked so happy, and he felt so happy that he didn't want to do anything to ruin this moment. But at the same time, he felt the pull of guilt as he thought about the interview he was going on later this week, and what that might mean. He knew he couldn't wait any longer to tell her, especially not after she'd just been so brave to lay all her cards out there on the table as well.

"Amanda, I want to make sure we're on the same page before we do this," Dominic said, leaning his elbow against the counter as he watched her fuss with one of the sunflowers in the vase she must have brought over.

She paused and her eyes cut to him quickly. "What do you mean?"

He licked his lips, trying to figure out how to word the news. "I really like you."

"I like you, too," she said, the tensions in her shoulders loosening some. "So, it sounds like we're on the same page."

"I mean about going forward," he continued. "I...I have an interview in New Jersey this week."

"What kind of interview?" she asked, her brows furrowed now.

"It's for a sportscaster position—exclusively MLB and baseball. It's kind of the perfect position for someone who is retired from the game. It's a way of still being actively involved in baseball without being a player on the field, and they are willing to accommodate any issues that happen with my sight. It's not guaranteed. There are other people interviewing as well, but my manager seems to think I have a pretty good shot at getting it."

Amanda dropped her hands from the sunflowers and focused on him. She took a deep breath before speaking. "It sounds like an incredible opportunity."

"It is," he admitted. "Selfishly, I do want it. I think you deserve to know that."

She shrugged, like it wasn't a big deal, but he could tell from the way she was avoiding eye contact that she felt more than that about it. "What's selfish about that? You've been pretty clear about missing being part of the game. This sounds like a great way to still be involved in whatever capacity you can be."

"Yeah, but I don't know what it might mean for my length of time in Heart Lake," he continued. "It's why I didn't make a long-term commit to Little League with Evan. I love it here, and I wouldn't have moved here if I'd known this was a possibility. But now it is. And it could be a reality."

Amanda tapped her fingers against the kitchen counter. "Well, we'd miss you here, of course. But you have to follow what you love. If you get this job, you have to take it."

"I know," he agreed, even though it felt like a

betrayal coming out of his mouth. "I think I would take it."

"So, do you still want to go out tonight?" Amanda asked after a quiet, tense moment passed between them.

"Of course, I do," he replied immediately. "But I guess I'm worried that that information might change your mind. And I would understand if it did. Absolutely no hard feelings."

Actually, it would be an incredible amount of painful, hard feelings, but he swallowed that fear.

She kept her eyes on her hand, her fingers still tapping against the counter. Finally, she let out a small sigh and licked her lips, then lifted her eyes to look at him. "I think I'd regret it if I didn't give it a chance. If I didn't give us a chance."

He nodded because he agreed. He wanted them to try, even if he couldn't guarantee where things were going or what any of it might mean. It was still a box he knew he wanted to check. If he took that job and never opened himself up to the possibility of Amanda, he'd think about her forever. "I think I'd like that, too."

"I'm going to go home and get dressed in something a little fancier," Amanda said, this time stepping toward him again and wrapping her arms around his waist in a tight hug. "I'll meet you out front in thirty minutes?"

Dominic agreed, hugging her back and then walking her to his front door.

Despite his best efforts to temper his excitement, he couldn't stop the butterflies from coming to life inside of him as he thought of spending the evening with her, of actually being on a date with her. Until right now, he hadn't considered this as a possibility. He'd hoped— he refused to even admit how much he'd hoped—but he had been sure she was not in the space to even be open to it. And frankly, he still wasn't sure he was, either.

But for Amanda...he was willing to try.

Chapter Nineteen

Amanda

I don't think you're an asshole," Dominic said to her as she relayed the story to him of what had transpired with Clayton and Mrs. Crawford. "It just sounds like a really hard situation. To be frank, Mrs. Crawford seems a little insensitive. I'll never understand how people can play with other people's lives like that just because they have money."

"I get how it might sound like that," Amanda replied, reaching forward to the platter of naan bread between them on the restaurant table. She grabbed a piece and ripped it in half before taking a bite. This was already her third piece, but it was delicious. She waited to swallow before she completed her thought. "But Mrs. Crawford really does have her heart in the right place. I know she was just trying her best to be helpful and make sure everyone gets what they want out of the situation—including herself."

"'Including herself' being the key words," he replied, scooping up the other half of the naan bread she hadn't taken. "You asked her to wait and let you handle it, but she didn't."

"Yeah," Amanda said with a sigh. "It definitely could have happened a lot smoother."

He nodded. "I'm sorry."

"But at least that whole thing brought me here," she continued. "I would never have asked you out if not for that whole experience."

Dominic lifted one brow. "You're going to have to walk me through that one."

"I hadn't expected him to be hurt. I hadn't expected him to care about me in the equation—just about the work I was taking away from him," she explained. "But he was *really* hurt."

"Clayton?" he clarified. "How do you know?"

Amanda swallowed another bite and then took a swig of the glass of red wine in front of her. "I mean, the look on his face in that moment said it all, but his follow-up email with continued offers to help me really made it hit home. I thought he was just saying that to be nice at first, like because Mrs. Crawford was there, and he wanted to save face. But now I think he actually means it."

Dominic frowned. "How long have you two known each other?"

"Maybe eight or nine years? Since right before he met Adam." Amanda had actually been at their wedding a few years after that, but he'd also invited other people at the firm. "I didn't meet him at the firm at first. We actually met when we were both volunteering at the Heart Lake High career fair. He was there talking about his firm and design work, of course."

"Were you, too?" Dominic asked.

She shook her head. "No, I was there with my mom. She works in hotel management and concierge. I was helping her present to the students about the hospitality world. She would float me different small design jobs at her hotel for a while before I found something more full-time with Clayton. Before him, I was doing free-lance here and there with design work after undergrad, but I was mostly working in events."

"Oh, wow. I guess that makes sense, given you doing the Heart Lake Boat Parade and all."

The waiter came and delivered both of their main courses at that moment, so they paused the conversation to take a few bites.

"I'm good at event management," she told him finally. "But it was never my passion. It just paid the bills. Getting the job with Clayton was a big break for me—finally in the field I wanted to work in."

"Sounds like he really took a chance on you," Dominic replied. "But it also sounds like you've been working hard toward this for a long time. You can't give Clayton all the credit for that."

"Maybe," she agreed, but the feeling of guilt was still alive and well inside her. She knew her talent was valid, and her success was based on that, but she also now knew that she had overlooked Clayton and his sup-port in the process. "But enough about my shitty job situation. This is supposed to be a date, not me com-plaining for an hour."

Dominic laughed and waved his hand. "No. Don't apologize. I love hearing about your job and the peo-ple in your life. Outside of you summarizing your dates recently, I don't know as much about you as I would like to."

She hadn't really considered that before, but he wasn't wrong. He had shared with her a lot about himself and his history, and she soaked all that in like a sponge. She loved learning about him, and yet, she hadn't returned the favor as often or nearly as deep. He was a good guy, and he'd probably understand her lack of sex drive and be kind about it, but really…it wasn't exactly a selling point, and she didn't want to see a polite expression on his face as he pulled away.

"Well, what do you want to know?" she asked. "I'll give you a one-night free pass to ask anything you want."

"One night?" he asked, raising one brow again. God, the way his entire face moved with his smile was exhilarating. She'd never met a man who so easily wore his emotions on his face. Plus, it was such a handsome face to look at. "I'm going to need more than one night of questions, Amanda."

She grinned, a warmth spreading across her belly at his words. "Let's start with one, and then we'll see where it goes from there."

"It's going to go to night two, and then to night three, and then maybe even night four," he replied, leaning forward against the table now. He placed his fork down and pressed his elbows down on the tabletop, focusing his gaze on her. "I'm having a good time, Amanda."

"I am, too," she admitted, her voice a little quieter.

"So, first question," he continued. "Why do you love sunflowers so goddamn much?"

She burst out laughing, tilting her head back at the unexpectedness of that question. "Jesus, you really can't get over the sunflowers, can you?"

"You brought them into my house," he reminded her. "It's like a weed spreading from next door and onto my kitchen counter."

"There are few environments that sunflowers can't grow in," she finally explained. "They are a very resilient flower—bad weather, terrible soil, whatever. They can still survive when planted in bad circumstances, and they do it by turning toward the sun. Even if everything around them is falling apart, they still turn toward the sun, and they survive. They thrive."

He was quiet for a moment, then exhaled loudly. "Shit. That's actually really cool. I didn't know that."

"We can have harsh winters here in Michigan," she continued. "But the sunflowers survive, and they come back stronger than ever."

"Sounds symbolic," he replied.

"It is," she agreed. "I like to think of them like a symbol for myself. No matter where I'm planted, or what I've been planted around, I know that I can turn toward the positive and find a way to survive."

He took another bite of his food, surveying her as she did the same.

"I guess that leads me to my second question," he said after swallowing.

She was ready and actually felt some excitement about opening up like this, even if it was just about flowers so far. It was still very meaningful to her. "Shoot."

He kept his eyes on her, and she felt a shiver run down her spine that felt both titillating and unnerving. "What was your worst day?"

The day came to her mind immediately, but it wasn't a story she'd shared with anyone. Her mother knew about it because she'd been there, but that's where it ended. She placed her fork down on the tabletop as well and tried to steady her heartbeat because she could hear the rush of blood in her ears.

"If it's too much to ask, you don't have to answer," Dominic added quietly.

"No, it's not too much to ask." Plus, she'd said she wanted to be more open and vulnerable, and this was the perfect opportunity to prove to herself that she could—and that she wanted to with him. "It's just not a story I've told before. I guess I'm realizing more and more lately how much I hold back from people in my life."

She took a deep breath and then lifted her gaze to look at him. "I was honestly relieved when my parents got divorced. I was about ten at that point, and they'd been fighting since before I could remember. Every day, sniping back and forth or full-blown shouting and screaming matches. I'd learned to tune it out as best I could, but it was jarring and scary and I still think that led to a lot of my anxiety and struggles calming my nervous system to this day."

Dominic grimaced. "That sounds really difficult to be around."

"It was," she agreed. "So like I said, the divorce was a relief. Things were suddenly quieter. My mom was actually happier in her day-to-day life in a way I hadn't seen before. She had all this space and freedom, and she engaged with me in new ways we never had before."

"What do you mean?" he asked.

Amanda loved that he seemed truly interested in her story and was actively engaged. "With my dad out of the house and still helping with child support, she didn't work as much as she had been before. I think she'd worked so much before because she just wanted to be away from him as much as possible, but that also meant she was away from me. After the divorce, there was this brief period of about a year where we actually spent a lot more time together."

That hadn't lasted, though, and she swallowed hard as she thought about it.

"My father found someone new almost immediately," she continued. "My stepmother had kids already, and then she got pregnant, and my dad stopped paying child support. He also stopped showing up for visitation. She tried to take him to court, but I don't really know what happened. All I know is that the money stopped coming in, so she had to go back to working overtime hours again."

"Meaning less time with you," Dominic finished her thought. "Shit. That sucks. I'm so sorry. I can understand why that would be your worst day."

"No, the court date wasn't it," she replied, shaking her head. "It was actually the talent show at school when I was twelve."

He looked surprised as he picked up his fork and took another bite of his food. "The talent show?"

"Yeah, every year the school has a talent show, and any student can sign up to be in it. I hadn't gotten to see my dad very often that year, which, as a kid, I really thought was my fault. I thought maybe I wasn't being who he wanted me to be, or I was boring him, or...I don't even know what my kid brain conjured up back then." Amanda had read multiple self-help books and listened to a few podcasts by psychologists at this point to realize that that was a normal thing for children to think, and that it wasn't her fault. But the feeling still sat deep in her gut. "So I made this plan that I was going to play his favorite song on the guitar for the talent show. He was the one to teach me to play the guitar. He was the absolute best at it, and he always wanted me to learn. I never put a lot of effort into it until then, but I was determined to learn how to play it finally."

"What song?" he asked.

" 'Blackbird.' The Beatles." It was still her favorite song to this day, even though it was kind of a sad song but in a hopeful, gentle sort of way. "It took me two months to learn all the notes, but I can still play it really well."

"That must have meant a lot to your dad," Dominic said.

She shrugged, looking down at her plate and trying to breathe through the lump forming in her throat. "I don't know if it would have or not. He never showed up. I never actually heard from him again."

Dominic's eyes widened. "What?"

"My mother told me that she found out he'd moved with his new family. Somewhere on the West Coast, but she wasn't sure where." She remembered the phone call where she'd told her father about the talent show, and how he'd promised to come. Now, looking back on it, she wasn't sure he'd even been listening. "I got on that stage, and I looked for him in the audience, but he wasn't there. I still played it—came in third place. But I never heard from him again."

"Was your mom there?" he asked after letting a quiet moment pass between them. "Did she hear you play?"

Amanda shook her head. "No. She thought he was going to be there. They didn't ever go to the same things because they couldn't stand to be around each other. So she'd picked up a shift at work."

She almost felt foolish talking about something as benign as a school talent show. She knew full well that there were people out there who'd experienced so much worse, but she was slowly trying to learn to stop comparing her experiences to others. She wanted to believe her feelings were valid, even if that felt like a foreign concept.

"That sounds like a really horrible day," Dominic confirmed. "I'm so sorry. And screw your dad. What an absolute idiot to miss out on getting to know you."

That brought a small smile to her lips. "Thanks. I keep trying to tell myself that. It's also why Rosie and Nola keep pushing for me to go to therapy. I'm pretty sure they think I don't date because I have daddy issues."

"Who doesn't have daddy issues, though?" Dominic joked, and she could tell he was trying to lighten the conversation a bit more. "I know I do. My therapist said it's why I put so much emphasis on baseball and success in sports. Like I was trying to prove my worth to this man who I didn't even know."

"I think it's the opposite for me in some ways," she replied, pondering the idea as she was talking. "It's like I refuse to prove my worth to anyone. I demand independence to an extreme, you know? So much so that I am now in a place where I've forgotten I need anyone at all."

He seemed to understand what she was saying as he nodded and finished the last few bites of food on his plate. Finally, he put his fork down on the empty plate and wiped at his mouth with the napkin. "Thanks for sharing that with me, Amanda. It means a lot to me that you'd trust me with that story."

"Really fun first-date conversation, right?" she teased, stabbing her fork into the last few bites of her own meal.

"I might not be the serial dater that you've been this summer," he teased back. "But I think that was actually perfect. I feel like I got to know you more tonight than I have all summer."

She placed her fork down on the plate when she was done as well, and the waiter swooped by quickly to pick them up, as well as offer dessert. They both declined, and Dominic picked up the check without hesitation, even though she made the play of pretending to reach for her wallet.

When they exited the restaurant, it was already dark outside, and he guided her toward his car. They chatted about lighter topics on the car ride back, and Amanda was grateful for that. She hadn't expected opening up to be so physically exhausting, but she honestly felt like she'd just run a marathon over their ninety-minute appetizer and main course.

Still, she didn't regret it at all. In fact, she felt full in a way she never had before. Satiated with validation and connection.

"I know this is a little forward to ask on a first date," Dominic began as he pulled the car into their shared driveway. "But do you want to come in?"

She absolutely wanted to come in, but she wasn't sure if that's all he was asking. "You mean like...for a drink?"

"Or more," he offered. "No pressure, of course. Whatever you're comfortable with. I just...I like being around you."

There was that flutter in her chest again. "Okay," she agreed. "I'll come in, but only because I haven't seen Tom in a while. She probably misses me."

Dominic laughed as he steered the car toward his house and came to a stop out front. "I'll take what I can get."

She grinned and tried not to think of the fact that he quite literally might have to if this was actually going to become a thing between them.

Chapter Twenty

Dominic

Amanda had been at his house plenty of times before, but as she sat down on his living room couch tonight, things felt abundantly different to Dominic.

There was a hesitancy in her movements that he'd not seen before, but he knew her long-term dating history was minimal and that her most recent dating experiences had been nothing less than shitty. He didn't know much more than that, frankly, but he was sure she'd talk to him more eventually. It had already felt like a huge leap of faith that she'd told him about her father tonight and the origins of her hyperindependence. He'd suspected something was behind how she kept so many people at arm's length, but it was helpful to understand the full picture more now.

And he didn't blame her one bit.

The absence of his father in his life had always been hard for him, but he couldn't imagine what it would have been like to have had him and then have him taken away. In some ways, he wondered if it was easier to never know what he'd lost than it was to have had it—or some version of it—for a short time.

"I only have beer," Dominic informed Amanda as he walked into the living room with two bottles of a pale ale he'd gotten in a six-pack at the farmer's market last weekend. "I thought I still had a bottle of white or red wine somewhere, but I guess not."

"I like beer," she replied, taking one of the bottles as he held it to her. She took a sip out of the top of it and gave a slight grimace. "This is great."

He laughed. "You look like you just drank vinegar."

"It's just an acquired taste," she replied with that smile he'd gotten to see so often tonight. He'd seen her fake smiles a few times over the last month, and those were all teeth and no eyes. Her real smiles, however, were barely on her lips at all. It was in the shine in her eyes and the way she lowered her lashes with this hint of shyness that he never saw in any other area of her life. "I promise I don't hate it."

"Okay, but don't drink it just to appease me," he said as he settled onto the couch next to her.

Tom had already taken up residence between them, and she was rolling around on her back, clearly hoping someone would play with her. Amanda gave in quicker, ruffling her fingers through Tom's hair and teasing her with darting her hand back and forth across the couch cushion.

"I promise I'm not," she said. "I probably won't have a second one, but one is fine. What's that saying? Wine before beer, you're in the clear. Beer before wine, never fine."

Dominic sipped at his beer. "I think I've heard like five different versions of that rhyme, and they all contradict each other."

Amanda raised her bottle in the air. "Well, cheers to the unknown, then."

He raised his bottle as well as let out a laugh. "That sounds so ominous."

"Admittedly, this is my first nonominous date of the summer," Amanda said, taking a larger swig of her beer this time. "It was a pretty low bar, but I will say, you have topped the other ones so far."

"So far?" He lifted a brow as he eyed her over the top of his beer. He wasn't about to let on how thrilled he was to hear that this date was better than her last four, and he tried to remind the alpha male part of him that none of those dates was a threat. "Does that mean I still have time to screw this up?"

"Of course," she teased, but he also heard a seriousness in her tone at the same time. Understandable, given all he knew about her now. "I once read a study that said it takes seven positive things to outweigh one negative in people's impressions."

"How many positives am I at so far?" he asked, now leaning his top half a little closer toward her on the couch.

"Well, there was the dinner conversation—that's one." She held up her hands and began to count it out on her fingers. "You paid for dinner, so that's two."

"I feel like dinner conversation deserves at least three positives," Dominic argued playfully. "Or one positive per topic."

She surveyed him for a moment like she was considering his suggestion carefully, and finally she nodded. "Okay, I'll give you three for that one. But that still only leaves you at four positives."

"Jeez, tough crowd."

Tom jumped off the couch, and suddenly the space between them was left empty.

Dominic glanced down at it at the same time as Amanda, and he could feel the question they weren't speaking. He wanted to move closer to her. He wanted to wrap his arms around her and kiss her and take her to his bedroom. He wanted to show her how much she meant to him in whatever way she wanted for as long as she wanted, but he didn't want to push her limits. She'd already revealed so much about herself tonight and asking for more just felt greedy.

So he didn't move. But she did.

Amanda scooted closer to him on the couch and tossed her legs up over his so that they were laid across his lap.

He placed his hand on her knee and then caressed down the length of her leg until he reached her ankle, then reversed directions and moved back up to her knee.

She leaned back into the couch and sighed, the beer still in her hand but now down at her side. Her eyes fluttered closed for a moment, and he just kept rubbing her legs. The pleasure on her face was undeniable, and he felt such a thrill at being able to give that to her. Sure, he could whisk her off to his room and show her pleasure of a completely different sort, but this alone felt more than enough for right now.

"When is the last time you had a massage?" Dominic finally asked her.

Her eyes opened slowly, lazily, heavy. "A massage?"

"Yeah," he repeated. "A massage."

She stared at him for a moment, like she genuinely wasn't able to pinpoint when. "I guess never, if you are talking professionally. I've never been one to be comfortable with strangers touching me, you know?"

He could understand that to an extent, but massage had been part of his postworkout routine and physical therapy while playing baseball, and he'd always loved it. "I guess that can be a bit weird sometimes, but the payout is more than worth it. We had a massage therapist on staff in the locker room around the clock, and Sergio knew what he was doing."

"Sergio?" She grinned and wiggled her brows. "He sounds like quite the gem."

He refused to be embarrassed. "He was a master at his craft."

"I love how in touch you are with yourself," Amanda commented as she closed her eyes again. "I don't think I've met a man who has the openness you do when it comes to emotions or your body or any of it."

"Blame it on the therapy," he joked, but he knew it was more than just that. "But also, my grandfather. I was blessed with a male role model who honestly had more emotional intelligence than I think I'll ever have. It's almost like it came naturally to him, but I know it didn't."

"What do you mean?" she asked with a small frown.

Dominic shrugged, continuing to rub her legs over her jeans. "I don't know for sure, but the little bits and pieces I've learned about his history were fragmented. He came from the generation that believed children were meant to be seen and not heard, and I think he refused to abide by that."

"Good for him," she commented. "Not that we need more outspoken men in the world."

"Right?" He laughed. "But in his day and age, a son of an immigrant, the first in his family to go to college…I'd imagine it was pretty meaningful for him, as well as difficult."

"I bet," she agreed, her voice falling off a bit into a murmur.

"My point in asking was to see if you wanted me to give you a massage," he tried again. "But I have to admit, I love how even a conversation like that leads to deeper topics between us. I don't think I've ever talked to anyone the way I talk to you."

She opened her eyes to look at him. "I really like our conversations, too."

He smiled. "So where did we land on the massage, then?"

Amanda glanced down at his hands, then back at him. There was clearly some concern around moving forward, and he didn't want to pressure her.

"You know what? Never mind," he said. "Honestly, I didn't mean to put any pressure on you. I just love touching you."

The apples of her cheeks tinged a darker red. "I like touching you, too. But I think we should move slowly. It *is* our first date, after all. Massages always mean something more."

He put his hands up in the air. "I promise I was legitimately only offering a foot massage, maybe some leg and calf muscles, too. Not sex."

She laughed lightly. "All guys say that, though."

"I don't want to be lumped in with all guys," he replied. "I know that's a common thing, but it's shitty. No judgment to anyone who does have sex on a first date—more power to them, you know? But that's not where I'm at right now."

"What does that mean?" she asked, now wiggling her toes into the crux of his elbow. "You actually just want to rub my feet?"

"Of course," he promised her. "My love language is physical touch. I think a lot of people confuse that with sex. Like if that is how you show or receive love, it must mean you're a horndog who needs to get it in all the time. That couldn't be further from the truth. Physical touch means just that...touch. It doesn't have to be sexual. Like right now, your legs across my lap...I feel connected to you."

She smiled at him. "I don't *hate* foot massages."

He placed his hands on her left foot and began massaging the arch softly. "I just want to be connected to you, Amanda."

"Even if that means sex is off the table?" she asked.

He honestly had not expected sex to be on the table tonight. Sure, he'd love to have sex with her at some point, but he wasn't in a rush. He'd had that before. Things with Melinda had always been sex heavy from the start, and that never seemed to fade, no matter what they went through. But it also didn't correlate to much more than that. It hadn't meant emotional connection, and it hadn't meant that they couldn't live without each other.

And right now, he felt like he couldn't picture a

future in which Amanda wasn't part of his evenings, his nights, and his mornings.

"You can try to seduce me as much as you want with those big brown eyes," he teased. "But as much as you might beg me to make love to you tonight, I'm not going to give in."

She laughed, her eyes fluttering closed again as he found a spot on her arch that was very tense, and he gently applied pressure until it released. "I'll try not to feel rejected."

"It's a compliment, if anything," he replied.

They were both quiet for a moment, until she finally sighed and opened her eyes again to look at him.

"Make love, huh?" she said, barely a whisper now.

He felt his rib cage freeze as his heart thundered louder in his chest. "Anything between us would be making love."

"It would be," she agreed. "I actually think it really would be."

She sounded like she was surprised or trying to understand something new. Either way, he wasn't sure, but he found it heartwarming. He wanted to prove to her that romance could be different than the experiences she'd clearly had before that were so negative.

He couldn't promise forever, but he could promise respect and kindness.

She deserved that more than anything, and he hated that she hadn't experienced that before.

Chapter Twenty-One

Amanda

Amanda felt like a glutton for punishment. Dominic had left early that morning to go to New Jersey for his interview, and Amanda couldn't stop checking her phone every few minutes to see if his plane had landed yet. He'd texted her when he got to the airport, when he'd been in his seat, and when the pilot had said everyone had to turn off their cell phones as they were about to take off. She'd wished him luck. She genuinely meant it, too, but the selfish part of her that had spent the last four straight days with him was also whispering in her ear that it wouldn't be the worst thing if he didn't get the job.

She hated that she was even thinking that, but the thought was there, nonetheless.

After their first date at Naan Sense, they hadn't stopped dating. Even though nothing physical had happened that night between them outside of a foot massage, she'd felt a physical intimacy with him that actually felt wonderful. Like there was a middle ground between no touch and full-blown sex that she could genuinely get behind. The way he'd touched her—just rubbing her legs and massaging her feet—had felt like she was being cared for in the best of ways. She almost began to wonder if she might be able to make a romantic relationship work. It wasn't sex, but it was physical touch, and, like Dominic had said, that meant a lot to him. And it didn't have to be sensual.

She felt the tiniest bit of hope blooming in her chest at the possibility that she might be enough without anything more, without sex and all that it entailed.

The following day, they had gone on a hike alone together and had a picnic on the edge of the lake. He'd put together an entire charcuterie tray and a bottle of her favorite wine, and she hadn't had to plan a single thing. The day after that, they'd gone kayaking and then gorged themselves on take-out pasta from the Italian restaurant in the next town. He'd slept over that night—just slept—and they'd woken up this morning and had bagels and coffee delivered. They ate them on her back porch, looking out on the lake and watching Tom run around in the yard, pouncing on different blades of grass and the occasional bug here or there. He wasn't an outdoor cat, but Dominic let him wander around when they were watching, and Tom was already getting used to coming back and forth between their two houses. So much so, in fact, that Amanda had put a pellet litter box in the front closet of her home for Tom.

There wasn't a topic that they hadn't covered at that point, it seemed. They talked about his childhood and what it was like growing up with his mom, and how their relationship had changed, and he'd grown closer with her now that he was an adult. She told him about her childhood also with a single mother, and how her relationship with her mother only seemed more distant with time. He told her about getting married and falling head over heels in love in a way that never seemed to make sense, like he and Melinda were always living a fairy-tale romance that looked perfect in the tabloids and from the outside looking in. But when it was just the two of them, things felt...forced. He actually described it as feeling like Melinda and he were the married version of "friends with benefits." They had had lots of physical chemistry for a time, and they had a strong friendship, but nothing between them was a partnership or based in deeper emotion. He admitted that he might not ever have pulled the plug on the two of them if Melinda hadn't initiated the divorce. It wasn't that he was still in love with her—or maybe he never had been—but rather that he felt a sense of loyalty he wouldn't have walked away from.

Amanda admired that part of him, and also his honesty about how things had transpired across his life. She wanted to open up and tell him about herself, too, and she did to an extent. She spoke about her family and her friends and her life here in Heart Lake. She told him about being lonely and wanting a partner and companion in the future, and how her dating history had been sparse and sporadic over the last fifteen years because she simply hadn't been very interested in getting out there. The part she didn't expand on, however, was why. She just left it at that—it hadn't been a priority for her. And that was true. But she tiptoed around the topic of sex and physical intimacy and that she was genuinely afraid she'd never be enough for a partner when she wasn't naturally interested in a sexual relationship like most women she knew were. After their physical intimacy on their first date night together, she knew that it was something Dominic wanted and that the conversation would have to happen eventually.

Despite that one omission, things felt like they'd gone from fast to hyperdrive overnight between her and Dominic. It was wild how quickly they'd settled into what a life together could look like. She knew she was getting ahead of herself, but it was like they'd been tempting that line for the last month, and now that they'd crossed it...things just were falling into place. She could picture this cadence for the rest of her life, and she couldn't help but hope he was thinking the same thing.

"Are you going to stop being glued to your phone at any point today?" Nola finally asked, refilling her passion fruit mimosa at Amanda's kitchen table.

Rosie glanced in their direction, polishing off her mimosa as well and holding out her glass for Nola to refill. "We've never seen Amanda in a relationship before, and clearly, this is why."

Both of her best friends had come over to keep her company that afternoon, mostly because she'd promised to fill them in on why she'd been missing in action the last few days. They knew she and Dominic were hitting it off and had been dying for the details.

Amanda shot them both a look. "I'm not *in* a relationship."

"Uh, the way you're staring at that phone since Dominic left says otherwise," Nola countered. "Not that I blame you one bit. Tanner never travels for work, and I prefer it that way."

"Evan does occasionally," Rosie volunteered, petting her hand across Tom's back as he was stretched out asleep in her lap. That cat was the biggest snuggle bug she'd ever met. "But the biggest issue with that is that it leaves me with four kids on my own, and that's some bullshit."

Amanda laughed and shook her head. "It's fine that he's traveling. I'm glad he's going. It's a great opportunity, and he needs to see it through."

"Yeah, he definitely does," Rosie agreed, sipping at her mimosa after Nola refilled it. "But have you two talked about what it means if he gets the job?"

She shook her head. "No. It seems too soon for a conversation like that, don't you think? It's just an interview. And he and I are just…I don't even know. He was honest about the interview before anything started. I can't blame him for any of that."

"Yeah," Nola agreed. "I know you two are just starting whatever this is between you guys, and this situation is kind of unavoidable, but the idea of it being time limited right from the start would really freak me out. My anxious attachment style would not allow me to open up to something like that."

Amanda remembered Nola's story with Tanner, and how she hadn't been sure if she'd stay in Heart Lake for quite some time.

"Same," Rosie agreed, then made a protesting sound as Tom jumped off her lap and walked over to a sun spot on the floor and stretched out his back. "I'd have my therapist on speed dial. Is it bad I hope he bombs the interview?"

Amanda tried to stifle her laugh but was unsuccessful. "I have been trying to push away those same thoughts."

"It's really hard," Nola said, sitting back down and picking up her own mimosa as well as a store-bought cookie from the small plate between them. "I can't imagine being in your position. I mean, I moved to be with Tanner, but it's not the same. I had roots here and knew people here. I can't imagine up and moving across the country to a strange new place at this point in my life."

"Wait, Amanda isn't moving. She *can't* move to New Jersey," Rosie said loudly, almost as if she were offended by the suggestion. "She just started the job for Mrs. Crawford. Her career is just taking off, and moving would completely derail that."

"Or moving now would be perfect because she's starting fresh," Nola countered. "She could start fresh there just as well she could here."

"Not with the wealthiest client in Heart Lake, she can't," Rosie argued back.

"There are wealthy clients in New Jersey, too, I'm sure," Nola replied.

Amanda put her hands up. "Guys, guys! Stop! No one is moving. Even if he does get the job, who says we can't make it work long distance? He still owns his house here, and those kinds of jobs aren't nine-to-five. Maybe he would split his time and fly back and forth, and I can, too. People live bicoastal all the time, and this is less than half that distance."

"That's a lot of frequent-flyer miles," Nola mused. "But yeah, you two could possibly make that work."

Rosie was quiet for a moment, staring at her thoughtfully. "You'd really do all that for Dominic? I know you'd do that for us and people you love. I'm not questioning that about you. But I've never seen you do anything remotely close to that for a man."

People you love. The comment struck Amanda deeply. There was absolutely no way she felt anything close to love for Dominic. She'd only known him for a month, and, technically, they'd only been dating for four days. Love would be absolutely ridiculous.

"I wish I knew how to describe to you both what I feel with Dominic," Amanda finally began, trying to make sense of it in her head at the same time. "It's not like what I hear you describe with Evan, Rosie. It's not like you and Tanner, Nola. I'm not sure I'm capable of feeling those things—that heat and passion and all-consuming fire you guys talked about when you first started dating them. It doesn't really exist inside of me—it never has. I think that has made me keep a lot of people at arm's length, because I honestly have spent a lot of time feeling ashamed that that part of me is missing. I see it everywhere—movies, television, books, in all my friends' lives . . . so it just feels isolating that that doesn't exist in me."

Rosie let out a heavy sigh. "Amanda, you don't know that it doesn't yet."

"Yeah," Nola agreed. "Maybe you just haven't met the right guy yet."

"Or maybe I'm just not a very sexual person, and

that's also okay," Amanda countered, because those types of responses were what she hated and why she rarely talked about this side of herself. She knew people would feel sympathy or pity or tell her she just had to hold out for the right situation or person or whatever, but it wasn't that. She knew in her gut that she was built differently than her friends. She was a romantic at heart, but it didn't extend past that.

Her friends traded nervous looks for a moment then returned their gaze to her. It was clear that neither of them knew how to respond, and, frankly, she didn't blame them. None of them had been raised in a world that embraced women as anything other than sexual beings, so the thought that maybe that wasn't a defining characteristic for her was going to be confusing.

But Amanda was finding her way to a place where she refused to be held back by that. She refused to think of it as a defect or something being wrong with her. She just wanted to be embraced for everything she was, as it was.

"Dominic feels like family," Amanda continued. "He feels like a teammate I was always meant to have. I know he's attractive—drop-dead handsome, even. I have eyes. But none of that pulls at me the way his heart does when he's talking to me about his insecurities or his fears for the future or the way he misses his grandfather. I honestly don't think I'd care if he looked like Quasimodo because I'm just so enamored by who he is on the inside, and I don't want to let go of that."

Nola reached a hand forward and placed it on top of Amanda's. "Sex is only one part of relationships—and it doesn't have to be a big part or any part. There are so many marriages out there that are super healthy with tons of sex and super healthy with none at all. The reverse is also true. You know Jessica from Mommy and Me Gymnastics? She brags about having sex with her husband twice a day, but I've never seen two people who hate each other more."

Amanda let out a laugh. "See? That's what I'm saying. I just want to embrace who I am, and whatever that looks like in a relationship. I don't know if that makes Dominic the person for me, or if a person for me even exists. I know it's something I'll need to keep talking to him about, but I'm okay with putting myself out there for now and giving this a try. I think . . . I think it could be something. I think he and I could be something, and after this job situation becomes clearer, I'm going to talk to him about it."

Rosie's phone buzzed on the tabletop with a new notification. She glanced down at it for only half a second but then quickly did a double take and picked it up to read more closely. "Oh my gosh . . ."

"What?" Nola removed her hand from Amanda and turned to Rosie. "What's wrong? What happened?"

Amanda grabbed at her phone, as if she might have the same notification, but her screen was blank.

Rosie lifted her eyes to Amanda, and her face had turned completely pale. "Amanda, I think this might be about Dominic."

"What?" Amanda could feel the air being squeezed from her lungs as she leaned forward and took Rosie's cell phone from her. She turned it to face her and read the recent local news notification that was on the locked screen: Former Detroit Tigers Player Suffers Medical Emergency on Flight, Emergency Landing Initiated in Cleveland, Ohio.

"Oh my God," Amanda gasped, quickly clicking on the notification to read the full article. It pulled up but literally only included maybe one more sentence than the title itself and had no additional information, including a name. "Wait…what? It doesn't say who or what happened. It just says it's an ongoing story. What the hell kind of reporting is this?"

Nola grabbed the phone from her and caught herself up on the sparse storyline. "I mean, there's no way it can be anyone else, though, can it? He got on a plane today, and Cleveland is only ninety miles from Detroit's airport. An emergency landing there would make sense if the medical issue happened right after takeoff."

"And it doesn't say current player. It says former," Rosie added. "What are the odds it could be about someone else?"

Amanda hoped beyond all hopes that it was talking about literally anyone else, but Rosie and Nola were both right. This was most likely about Dominic. "I need to call him."

"Yeah," Rosie agreed, wide-eyed.

Both she and Nola leaned forward as Amanda picked up her cell phone and quickly clicked on Dominic's contact information. His number came up and she hit the call button, holding it up to her ear. It rang six or seven times, but no one answered. Instead, it clicked over to voicemail and Dominic's prerecorded voice came on.

"He's not answering," Amanda said, hanging up the phone without leaving a message. Instead, she typed out a quick text message to him asking him to check in and saying she'd seen a news story that was concerning. "I don't know what to do. Do I keep calling him? Do I call his mom?"

"Maybe the news channel's social media has more news," Rosie said, picking up her cell phone again and tapping away at it like it was her job. "Social media always has the latest information even if the news websites aren't updated yet."

"If theirs doesn't, someone else's might. Maybe someone on the flight is posting about it," Nola offered. "Not that that would be good, either. I mean, I can't imagine my personal medical information or emergency being put out on the World Wide Web like that."

Amanda knew that Dominic would absolutely hate that but that he was also accustomed to the lack of privacy his lifestyle had given him. He'd told her before that the large paycheck wasn't worth the invasion on every part of who he was, and she hated to think that might be happening to him again today, even almost eighteen months out from that life.

"Oh, God." Rosie groaned loudly and turned her phone screen around to face Amanda and Nola. "There's a video. It's Dominic."

Amanda grabbed at her phone and quickly hit play on the short cell phone video that another passenger on the flight had shot of Dominic. He was standing up in the middle of an airplane aisle and shouting for a doctor, holding the palms of his hands over his eyes. A half-open suitcase with clothes strewn about was lop-sided on the seat in front of him and the overhead bin was wide-open, like it had just fallen from there. She couldn't make out what he was saying in the garbled video, but it was definitely Dominic. The person taking the video was laughing in the background and joking that "a passenger got hit in the head with a suitcase."

Amanda felt her entire body fill with rage at the poster and she tossed Rosie's cell phone back down onto the tabletop. "I have to get to Cleveland right now."

"You don't even know where he is," Nola reminded her. "It's not like they're going to keep him at the airport if there's a medical emergency. Plus, it looks like a suitcase fell on him. I don't know how that would constitute a medical emergency."

Amanda had an idea but didn't want to say it out loud in case that might make it real.

"So I'll go to the closest hospital, then," Amanda said. "They'd bring him there if he landed in Cleveland."

"It's still a five-hour drive, Amanda," Rosie added. "What if he's not there by the time you arrive?"

She pushed her chair back and stood up quickly. "I can't just sit here, Rosie. I can't just do nothing. Look at him! He's clearly in pain, and people are laughing at him!"

Rosie didn't respond, closing her mouth and nodding instead.

Nola stood up, too, reaching into her pocket and pulling out a set of car keys. "Okay, but take my car.

It's faster and has better gas mileage. Plus, if you have to drive him back, it has more space for him to lay out than your sedan does. There's also a bunch of bags of Goldfish crackers in the center console if you get hungry. And a secret stash of Hershey's Kisses in the glove box."

Amanda took the keys to Nola's SUV and nodded, her brain feeling like it was going into autopilot. "I will text the group chat when I get there. If you hear anything in the meantime, let me know immediately. And can one of you watch Tom?"

Rosie saluted her like she was in the military. "On it. I'll take Tom to my house for the night, or until whenever you get back. I'll take his litter box, too. The kids will be ecstatic. They've been begging for a pet, so maybe this will shut them up until Christmas."

Amanda just nodded, not really able to meet Rosie or Nola at their humor right now. She shoved her own cell phone in her pocket and grabbed a bottle of water out of the fridge and her purse off the kitchen counter, then headed out the front door to Nola's SUV in the driveway.

As she started the car up and put in directions to the hospital closest to the Cleveland airport, she couldn't stop replaying the image of Dominic standing up in the center aisle of the airplane and screaming in pain. If anything happened to him, she wasn't even sure how she'd react.

All she did know was that she needed to be there with him, and she needed to be there now.

Chapter Twenty-Two

Dominic

Honey, it could have happened to anyone," Ellen said from the small folding chair she was in next to her son's hospital bed. "There was no way for you to know that suitcase was going to hit you."

"I should have been being more careful," Dominic disagreed as he stared up at the ceiling over his hospital bed with one eye, a giant patch over the other. Even in the eye that wasn't covered and hadn't sustained the direct impact, there were squiggles and floaters in his vision that looked like they were dancing on the ceiling, and the edges of his vision were dark and blurred. The emergency room doctor had confirmed that his retina had become detached again with the latest injury, and it looked like there was blunt trauma to his other eye as well but not a full detachment.

A fucking suitcase falling out of an overhead bin onto his face.

How absolutely humiliating.

Especially in today's world, where everyone had a camera and access to the rest of the world instantly, and some jackass had posted a video of him reeling in pain as if it were funny. Eric was already working hard with a tech friend on scrubbing the video from the internet and sending out cease and desist letters to media outlets who were trying to share it, but once something like that was out there, it's impossible to get rid of entirely.

He felt like a fucking laughingstock. Hell, he *was* a laughingstock. And even that would be tolerable if it meant he wasn't possibly losing his sight altogether.

Ellen sighed and patted his hand with hers. "Dom, you're so hard on yourself. I wish you'd lighten up some. Dr. Ahn said that there was a possibility of this happening again with even a small injury or bump. You might not have been able to avoid it entirely, and it helps no one to blame yourself. We were already working on borrowed time."

He knew that she was right, but he was seething with so much anger inside right now that he couldn't even think about her perspective. He was just pissed off at that fucking suitcase, at the faulty latch on the damn overhead bin, at the passenger who hadn't been more careful with how they packed their luggage, and with himself for not ducking out of the way instead of turning to look up directly at the incoming blunt trauma.

First, he'd lost his entire career in front of the entire world, and now he couldn't even go gracefully into retirement. It felt like…what was even the fucking point anymore? What did he even have to look forward to?

"Dominic Gage?" A tall man in a white doctor's coat walked into the room. "We're going to get you transferred from the ER and up to pre-op. Your blood work and everything look great, so we feel comfortable moving forward. I've got some releases here for you to sign and look over, and I want to talk to you a bit about the surgery and potential complications, as well as aftercare. You won't be able to get on a plane after this for at least six weeks, or drive a car yourself, so it'll be important to have a ride available to take you home."

"I'll take him home," his mother responded to the doctor. "I'm his mother. Whatever he needs, we'll make sure he has it."

Dominic looked away toward the unit of shelves and cupboards on the wall, some of which had peeled stickers on them or paper notices about procedures and wait times. The doctor kept talking and describing the upcoming surgery in detail to him, and he nodded along like he was following, but he wasn't even the slightest bit. Instead, he was thinking of last night, before he'd ever gotten on that flight, when he'd been laid out on Amanda's couch, her body curled into his side, as they watched a Hallmark movie that she swore would bring him to tears. It didn't, but he loved that she got so invested in films and stories like that. He wondered what it would be like to sit on that couch with her and listen to the movie but not be able to actually watch it. A lump formed in his throat as he considered what it might feel like holding her but not being able to see into her perfectly brown eyes again or remember what her smile looked like when she completely lit up a room with her laughter. He wondered what it would feel like to walk into a home he only had visual memories of but couldn't actually see anymore.

His entire life had been dedicated to baseball, to coaches and spectators and other people. This was supposed to be the time he got for himself—to live out his dreams that he'd spent his entire career earning. And he wasn't going to see any of it.

"Dom, did you hear what the doctor said?" Ellen asked gently, prodding his arm to get his attention.

He turned to look at her and the doctor, who had a clipboard stretched out toward him with consent paperwork on top. Dominic just nodded and took the forms, signing them one by one, then handing them back to the doctor.

"I'm going to stay with you the whole time, okay?" His mother was talking to him, but he was back to staring at the wall.

For some reason, he wanted to remember what these cabinets looked like. He carefully studied the corners and edges, the handles, and the different notices posted on each side. He tried to read some of them, but most of the typography was too small for him to make out the words anymore.

"Is he in here?" Her voice was soft from somewhere behind him, but he recognized Amanda immediately.

He turned to look toward the entrance to the room to see her standing there, car keys in one hand, her hair in a messy bun on top of her head, wearing her signature T-shirt and skinny jeans that she always wore on her days off.

"What are you doing here?" he asked, because he'd told his mother to contact her and let her know what happened, but he certainly hadn't expected her to drive all the way down here. "You must have broken every speed record getting here since my mom called you."

"Actually, I was already halfway here when she called," Amanda said, walking over to the edge of the hospital bed and placing her hand on his shin.

"I'll give you two a few minutes alone," Ellen said, standing up and slipping Amanda a quick hug. "I need the bathroom and some water anyway. I'll be back in a few, but I have my cell phone on me if the doctors come back sooner. They said about an hour until they'll take him to pre-op for the surgery."

Amanda nodded and thanked her, then took a seat in the chair she'd been in. She scooted it closer to Dominic so she was right up against the bed, leaning her elbows on the thin mattress. "How are you doing?"

He let out a huff of air and gestured to the room around him. "How do you think I'm doing?"

His tone came out a lot more aggressive than he meant it to, but he didn't want to take it back, either.

"This is the only way I know how to process what's essentially my worst nightmare."

She cast her eyes down, her mouth in a firm line. "I'm so sorry, Dominic. That was an insensitive question. I can't imagine what you're going through. Your mother told me about the diagnosis and the surgery, and I booked a hotel nearby for the night. I told your mother I'd drive you back to Heart Lake when you get discharged, unless you'd rather she be with you. Whatever you're more comfortable with."

"To be honest, I don't care that much," he replied. "I just want to get this over with."

Amanda nodded like she understood, but of course, there was no way that she could. No one could understand what he was feeling right now, and he couldn't even figure out how to vocalize it.

But deep down, underneath all the fear and shit, he was glad she was there.

"Have you uh…have you called your therapist?" Amanda asked gingerly, and he could tell she felt like she was walking on eggshells around him. That only made him feel worse, and the guilt was absorbed into his anger and resentment, only tripling the entire thing. "Maybe we get an appointment on the books for after the surgery? I can do it for you if you tell me where to find him."

"Oh, now *you're* the one telling *me* to go to therapy?" He let out a wry, unmeaning laugh. "That's a turn of events."

"Hey," she replied defensively. "Dominic, I'm just trying to help."

"Well, it's not very helpful," he snapped back, immediately hating himself more for doing it. He wanted to just shut up, but it was like he couldn't keep his venom inside in that moment, and she was the one who happened to be standing there when the floodgates unlocked. "I didn't ask you to come here. I didn't ask you to drive me home or take care of me. I'm a grown man, and I don't need my girlfriend to come be my nurse or my mother. I don't need anyone at all."

Amanda stood up from the chair and took a step back. "I'm going to go out into the hall and get myself some water and give you a few minutes to think about why you're being such an asshole right now."

Good, she was fighting back. That's exactly what he wanted. He wanted to fight. He wanted to slam his fists into a wall and feel the crack of his knuckles against the Sheetrock, the stream of warm blood against his skin. He wanted the pain, and he wanted to suffer.

He was already suffering so much.

"How about you just get back in your car and go home, and leave me alone instead?" he replied, resorting to the only option he had left—emotional pain and isolating himself from the people who cared about him. Because that's what he deserved right now.

"Maybe I will," she said, her tone louder now. "And, by the way, we never put labels on things yet, so don't call me your girlfriend because this is *not* how someone should treat a girlfriend."

"You'd rather me call you a fuck buddy?" he shot back. "That's romantic."

"We haven't had sex," she reminded him, her voice even louder now. "And we're not going to now because you're an asshole, and I'm leaving."

With that, she stormed out of the room and right past his mother who was walking back in, eyes wide with a cup of ice water in her hand.

"Jesus, I was gone for three minutes, and I could hear the yelling down the hall," Ellen said. "What the hell, Dom? Since when do you yell?"

He turned back to look at the cabinets, refusing to answer her, refusing to answer anyone.

"Fine," Ellen continued, putting her cup of water down on a side table and heading back in the direction that Amanda had just gone. "Throw yourself your little pity party. I'll go find Amanda and apologize to her for your asinine behavior, but you owe me—and you absolutely owe her now, too."

He didn't watch her leave but kept studying the cabinets instead. His cell phone vibrated on the bed next to him and audibly announced the name of who was calling so he didn't have to look at the screen—Eric Minton.

Dominic answered the call. "Hello?"

"Buddy, I've got good news and bad news," Eric started the call with his usual jumping-right-in style. "Are you sitting down?"

"I'm lying in a hospital bed, dumbass," he replied. "You know that."

"Oh, right. I just got an update from your mother and heard all about the surgery," Eric replied. "Everything is set for discharge tomorrow. They wanted to do it outpatient—in and out same day—but I told your mother to tell them absolutely not. Give you some time to recoup and I'd pay for the upgrade to a private room."

He only grunted in response to that.

"But the other news is," Eric continued. "You got the fucking job."

"What?" He perked up slightly at that news, confused as all hell. "The commentator position? At MLB Strike Zone? I never even made it there for the interview."

"Yeah, but it was between you and one other person, and they apparently didn't like the other guy's interview, so they offered it to you instead," Eric explained with more enthusiasm than Dominic could muster in that moment. "They said no need to even come in to interview, just take time to rest. They want you to start in two months, which gives you more than enough time to heal and move."

"Holy shit," he replied. That was absolutely the last news he'd been expecting to hear, and it honestly did dissipate some of his anger the smallest amount. It was like a path forward was opening up in a moment where he felt so hopelessly deadlocked. "I'll take it."

"Really?" Eric let out a holler and clapped his hands from the other end of the phone. "That's perfect, D. I'll call them right after this and let them know. This is big—we're doing big things together, man!"

"Sure," he replied with a half-hearted chuckle at Eric's excitement. He still couldn't forget that he had a surgery to complete and heal from before then, as well as an entire move across the country. Plus, he'd have to tell Amanda that he was leaving, which would probably be a lot easier now that she certainly disliked him.

Honestly, it was probably for the best. He hated hurting her, but a future with him would ultimately hurt her far more. She hadn't signed up to be his caretaker, and he wasn't about to put that kind of burden on her. She deserved a relationship with someone who could actually give her the life she wanted, and that clearly wasn't going to be him after all this was over.

"You said there was also bad news?" Dominic asked.

"Yeah," Eric replied. "TMZ picked up the video. I got them to take it down within twenty minutes of it going up, but the views are already out there, and people screen-recorded it. It's looking like it's going to be a lot harder to scrub it entirely."

Dominic didn't even care anymore. "Well, I won't be able to see it soon anyway, so whatever. People are assholes."

"Morbid joke, but I hear you," Eric agreed. "But also, any publicity before a job like this is good publicity. It will bring in the viewers, which will make Strike Zone happy, and you'll look like a superstar who sky-rocketed their ratings."

"Great. Can't wait," he replied sarcastically. "My misery can be their gain."

"There's always a light at the end of the tunnel, D," Eric tried to soften things.

He scoffed again. "Not when you're blind. Bye, Eric."

With that, he hung up the phone, closed his eye, and tried to block out every memory from today.

Chapter Twenty-Three

Amanda

He was way out of line, Amanda," Ellen said as she caught up to her at the far end of the hospital hallway after she'd stormed out of Dominic's room. "I don't even know what he said, but from his tone and volume alone—I am so sorry. That is not the man I raised. I've never heard him talk to a woman like that before, or anyone actually."

"You don't need to apologize for him," Amanda told Dominic's mother. She certainly didn't blame Ellen for how Dominic had just spoken to her, and she could see how horrified the older woman was at the entire exchange. "I should be the one apologizing."

"What?" Ellen furrowed her brow as she looked at her. "For what? What happened in there?"

She honestly didn't even know how to answer that question except to say that Dominic had somehow known how to hit all of her more reactive buttons, and she'd completely spiraled—fast.

"I think I just let my emotions get the better of me," she finally said. "Given everything he's going through, I know I should be more patient."

"I mean, you can be patient and still not be a punching bag," Ellen told her, now linking her arm around Amanda's elbow and guiding her toward one of the small sitting area alcoves for families and guests.

Amanda took a seat on one of the stiff, plastic-like couches and Ellen poured them each a glass of water from the machine against the wall that had ice on one side and a water fountain on the other. She handed Amanda a cup, and she drank half of it quickly, letting the frigid liquid shock her system into calming down.

"Should I stay?" Amanda finally asked, running her finger absentmindedly on the rim of the cup. "I mean, he very clearly told me to leave. But he's going to need help after this surgery. I'd feel like an asshole abandoning him right now."

Ellen sat down on the couch that was perpendicular to hers. "Listen, Amanda, I like you and Dominic together. Really, I do. He's been talking about you nonstop the last month, and I'm glad that he found you. He needs someone like you in his life, but this isn't just about him or what he needs. This is your life, too."

"I know, but I...I do like being with him," she admitted. "I mean, the whole last ten minutes aside."

"But it's not just going to be ten minutes, Amanda," Ellen continued. "The doctor said after this surgery, his vision is going to be pretty bad. Not entirely blind, most likely—still some shapes and shadows, we're guessing—but there's a lot he's going to have to relearn how to do without the help of visual stimuli. I can't even imagine what kind of learning curve that is going to be, but I know it's going to be hard. I also don't know where he'll land on the other side of that. It would be completely understandable if that's not a journey you want to take on for yourself."

Amanda frowned and shook her head. "I don't care about any of that. He's been open with me from the start that his vision wasn't guaranteed long-term. I might not know a lot about how to deal with that or what to do, but I'm willing to learn alongside him. We all have things we bring into relationships—I do, too."

She wasn't about to explain to his mother that she saw her lack of libido as what she was bringing to a relationship because that was a lot of unnecessary information. She also didn't really like that she was even thinking about her sex drive as baggage, because it shouldn't be. She didn't think of Dominic's vision as baggage—it was just part of who he was now and going forward. She was so freaking tired of everyone having to mask and put on these pretend shows of having it all together and being perfect.

She wanted to be accepted for who she was, not despite of who she was, or tolerating who she was, or any of that shit. Just love and acceptance. If she knew she could do that for another person, she also was beginning to know that she deserved that for herself, too.

"Well, I'm glad to hear that," Ellen replied. "I'll come up for the summer to Heart Lake. I pushed back my internship over the summer to the fall, so we can help him get settled together. But again, no pressure. Also, he owes you an apology."

Amanda let out a small laugh. "He does."

Ellen finished her cup of water and stood up. "Why

don't you hang out here a bit until he gets transferred upstairs? I'll keep you updated on what's happening."

She nodded in agreement, settling back onto the couch as she watched Ellen leave and walk down the hallway. There wasn't a solid plan on next steps, but she'd already driven five hours to get here, so she wasn't going to just turn around now. At the very least, she'd give him some time to calm down and try to reengage with him once he was out of surgery and feeling up to it.

The fight replayed in her head, though, and she couldn't help but cringe at everything they'd said. He'd been mean, without a doubt, and she knew that wasn't who he was. But his comments about sex, or her being a fuck buddy, had been jarring. She wanted to be here for him and to help him, but if she did go through all of that and then he still didn't want to be with her because of her lack of sex drive . . . well, that would really sting.

At the same time, she wasn't here to help with strings attached.

Her being here was because she genuinely cared and wanted to help, not because she was trying to convince him to be with her. So as mad as she was at him, and as scared as she was of the future, she wasn't going anywhere.

She pulled out her cell phone and sent the girls an update on having arrived and the plans for surgery and discharge tomorrow. They both immediately responded with well wishes and that they were sending prayers. Rosie also sent a picture of Tom playing with the twins and assured her that she was settling into their house well.

There were a few missed emails in her inbox, and she clicked on them haphazardly even though she had no actual desire to catch up on work right now. However, an email from her now former boss caught her eye.

claytondesigns69@gmail.com: Exit Project

Hey Amanda,

Thanks for sending in all the exit paperwork. Everything looks squared away. I'm excited to see what you do out there with your new ventures and am happy to help in any way I can. As you may know, our firm won the bid for the Culver farmhouse at the end of Main Street. When I was bidding on this project, I always had envisioned it being your project, and I'd like to stay true to that vision. If you're willing to take it on, I'd like to give you the contract as a parting gift and your first official contract in your new business venture. If that feels like too much, just let me know, and I'd be happy to help walk you through any parts of it. However, I think you are more than equipped to handle this level of project, and I'm excited to see what you do with that venue.

Let me know if you have any questions. I'll have Brenda send over the measurements and blueprints as soon as possible.

With all my admiration,
Clayton

She felt like her chest was seizing up as she read his words. The Culver farmhouse was a dream project—her dream. She hadn't even known to wish for it, let alone known that Clayton had won the bid for the project.

Amanda opened up an email in reply to him but hesitated over typing out any words. She couldn't think of what to say to accurately express her thanks. She couldn't think of how to apologize for everything, either. She had completed the design recently for Mrs. Crawford's hall bathroom, and it was currently under construction with the contractor. As thrilled as she was about working on that project, she still felt the overwhelming sense of guilt in her gut at how she'd obtained it.

And now Clayton—the person she'd betrayed to do all that—was giving her another huge project. Free of any strings attached. Just because he believed in her and her vision.

Which, apparently, he always had.

She wondered why she hadn't been able to see that before, but she wasn't sure she'd even been open to the possibility. It hadn't even crossed her mind as an option before—he was her competition. She'd put him in that category from the first day, and that hadn't changed once. Maybe he'd tried to make it change over the years she'd worked there, but she knew she'd never been open to even acknowledging that.

God, she needed to apologize to him, but she wasn't ready right now.

A text message from her mother popped up right as she was about to put her phone away, and she clicked on it automatically because it wasn't often that her mother reached out. Plus, she was already in a self-punishing mood, so why not see what her mother had to add to it today?

Hey, baby girl! I've got the weekend off this week. The hotel is being closed for renovations, so all the staff gets two days paid leave. I'd love to see you!

Amanda felt both excited at the prospect of spending time with her mother and also frustrated that she only got opportunities to do so when her mom's work allowed. She took a deep breath, trying not to focus on the negative right now. Instead, she clicked the call button next to her mom's name and lifted the phone to her ear.

"Amanda!" Her mother's voice came on the line after the first ring. "I'm so glad I caught you at a free moment. How are you?"

"I'm okay," she replied, but an unexpected tremor in her voice said otherwise. She cleared her throat, pushing it away. "I'm, uh, I'm out of town right now. Just a lot going on. I'll be back tomorrow night."

"Oh, fun!" Her mother didn't seem to notice the emotion in her voice. "Any plans this weekend? Do you want to grab lunch? Dinner? My treat. I also just found out I'm getting a raise in the new fiscal year, so we've got to celebrate."

"That's great, Mom," she replied, even though she wished her mother would just retire. "Congratulations."

"It speeds up my timeline, too," her mother continued. "At that rate, I can pay off the house within seven years instead of nine. Then I can actually slow down and relax."

"Mom, you can slow down and relax now," she countered. "I've offered multiple times to help you with those payments, and you have money in your retirement account. You deserve to rest."

"That money is for you, baby," her mother replied. "I want to leave you something when I'm gone. It's the least I can do—that's my job as a mother, to take care of you."

Financially but not emotionally? Amanda didn't say that thought out loud.

"Yeah, Mom," she agreed, her voice lackluster. "You've always taken great care of me and made sure I was provided for. But I'm an adult now, and I really just want to spend more time with you. If there's anything I'm learning more and more in recent months, it's that I want to just spend time with the people I care about without strings attached or keeping walls up between me and everyone."

Her mother paused for a moment. "What walls? What do you mean?"

"I think I'm going to start going to therapy, Mom," she replied.

There was a groan from the other end of the line. "Oh my God, did I screw you up that bad? Amanda, you don't have to pay a stranger to complain about me. I'm here to listen. If you hate me, just say it. I can take it."

"Jesus, Mom." Amanda rolled her eyes and let out a sigh. "I don't think that's the point of therapy. I think it's about bringing people closer together—not telling someone how much you hate your mother."

"So you do hate me, then?" her mother replied. "I knew it. I knew I should have done more. I could have done more. Listen, I'm sending you a check right now. I'm going to drop it off at your door this afternoon, and you do something with it to make you feel better. I only want to ever take care of you, Amanda. I wasn't perfect—I know that. But I've always tried my best."

"Mom, of course I don't hate you. But if you drop off a check at my door, I'm going to spend it on therapy," she said.

Her mother seemed fine with that idea. "Can you tell that to the therapist? Tell them I help. Tell them I have always made sure you had a roof over your head and food in your belly. You went to a good school, and you wanted for nothing."

Except her time and attention.

Again, she didn't say that part out loud.

"Mom, I have to go. I'm helping a friend who is sick," she finally said, because there was no point in continuing this conversation. "I'll call you when I get back to town, okay?"

"Okay, baby. I love you so much," her mother replied. "Seriously, Amanda. You are my reason for living. You know that, right?"

"I know, Mom," she replied. "Talk to you soon."

With that, she hung up the phone and placed it down on the couch beside her.

Everything in her life had felt so stable and calm before a month ago, before meeting Dominic. She worked a job she mostly liked, even if it wasn't her forever plan. She had a home full of sunflowers that she was so proud of and had spent years turning into her space. She had a small group of friends whom she saw regularly and considered family. Everything had been...fine.

And then she'd met Dominic, and somehow it had been both the best and worst time of her life since then. She barely even recognized her life today from where she had been, and she was simultaneously happy about that and...not.

Going forward, she had no idea what to expect or what she wanted, but what she did know was that things were going to change even more. The further she let herself get absorbed into Dominic's orbit, the more she was going to unlock parts of herself she'd worked really hard to keep under wraps.

And that was a terrifying and exhilarating thought.

Chapter Twenty-Four

Dominic

The discharge nurse insisted that Dominic be wheeled out to the car in a wheelchair even though he could full well walk. Sure, he would definitely need someone to guide him because his sight was out for the count at the moment, but his legs worked just fine.

Didn't matter, they said. Hospital policy.

So he sat in the chair and felt the breeze of stale hospital air whip past his skin as he was rolled through the hallways. His mother was walking alongside him chatting about the traffic on the drive back that she'd seen on the GPS, and that there was apparently an accident that was going to set them back at least twenty extra minutes. He wasn't particularly in a rush, though, so it didn't bother him.

Cold air hit him in a whoosh as the sounds of automatic doors opened, and he realized they'd just stepped outside. It was wild how much he could sense and interpret around him without his sight. Honestly, he'd never considered before how many different sounds he would already recognize and ways to orient himself with the space around him. It was strange, and he definitely felt very off balance, but it didn't feel impossible.

Plus, he was going to get some sight back over the next few days and weeks as he healed from the surgery. Right now, he had patches over both eyes and was just seeing black, but the doctor had told him that it was likely he'd start to regain some vision by the end of the week if he let his eyes rest and took care of himself properly. While he might have been stubborn before, he was absolutely going to take the doctor's advice like the letter of the law. Whatever he could do to assure he had as much vision back as possible, he was going to do that.

"Amanda, do you want to drive? Or should I?" He heard his mother say.

"Amanda's here?" he asked, turning his head toward the sound of someone walking up to them.

"Yeah, I'm here," she replied. "I told you I would be."

"Oh." He didn't know how to respond to that, because he'd honestly thought she left yesterday after he'd quite literally yelled at her. And she should have. He wanted her to leave.

And yet, he couldn't deny that the warmth spreading across his chest and in his gut right now was absolute relief that she'd stayed.

"I can drive," she said to his mother. "Do you need help getting him in the car? Dominic, we're putting you in the back seat just because we don't want the sun glare through the windshield to bother your eyes. I've got you a cup holder back there with water and a bag of chips and some granola bars. Also a pack of M&M's in case you were in a sugar mood. It's a long drive."

"Thank you," he replied tentatively. "You, uh, you didn't have to do all that. I really appreciate it."

He felt a hand on his, and she squeezed gently. He didn't let go for a moment and squeezed back.

"I've already got my suitcases in the trunk," Ellen said as he heard car doors opening and people moving around him. "Enough for at least two weeks. I'll go back and restock on supplies if I need to, but I should be good to go for a while."

When he'd decided to make sure his mother had a room at his new house, he hadn't expected her to come live with him so soon, but now he was so glad she was. He felt guilty that she was pushing her school schedule back a semester for him—she'd already sacrificed so much of her life for him. But he did really need her right now, and he knew how blessed and lucky he was to have that support.

The nurse finally allowed him to get out of the wheelchair and, with a hand from Ellen, he climbed into the back seat of the car.

"How's the temperature in here?" Amanda asked from in front of him inside the car. "Do you want me to turn up the cold air? Warm air?"

"It's fine," he assured her, feeling a twinge of embarrassment at the fact that she was being so caring toward him right now. He absolutely did not deserve it after how he'd talked to her yesterday, but she didn't even seem fazed by any of that.

Still, he was going to apologize. Just maybe not with his mother in the next seat.

The car ride in total was about five and a half hours,

and they kept the conversation light and surface level the entire time. There were also a few breaks of just listening to music on the radio and a couple songs that Amanda and his mother sang along to together. He didn't join in even though he did know the songs, but he liked listening to the camaraderie between them. He'd underestimated their friendship, because it was clear that they communicated regularly outside of him and the interactions he'd seen them have. They chatted like they'd known each other for years, and he was glad that Amanda had that with his mother because he knew she didn't have that with her own.

That thought only made him feel more guilty about the fact that he was going to rip it all away in two months, though. Not that she knew that yet, and he'd certainly never tell his mom to stop talking to Amanda after he moved. In fact, he hoped they'd maintain contact. It sounded like they both needed the other in some manner, and him taking a job on the East Coast shouldn't get in the way of that.

But there was no chance he and Amanda could continue whatever it was they were.

He wasn't about to ask her to leave her home and her career just as it was taking off to move to New Jersey with him. Long distance was absolutely not going to work given his current health and vision issues. It just wasn't feasible or safe for him to be flying back and forth to see her regularly, and he couldn't ask her to be the one who did all the traveling. None of it was fair to her, or to either one of them. It just wasn't sustainable, and the resentment would break them both. If there was one thing he wasn't willing to do, it was leave things on a bad note.

Heart Lake had always been a place of good memories for him his entire life. He didn't want to lose that by burning bridges behind him. He couldn't lose that. He needed the emotional safe haven that Heart Lake had given him, especially if he was going to move to a place where he knew no one to do a very public facing job. He'd be under constant scrutiny and have to figure out how to build a network and community out there from scratch—all while also navigating partial blindness.

Jesus, the entire plan sounded crazy, even to him.

But he had to do it. He had to do something with his life. Yesterday, he'd spent the day down in the dumps feeling sorry for himself, feeling helpless and hopeless. But the surgery had gone well, all things considered. It wasn't a cure or perfect fix, but they'd reattached his retina and removed some of the scarring in the other eye. It didn't mean he'd get perfect vision back, but he should eventually be able to see shapes and shadows and movement once he healed. It would be at least enough to move around a bit more independently than he'd thought he'd be able to.

Beauty, nuance, colors… they couldn't promise him any of that going forward.

"We're home!" his mother announced as he felt the familiar rumble of the gravel driveway underneath the car.

He immediately felt an ache—something akin to homesickness, maybe?—at being here and sat up in his seat. "How's it look?"

Technically, he'd been here yesterday morning, so he doubted the house had changed in that amount of time, but he still wanted to know.

"There's definitely not enough sunflowers," Amanda commented. "But it looks fine outside of that."

He laughed and shook his head. "And Tom? Is she okay?"

"Tom's great," Amanda informed him. "Rosie said that she will bring her over after the kids go to bed. That's the only way she can sneak her out because the twins are obsessed with her."

Dominic grinned at that and remembered what it had been like to be a kid with a new pet. His childhood pet had been a turtle that he got from the state fair, but either way, he'd loved it until he'd gone to college and given it away to another much younger kid in his neighborhood.

Turns out, box turtles live a very long time, and college dorms aren't about them.

"Maybe ask Rosie to keep her a while longer," Dominic found himself saying, despite the pang in his chest at the idea of letting her go. He had grown very fond of Tom, for sure, but he was also not in a position to care for a kitten right now. And if he was going to move... well, he just wasn't sure he could do that to Tom if she was happy with Rosie's family. "It might be better to let her stay there until I can do more, you know?"

Amanda seemed to understand that explanation. "Okay, I'll tell her. I guess that makes sense, but if you want her back here, I'll be happy to feed her and whatever. You don't have to worry about any of that stuff right now."

"Sounds like the kids are enjoying her, and I bet Tom is enjoying them," he continued. "That sounds best for now."

No one argued with him.

Instead, they both helped him into the house. The first thing he requested was a hot shower to get the hospital smell off of him, and his mother awkwardly excused herself, clearly deciding to let Amanda handle that, giving the excuse that she needed to go to the grocery store to make sure they were stocked up on food for the week.

He knew his fridge was full, but he didn't say that to her. He wanted the time alone with Amanda.

"How much help do you want?" Amanda asked as she held his arm and walked him toward the bathroom. "I can turn on the shower and show you where all the soaps and shampoos are, leave a towel on the door. Whatever makes you the most comfortable."

He stepped from carpet onto cold tile and knew they'd arrived in the master bathroom. "Can you turn on the shower? Really warm, but not scalding?"

"Absolutely," she said, guiding him to the counter and putting his hands down on the marble top. "Give me a second to do that and grab a towel."

When she walked away and let go of him, he stood up straighter and reached for the bottom hem of his T-shirt. He wasn't even sure what T-shirt he was wearing— something his mother had brought him—but he pulled it carefully over his head, minding that it didn't make contact with the patches on his eyes. He dropped it onto the floor beside him and reached for the hem of his pants next, sliding both his sweatpants and his boxers down in one go.

"Oh." Amanda's voice came behind him, the sound of the shower now on as well. "You are naked."

"I mean, that is usually how people shower," he commented with a small laugh. "Sorry. I should have warned you. Do you want to leave?"

"Do you still need help?" she asked.

The last thing he wanted was for her to be his nurse or caretaker. "I'll manage fine on my own. I remember the layout. Where did you put the towel?"

"On the closed toilet lid," she told him. "But I can stay."

"You don't have to," he replied, turning his body in the direction of the shower and reaching a hand out to guide him toward it.

"But if I want to?" she asked, her voice quieter.

He might be in recovery from surgery, but he was still a red-blooded male, and her response caused an immediate reaction in his body. He reached both hands down to quickly cover himself. "Uh, well, you can stay. Of course you can stay."

She giggled lightly and he could feel the heat rushing to his cheeks. "I can see you'd be okay with that."

"Sorry," he said with a chuckle. "I couldn't help it, but it'll go away. Ignore me."

"Actually, maybe I shouldn't," she continued just as he was reaching one hand into the water stream, testing the temperature. "I think this is the perfect time to talk."

He wasn't sure he entirely agreed with that assessment,

but he focused on returning the blood to his brain anyway. "You want to talk while I'm naked with a stiff dick and can't see you?"

"I didn't say it was ideal circumstances," she continued, laughing again. "Get in the shower. I'll sit out here, and we can just talk. We have a lot to talk about."

That part was definitely true, but he only felt dread at how that conversation was going to go. He didn't argue with her, though, and stepped into the shower completely. Making sure that the water didn't touch the bandages on his face, he dipped his hair back into the stream and began lathering himself with soap.

"Okay, so let's talk," he finally said. "Can I start?"

"Go for it," she said. He was pretty sure she was sitting on the bathroom counter from the direction of her voice from somewhere behind the shower curtain. "I'm all ears."

"I was way out of line yesterday with how I spoke to you," he said. "Honestly, I'm embarrassed. That's not like me."

"You were really hurting," she said, letting him off the hook. "Physically, emotionally. I get it. Sort of. I mean, I'll never fully get what you're going through, but I can forgive that moment."

That meant a lot to him, but he wasn't sure he agreed with her. He didn't feel like he should be let off the hook for any of it.

"Just never talk to me that way again," she continued. "Because that's a one-time pass for being bedridden in the hospital. Any other incident like that, and I'm going to knee you in the balls."

He laughed and almost lost his grip on the bottle of shower gel he was holding. "Totally fair. I'll keep that warning in mind."

"So are we good?" she asked. "Discussion over?"

Not even close, but this next part felt like he was going to hurt himself as much as he was going to hurt her.

"I think we need to discuss the future," he said over the water rushing down his back. "I got some news."

"The job," she finished the thought for him. "You got it? I thought you didn't even make it to the interview."

"I didn't," he explained, rinsing the last bit of shampoo out of his hair until he could hear the squeak of his fingers against his scalp. "But Eric called, and they offered it to me anyway. I start in two months."

"September? Wow." Amanda's voice lacked any emotion, and he knew that meant she was experiencing all the emotions. "That's really soon."

"It's actually further off than I thought they'd allow," he said. "But they're giving me time to heal and move."

"Move?" Her voice was a slightly higher pitch than it had been a moment ago. "To New Jersey?"

"I'm not sure that there's any other option," he replied, rinsing the shower gel off his body now. "I can't make the trip back and forth when my health is like this, Amanda. And I can't ask you to move out there or be the one traveling back and forth all the time."

"Yeah, that would be really unfair," she replied, and he was actually surprised to hear her say that.

"You agree?" he asked, pausing for a moment and letting the water just wash over his shoulders.

She didn't respond immediately, but he heard her clear her throat. "Dominic, if this was...if this was forever, I'd do all of that. More, even. But I think we don't know enough about each other to make a claim like that yet. And if we did, I'm not sure this would be forever."

He wasn't sure why that comment stung so much, but he finished rinsing himself and turned off the faucet before responding.

A soft towel was being pressed into his hands almost immediately, and he took it, quickly rubbing the water out of his hair and off his skin before wrapping it around the lower half of his body. She gripped his arm right above his elbow and helped guide him as he stepped out of the shower and onto the bath mat.

"I put some clothes out on the bed—T-shirt and sweatpants. Does that work?" Amanda asked as she walked with him, arm in arm, out of the bathroom and onto the carpet of his bedroom. "I can help you get dressed."

"I can pull a shirt over my head," he told her, a little more brusquely than he'd meant to. "Sorry, I just mean... I can do it."

She placed the fabric in his hands, and he maneuvered it over his head by himself. When he was done, she placed another piece of clothing in his hands.

"Boxers," she informed him. "I'll turn around."

He wanted to tell her she didn't have to, but everything about their conversation right now felt like things were coming to a close. He felt like he was saying goodbye, and he didn't want to. But he didn't know what else to say, and it sounded like she wanted the exit.

"What don't I know about you?" he asked quietly after pulling his boxers on and she'd handed him a pair of sweatpants. "You said we don't know enough about each other, but I haven't held anything back from you."

She helped him take a step back until he was seated on the edge of the bed and could lean forward to pull his sweatpants up his legs.

"I'm not hiding anything. It's not like that," she promised. "I just think you have needs that I won't be able to meet. I told you that before, remember? At the Boat Parade."

He swallowed hard, knowing she was talking about his vision and all the help she was currently providing him just to take a shower and get dressed. Of course, she didn't want to sign up for meeting those needs for the rest of her life. That was completely reasonable, even if it felt like a dagger to the chest to actually hear out loud. He tried to still his breathing and keep his focus on getting dressed so she wouldn't see the impact her words had just had on him.

"Oh," he replied. "Yeah. I remember. I guess that makes sense. I mean, not 'I guess.' It *does* make sense. You deserve someone who doesn't need to be taken care of every day."

"And you deserve someone who can give that to you," she countered, her voice sounding kind while everything coming out of it . . . wasn't. "I wish that was something I could give you, but I think I'd be lying about myself if I did. It would be . . . performative."

Jesus, the woman did not mince words. Sure, nursing him back to health or whatever that looked like for him was a hard ask, but saying she'd only be able to phone it in? Damn.

He pulled his sweatpants up entirely and nodded his head. "Yeah, I get it. I'm going to take a nap, okay? Could I be alone for a bit?"

"Of course," she said instantly. "I'll go prep something for dinner, okay? Take some time to sleep."

"Thanks, Amanda." He felt for the edge of the sheets and pulled them down, crawling underneath. Once the blanket was over him and he was curled into a pillow, he let out a sigh. "For everything, Amanda. Not just today. Everything has been…it's been one of the best months of my life."

There wasn't an immediate response, but he could hear her breathing a little farther away now, like she was on her way toward the bedroom door.

"Me, too, Dom," she finally said, barely above a whisper, before he heard the bedroom door open and then close.

He waited until he could hear someone moving items around in the kitchen before he let himself pull the covers up to his chin and shut the entire world out.

Chapter Twenty-Five

Amanda

Amanda wasn't naturally a liar. In fact, she actually had a pretty big personal policy against lying, but there she was, flat out lying to Dominic. She had all but directly said that she didn't want to continue a relationship with him, and there was nothing further from the truth. But she'd told him—in not so many words—that she wasn't going to be able to meet all his daily needs, and he'd agreed that that didn't make them a match.

That had become abundantly clear in the bathroom when she'd seen how quickly he'd been physically turned on by her. Sure, she was flattered. It was quite an ego boost to know that someone as handsome and wonderful as Dominic felt that strongly about her, but it was also a very—*very*—large reminder of what she wasn't going to be able to give him. Of course, he'd want physical intimacy to be a big part of his life going forward, and he deserved that, just like she told him.

He'd already lost so much, she wasn't going to ask him to give that up, too.

Add to all of that that he was also moving in less than two months, and it was a pretty clear reason to cut things off romantically now, before even more feelings got involved.

Yet here she was in his kitchen, cooking a pot of spaghetti for him for dinner and feeling like her heart had been shattered into a million pieces. Literal tears were streaming down her cheeks as she stirred the noodles in boiling water and tried to convince herself to buck up and give it a rest.

She was *not* someone who cried over a man. Hell, she couldn't even understand what she was crying about. This had been her decision just as much as it had been his.

"Okay, so I got some garlic bread," Ellen's voice came through the hallway behind her and into the kitchen.

She didn't turn around, because she wasn't about to let the older woman see her crying. Instead, she quickly and surreptitiously wiped at her cheeks and leaned her face over the steam from the pot. She could blame her red cheeks on that easily if Ellen noticed anything.

"But I also got some eggs, veggies, and other staples like milk. Dominic always goes through so much milk," Ellen continued. "Plus, some ice cream for me. I'm going to write my name on it, so he doesn't steal any."

"I don't think you have to worry about that," Amanda commented quietly, still not turning around fully.

"Oh, shit." Ellen sighed. "Yeah, I guess he can't read that. That's going to take some getting used to. Well, just don't tell him I bought ice cream, I guess."

"My lips are sealed," she replied, steadying her voice.

"This is . . . this is all really hard," Ellen admitted out loud, though it didn't seem like she was talking directly to Amanda. More so like she was processing everything on her own. She placed the bags of groceries down on the kitchen island and began unpacking them. "Oh, by the way—are we expecting company? There was a car coming up the driveway as I was unloading."

"Really?" Amanda pulled away from the stove and turned off the burner, the noodles fully cooked through now. "Let me go check."

She walked past Ellen and looked at herself in the hall mirror before getting to the front door. Any hint of tears was gone, and aside from some red cheeks and sweat on her brow and upper lip, she looked fine. She wiped at the sweat anyway, then opened the front door and walked out onto the porch.

Sure enough, a small red sports car was pulling up right next to where Ellen had parked Nola's car that she'd taken to the grocery store. A woman with bright blonde hair was behind the steering wheel and didn't move to get out, but the woman in the passenger seat immediately opened her door and stepped onto the gravel.

She was extremely tall and beautiful and wearing a pair of stiletto heels. She spotted Amanda on the porch and waved to her. "Hello?"

"Hi?" Amanda called back, unsure who this was.

"Is this Dominic Gage's house?" the woman asked.

Shit, the tabloids had figured out where he lived. She was not about to let his privacy be even further invaded after that damn video from yesterday had gone viral.

"Who?" she replied. "I don't know who that is. I think you have the wrong place."

"Shit." The woman looked perplexed and pulled out her phone, scrolling through it. "Let me call him. I must have the wrong address."

She had his phone number? "How do you know him?" Amanda asked, stepping down the porch steps.

"I used to be married to him," she replied with a slight laugh. "I promise, I'm not a stalker."

"Wait, you're Melinda?" Amanda stood up straighter.

Melinda lifted one brow. "So, this *is* where Dominic lives?"

"Yes," Amanda admitted. "Sorry, I thought you might be the tabloids."

She nodded her head and walked toward the porch steps carefully, her stiletto heels getting repeatedly stuck in the gravel. "Fair thought. It makes me feel a lot better to know he has people like you watching out for him."

Amanda hadn't thought much about what Melinda might be like or what she might look like, but meeting her in person exceeded any expectations. This woman was drop-dead gorgeous. Literally an absolute bombshell. Plus, she seemed genuinely nice and kind, at least from first impressions.

"Is he expecting you?" Amanda asked as Melinda finally made it to the porch steps. "He just fell asleep."

"Definitely don't wake him up," Melinda said. "And, no, he's probably not expecting me. I texted and called him, said I was coming here to check on him. But he didn't respond."

"I think Ellen has his phone, actually," Amanda commented, opening the front door for her. "She's in the kitchen."

"Oh, his mom is here?" Melinda's face split into a huge smile. "I love her."

A pit was slowly starting to form in Amanda's gut as the small-town hospitality side of her began battling with the protective, girlfriend/not-a-girlfriend side of her.

"Does your friend want to come in, too?" Amanda asked, gesturing toward the woman sitting in the car still. "She doesn't have to stay out here. You guys can wait inside until he wakes up."

"They, not she," Melinda corrected her use of pronouns. "That's my partner; and yeah, I'll ask them to come in. Dominic hasn't met them yet, so this might be a little weird. But I think he'd be okay with it from talking to him on the phone about it."

"Oh!" Amanda looked back out toward the car, which Melinda was waving to and gesturing for the person to come in. "That's your partner? Like…like romantically?"

"Yeah, this is Emmy Jac," Melinda introduced her partner as they stepped out of the driver's seat of the car and walked up toward the porch.

Emmy Jac was actually wearing sensible shoes on gravel—a pair of colorful Toms with blue unicorns on them. They perfectly complemented the blue vest they were wearing over a pair of skintight black jeans, with dangly hoop earrings.

"I'm sorry," Melinda continued. "I never actually got your name."

"I'm Amanda," she told her, offering her hand. "I live in the yellow house next door."

Melinda shook her hand as Emmy Jac got onto the porch, and they exchanged a handshake with Amanda as well.

"It's great to meet you, Amanda," Emmy Jac said.

"I feel like I've seen you before," Amanda commented, narrowing her eyes and racking her brain. Emmy Jac's face looked so familiar, and the way their slicked-back hair was styled was too unique to forget. "Are you in a band? Wait…oh my God, the Kinetic Kind! You're in the Kinetic Kind, aren't you?"

Emmy Jac grinned and let out a small laugh. "Yeah, I'm the lead singer."

"That's actually how we met," Melinda added, sliding her hand around Emmy Jac's back and pulling them against her side. "I had meet and greet tickets to a concert, and I was just enamored. They are so incredible. If you haven't seen them perform live, you absolutely have to. Emmy, can we get Amanda tickets to the Cleveland show this fall?"

"Of course," Emmy Jac agreed, placing a soft kiss on Melinda's cheek. It was actually really endearing to see the affection between them, but it made Amanda all the more aware of the disparity in her own life right now. "I'll make sure my assistant gets them to you, Amanda. Any friend of Melinda's is a friend of mine."

"Actually, this is Dominic's neighbor," Melinda

corrected them. "We just met, but I can absolutely see us being friends. Right, Amanda?"

The way Melinda said that would have felt phony from anyone else, but there was an authenticity in Melinda's tone and mannerisms that was beyond charismatic; she was actually connecting. Amanda wanted not to love the ex of the man she was clearly hung up on, but there was nothing unlikable about Melinda so far.

"Uh...yes, of course," Amanda replied, ushering them into the house. She wasn't sure if she should clarify to Melinda and Emmy Jac that she was not *just* a neighbor. But she also kind of was *just* a neighbor now.

"Is that Melinda?" Ellen's voice called out from the kitchen. She popped out into the hallway with the biggest smile on her face. "Oh my God! Come here and give me a hug!"

Melinda threw her arms up in the air. "Mom!"

Amanda was pretty sure that this was the moment she should either disappear or melt into the floor, but instead she was frozen in place like a deer in the headlights, like she'd intruded on someone else's family reunion.

Melinda and Ellen hugged tightly before Melinda pulled away and motioned toward her partner. "Ellen, this is Emmy Jac."

"I've been reading about you two in all the tabloids," Ellen confessed, throwing her arms around Emmy Jac's shoulders for a hug. "Don't tell Dominic that I read the tabloids. He thinks they are garbage, but they have the best photos of you two. I swear, I've never seen a sexier couple. I told everyone at my new internship that my daughter is a lesbian now. Gives me street cred."

"That's not exactly how this works," Melinda said, shaking her head but laughing all the same. "But I'll let you have that."

Amanda furrowed her brows at the spectacle she was watching. *What in the ever-loving hell was going on here?*

"I've heard so much about you," Emmy Jac replied to Ellen. "Melinda can't stop talking about her chosen mom."

Am I in the twilight zone? Yep, this had to be the twilight zone. Amanda made a mental note to pinch herself in case she was actually disassociating right now, which was a very real possibility given all she was witnessing.

"I was trying to nap, you know." Dominic walked out of the bedroom, his hands on the wall for support but turning his face in their direction. "Jesus, Melinda, you're like a goddamn freight train coming into places. I could hear you the second you walked in the house."

She should leave right now, right? Amanda was pretty sure that this was her cue. Pack up her shit and go because she did not belong in what appeared to be some sort of weird fucking family reunion that she was clearly not a part of.

"There he is! Dom, you look amazing—eye patches and all," Melinda said as she pounced on him, wrapping him in a huge hug and kissing him on the cheek.

He looked startled at first from the sudden physical contact, but then he returned her hug. "Like I said,

I was trying to nap. I just had surgery yesterday, you know. Be gentle with me."

"Why do you think I'm here?" she replied. "Plus, you have to meet my partner. I brought them with me because you know I won't make this long of a drive alone."

"I just had a second devastating eye injury, then surgery, and then my very recently ex-wife brings over her boyfriend to meet me the next day?" Dominic summed up the situation not so accurately. "Well, that's just fucked up. What kind of karmic retribution is this?"

Melinda smacked Dominic's upper arm and let out a loud bellowing laugh. "Still the best humor I know. We may be divorced, but you know I love you, Dom, and it's important to me that we don't lose that family, even if we're divorced."

He wrapped his arm around Melinda's shoulders. "I love you, too, Mindy. Family first, always. So where's the guy? I can't see shit."

Yeah, she should definitely leave. Honestly, she wasn't even sure Dominic remembered that she was still here. Now it was just beginning to feel awkward, like if she announced she was still here...would he be still acting so loving toward Melinda?

"I don't have a boyfriend, Dom," Melinda clarified. "Did you not actually read the article? I'm dating Emmy Jac, lead singer from the Kinetic Kind."

Okay, that was it. She'd been punished enough. She was out of here.

"You know what," Amanda announced loudly, ready to cut her losses and run. "You guys have a lot of catch-up to do, lots of stuff happening here. I'm just going to head on home. I'll see you tomorrow, Dominic. Let me know if you need any help sooner."

Dominic turned his face in her direction, and she could tell he definitely was surprised to hear her voice.

Ellen fussed immediately. "What? So soon? Amanda, stay with us. Let's have some wine and all get to know each other."

Absolutely not. No, thank you. That was enough heartbreak for one day.

"I'm so tired," she lied, even though it did feel like a blanket of existential exhaustion was weighing her down. "It was a long drive, you know? I'm going to head home."

"Amanda, are you sure?" Dominic asked. He reached his hand out, even if he couldn't see her. "You are absolutely welcome to stay."

She touched his hand, holding it for a brief moment and giving it a squeeze. "Dom, you've got a great support system here. I'll see you tomorrow."

"You really do have the nicest neighbors here, Dom," Melinda said in her seemingly naturally cooing tone. "Completely get why you moved here."

Amanda walked toward the front door and opened it quickly, stepping out onto the porch. Part of her almost wanted people to chase after her, beg her to stay. And by people, she meant Dominic. She wanted Dominic to beg her to stay, to beg her to be his actual girlfriend and kick his ex-wife to the curb.

Shit, she didn't even mean that. She actually really liked Melinda so far, and Emmy Jac seemed cool as hell. But she also hated that she felt so superfluous in the equation right now. And yet, she also knew that that made the most sense. They *weren't* together. They'd just made that very clear.

Why did love and life have to be so complicated? Heartbreak certainly wasn't.

Chapter Twenty-Six

Dominic

Mom, you have to take me over there," Dominic said to his mother after Melinda and Emmy Jac had settled for the night in the spare bedroom toward the back of the house. "I need to talk to her."

He'd spent the rest of the evening anxiously thinking about where Amanda had gone to and what she must have been thinking. He hadn't even known she was there when he'd first walked out and discovered his ex-wife was visiting.

He shouldn't have been surprised that she'd shown up, honestly. One of the things they'd talked about in couples counseling as they were separating was how guilty she'd felt for not being there more after his initial injury. It made sense to him that when she had seen the news about everything, she'd do something like this to prove to herself she wasn't that person. It was a really nice gesture, but that's all it was.

A gesture that was more about appeasing her own guilt than actually taking care of or comforting him.

But though he knew that, he couldn't begin to imagine how all that had looked to Amanda. Not that he owed her an explanation—she'd very clearly broken things off with him—but she deserved one anyway.

"Dom, you need to think about this a bit more," his mother replied, cautioning him with her hand on his forearm as they stood next to the kitchen island. "You can't just be playing around with that girl."

He couldn't see her as she was cautioning him, but he could easily picture his mother's face when she was scolding him—the way her brows furrowed, and she always turned up the corners of her lips, not in a smile but more in a judgmental manner.

"What are you talking about?" he asked. "I'm not playing around with anyone. I need to explain to her..."

"Explain what?" Ellen asked. "Because if it's anything short of 'I love you, and I want to be with you no matter what,' then you need to walk away and let her go."

His body stilled, and his mother's words rolled around in his head. Did he love Amanda? It sounded so real, so true when he thought about it... but how was that even possible? They still barely knew one another.

"I see the way that girl looks at you, and she adores you," Ellen continued. "She's all in if you let her be, but you need to think very carefully about if that's something you want. If you are just going to move to New Jersey in a few months, then don't put her through any of that. Be kind, Dom."

New Jersey. *Shit*. He'd completely forgotten about that.

"What if I don't?" he found himself saying, unsure

of where that line of thinking was even taking him. "What if I don't take the job?"

"Taking that job is all you've been talking about since you found out about it," his mother reminded him.

Except he'd just completely forgotten about it. "Yeah, but that's only because it was something to look forward to. It was a future to picture for myself, something to give me purpose. But I don't know if I need that in the same way anymore. I can picture my life here in Heart Lake just as well as that job—maybe even more. There's a future here for me if I want it, I know it."

Ellen was quiet for a moment, then cleared her throat. "I think that's the question then, Dom. Do you want it?"

"Can you type out an email for me to Eric?" Dominic asked his mother, then dictated to her what to say in it.

She typed it up quickly on his cell phone and read it back to him, then paused. "Should I hit send? If I hit send, that job goes away."

"Hit send," he confirmed, because nothing felt truer in that moment than the fact that he didn't need to move to New Jersey to find a future.

He had one right here in Heart Lake, whether Amanda wanted to be with him or not. But God, he hoped she did. He hoped he could change her mind and beg her to give them a chance.

"Let's go, then," Ellen said, wrapping her arm around his elbow and guiding him toward the back door.

She helped him down the porch steps and across the

yard. He could hear the sounds of the lake to his right and the crickets in the grass around him. The view of the lake was half the reason he'd moved here, but he hadn't realized until right then how beautiful the lake also sounded. The feeling of the chill, crisp air against his skin that had that freshwater smell to it, and there was a hint of pine trees just beyond that. The closer they got to Amanda's house, the more he could smell the sunflowers, and he hadn't realized how much they smelled like her.

When they reached the Sunflower Cottage's back porch, Ellen helped him up and then knocked hard on Amanda's kitchen's sliding glass door.

"Should I wait until she answers to leave?" Ellen asked him.

"No, it's fine," he replied. "She'll come. You can go."

Probably more romantic not having his mother chaperone the moment.

"Okay, but my contact information is pulled up on your phone in your pocket. Call me to come get you anytime. I'll watch out the window, too." Ellen fussed with him, guiding his hand to the siding of the back wall of the house. "Be careful, okay?"

"Mom, I promise I'll be okay," he assured her. "Thank you."

She gave him a quick hug, and then he heard her steps retreating down the porch steps. He waited a few moments longer before he reached his hand up and knocked again on the glass door.

A sudden whooshing sound in front of him made him take a step back.

"Dominic?" Amanda asked, and he figured that sound must have been her opening the door. "Are you okay? How did you get over here?"

"My mom helped," he told her. "Can I come in?"

He felt her hand on his arm and let her guide him into her house. He recognized the path they were taking to Amanda's living room, and when he felt her couch at the back of his legs, he carefully sat down on it. The cushions sagged next to him as Amanda sat beside him.

"What's going on, Dom?" she asked quietly.

He turned his body to face her and reached out a hand, placing it on what felt like her leg. "I turned down the job in New Jersey. I'm staying here, Amanda, and I want it to be with you. I can hire a nurse or someone to be here to help around the clock with my healthcare needs. I would never want you to feel like you'd have to do everything or be the one responsible for taking care of me."

"You're staying? Wait, what are you talking about? A nurse?" she asked, her hand now on top of his and squeezing it. "I feel like I'm missing some context here."

Dominic backed up his train of thought. "Earlier, you said that we couldn't be together because you can't meet my needs. Amanda, the last month of getting to know you and this last week of actually dating, they've been the best moments of my life. I don't want to just walk away from that without knowing I tried everything. That *we* tried everything. I know that being with someone with limited sight is going to be a challenge. It's a lot to ask, and I know it's frankly unfair of me to ask you to be with me, with all I can't give you. I know that there will be things I can't plan for, and there will be things that I can't do, and I know money isn't the solution to everything, but it can offer help. I would never want you to feel like you have to be my caretaker, and I'll hire a whole staff of nurses or a house manager or whatever it takes to make you feel like that burden isn't yours to carry."

"Dom, you are not a burden. You're not a burden at all," Amanda said softly, her hand on his chest now. She moved it up to his neck and then cupped his cheek. "I'm so sorry you thought that was what I meant."

He leaned his face into her hand, relishing the feeling of it. The comfort and softness of her touch was a remedy he hadn't even known he'd needed in that moment, and then when her arms wrapped around his neck in an embrace, he felt like he was melting into her.

His arms circled her waist, and he pulled her torso against his, hugging her tightly. Her hair smelled like flowers and tickled his cheek, but he didn't let go. He couldn't...wouldn't.

Still, he didn't understand where that left them. "What did you mean, then?" he finally asked.

She pulled back now, her hands running down his arms until they found his hands. She held both of his hands in hers and squeezed tightly. "Dominic, you're clearly a physical person. You said it yourself—your marriage was all about sex. And I met Melinda today, and she's freaking gorgeous."

"Okay?" He wasn't sure where she was going with this. "Why does that matter?"

"When you were in the shower, you…you were…" she continued. "And it really just hit home for me that I can't meet that need for you. You deserve someone like Melinda who can."

He furrowed his brow, which was pretty hard to do with bandages on his eyes. "This is about sex?"

"Yeah," Amanda replied. "What did you think it was about?"

"Honestly, I've never been more confused in my life," he replied, now laughing slightly. "Are you upset I got hard in the shower? I'm really sorry if that was offensive. It was a bit of an unusual situation."

This was absolutely not where he'd seen this conversation going tonight.

"No," Amanda said, her voice strained now, and he could tell she was getting frustrated. "Do I just need to say it? Are you just going to make me say it?"

"Well, you're going to have to say something because I'm absolutely in the dark over here," he replied. "Both literally and figuratively."

She chuckled. "Morbid joke, but fine. Dominic, I don't want to have sex."

Had he asked her to have sex? He felt like he'd missed a few pages in this story.

"Okay, that's fine," he replied. "I promise, me coming over here tonight was not at all with that intention."

"I don't mean tonight, Dom," she continued. "I mean, I've never been someone who wants to have sex…with anyone. And I don't think I'll ever be that person. If you're giving up this job, then it can't be for me."

Suddenly, a lot of the things she'd alluded to over their time together were starting to fall into place. "Oh. You mean, you mean you're a virgin?"

"No," she countered. "I've had sex before, and it's fine. It's not like it's terrible or anything. I just...it's not really interesting to me. Doesn't hold a lot of appeal."

"Wow," he said, rubbing his hand across the back of his neck. He was trying to put together all these pieces, but, damn, it was a lot. "When you said you couldn't meet my needs, you meant sexually."

She sighed. "It's not fair for us to get romantically involved in something where you're always going to want something I can't give you very often, or ever at all. You have to call them back and take that job. You've worked so hard for it."

"I'm not taking the job whether we're together or not," he assured her. "I don't want to leave Heart Lake. I don't want to leave the life I'm creating here. I don't want to leave you even if it's only friendship."

She looked like she didn't believe him. "That's... That's really sweet, Dom."

"It's just how I feel." But, he felt like his brain was on a conveyor belt going through a machine as he pieced together everything she was talking about. "Okay, so wait. Let's back up. Can I ask some questions? Not to be rude or obtrusive; you don't have to answer them. I just, I'm trying to understand this whole no-sex thing."

"Of course," Amanda replied. "If I can answer it, I will."

"You don't want to have sex ever in your life?" he asked.

"It's not that extreme," she replied. "It's more like, if I were to have sex, it would be for the other person. It wouldn't be something I particularly enjoy myself. I've had it before, and it's fine."

"But you don't want someone you're with to have it as an expectation, right?" he continued.

"Right," she agreed. "Because I think I'd get resentful if it was supposed to be this big, important thing I always had to perform or do or whatever. It wouldn't feel authentic. And I think the other person would also get resentful because they'd be asking all the time."

That made sense, and he could see her line of thinking. It wasn't something that had come up in his marriage to Melinda because they were the type to not talk about things deeply and avoid feelings with physical intimacy and sex. The opposite was true with Amanda, however, in that everything between them was deep and intimate on an emotional and connective level. He had been looking forward to having sex with her at some point—she was beautiful and he enjoyed sex and sexual release—but he also hadn't seen it as some sort of mandatory checkpoint for them.

"Two more questions," he continued. "Does that mean you don't want anything physical? Kissing, cuddling, everything?"

"What? No!" Amanda leaned closer to him on the couch and her hand squeezed his knee. "I'm always touching you. I love cuddling, and any sort of physical touch that is affectionate."

"Kissing, too?" he clarified.

"That's a newer one for me," she admitted. "I think

I've always lumped kissing in with sexual activities, but kissing you has felt... well, it's actually felt really nice. I guess I'm just worried it couldn't, or wouldn't, stay at just kissing."

"Last question then," he said. "Do you care if I still take care of myself from time to time on my own?"

"You mean like..." He could practically hear her discomfort in the way her body shifted, and he imagined her cheeks were turning red. "Oh, God. Of course. I would never tell someone not to do that. That's your business. I'd be completely fine with that."

He thought about it for a minute, weighing the possible outcomes she was presenting him. Honestly, though, it didn't seem like a hard decision. A surprising one, for sure. Definitely not what he'd been expecting to talk about tonight, but he was actually relieved that it was something much smaller than he'd expected.

"Okay, deal," he said, reaching a hand out to her like he was offering a handshake.

"What deal?" Amanda sounded confused, not taking his hand.

"I'm fine with us being together, with or without sex," he continued. "I just want to be with you, Amanda. I never wanted you just for your body or for what you can give me. I want you because you make me laugh, things are absolutely never boring around you, and I feel like I can talk to you about anything. I wake up thinking about you, and I miss you when I go to bed at night and you're not there. Sex is great, but it means nothing if I can't have you."

Amanda's hand held his, and she lowered it to her

lap, holding his one hand in between both of hers. "Dominic, are you sure?"

Her voice was soft and nervous, but there was nothing he was surer of in his life. If that was all she needed, to feel safe and comfortable not being pressured into a physical relationship, then he could absolutely give that to her. She'd already given him so much more.

"It's not even a question, Amanda. I'm sure," he repeated. He lifted his other hand to her shoulder, feeling for her neck and then coming to a stop on her cheek. "I would like to kiss you right now, though."

He heard her giggle, and she moved closer to him. "I'd like that, too. A lot."

Her lips pressed against his and she climbed onto his lap, wrapping her arms around his neck.

He held her against him, his hands on the small of her back. As their kiss deepened, he knew that this was everything he'd ever wanted. There was a feeling of belonging here in her arms that he'd never felt before—this was what he'd been looking for all along, and he didn't care that he was making sacrifices because she was, too. They were in this together, and there was a commitment here that felt like it was going to be forever.

It was strange to feel so found after going through a time when he'd been so lost.

Amanda pulled back slightly, her forehead resting against his. "You know," she whispered, "I've never felt this way ever before. Here, with you, I can truly be myself. I don't have to pretend or hide any part of who I am. It's like you see me, the real me, and you love me for it, and that's so wild to think about."

Dominic smiled, his heart swelling. "That's because I do love you for who you are, Amanda. Every quirk, every imperfection, every dream, and every fear. I love all of it because it's what makes you, you."

Amanda's eyes glistened with unshed tears. "I've spent so long trying to fit into other people's expectations, trying to be who they wanted me to be. But with you, I can just be Amanda. And that's enough. That's more than enough."

Dominic pulled her close, holding her tightly, and knowing he'd never let go. "You will always be enough, Amanda. You are everything I've ever wanted and more."

Epilogue

One Year Later

Amanda

Forty is a not just a number," Rosie informed them as she stood up in front of the partygoers at Dominic's fortieth birthday party with her champagne glass extended in the air for a toast. "It's a mindset, and, Dominic, I've never met anyone who thinks more like someone over the hill than you. You are an old soul, through and through."

Dominic lifted his glass in the air from where he was sitting in one of the Adirondack chairs Amanda had fixed up for their backyard. "Cheers to being over the hill!"

Everyone else at the party in the backyard of their houses lifted their glasses as well.

"I'm honestly just insulted that you think forty is over the hill," his mother said from somewhere behind them.

Amanda turned to look at Ellen with a smile, laughing. "Don't listen to Rosie. She has a complete anxiety spiral anytime she thinks about aging."

"No, I don't!" Rosie called out, but then Nola shot

her a look, and she laughed. "I'm just going to stay thirty-nine. Forever."

"That's what I said at forty-nine." Ellen downed the rest of her glass of champagne. The raspberry at the bottom of the glass hit her in the nose as she drank it. "Enjoy the forties, Rosie. You'll have some of the best sex of your life at that age. It's a woman's sexual prime, you know?"

"Mom, Jesus," Dominic called out. "Save that conversation for Richard."

A tall man with salt-and-pepper hair circled his arm around Ellen, nuzzling his nose into the side of her neck. She giggled and batted him away but then twisted her hand in the front of his shirt and pulled him closer for a kiss.

Ellen had spent the last two months since graduation in a whirlwind romance with her former professor, and Amanda had never seen anything grosser or cuter at the same time. The two of them were over the top with all the PDA, but thankfully, she was only in town for the weekend to celebrate Dominic's birthday.

"Amanda, we have a big problem." Marvel grabbed her by her elbow and pulled her toward the house.

"What?" she asked, letting herself get pulled along through the crowd of partygoers by the older woman. "What happened?"

"I mixed up the brownies with the shrooms in them with the brownies that aren't psychedelic," she informed her. "My sense of smell is shot to hell, so I need you to decipher which is which before I give them to the kids."

"The kids?" Amanda balked and stopped in her tracks. "Marvel, absolutely not. Throw them all out. Just toss both batches, and we can play it safe with the cookies and cake only."

Marvel frowned, hands on her hips. "But then how are we going to do shrooms?"

"Uh, we're not?" she replied.

"This is a terrible birthday party," Marvel informed her, leaving her with a wave.

Amanda laughed and shook her head, turning back toward the party. Just as she did, she nearly collided with Clayton and Adam.

"Hey! Are you guys having fun?" she asked.

"I heard there were shrooms here?" Adam asked with a teasing grin. "Because then we'd be having more fun."

Clayton gently smacked his partner's arm. "We don't do shrooms. Adam, don't spread rumors like that. Amanda, can we put something on the calendar this week to discuss the new condo development on the lakefront?"

Her firm was a lot smaller than Clayton's—she'd only just hired her first-time employee this past month—but they'd won the bid together on a new housing development. This was the first time they'd be working together again since she'd left, and she was actually excited about it. Things had already been col-laborative and open between them, and she did appre-ciate his help, since the scale of the project was huge.

"Absolutely. I'll send you an email. And we're still on for the double date next weekend, right?" she asked, pointing between the two of them. "This time we're paying. You guys picked up the tab at Lord of the Fries last time."

"Can't wait," Clayton confirmed. "I want to try that new seafood place, the Codfather."

She had been wanting to try that place as well. "Dom and I are in!"

"Oh, and I invited Melinda and Emmy Jac—is that okay?" Clayton added, then pointed and waved over to the couple where they were standing and talking to Mrs. Crawford and her husband, along with Nola, Tanner, Rosie, and Evan. "They are really great and are staying in town another week before Emmy Jac goes on tour."

A triple date with her old boss and her boyfriend's ex-wife—sure, sounded like a typical day in their life.

Amanda laughed and gave him a thumbs-up, making herself a mental note to schedule a girl's night with Rosie and Nola immediately after that to debrief. "Yeah, they're great. We'll have a great time."

She headed back to where Dominic was to check in on him. "Babe, do you need another beer?"

Dominic reached out a hand for her and she gave it to him, letting him pull her down onto his lap. "I'm great. I just need you."

Amanda curled into his lap and kissed his cheek. "You've got me."

Gary's head nuzzled onto both of their laps, and she reached out to pet the large Labrador. They'd finally finished the approval process to get a guide dog for Dominic about six months ago, and he was part of their family now. His temperament was perfect and gentle, and he never left Dominic's side. While Dominic's vision had slightly improved postsurgery, he had settled into his life now as someone who was considered legally blind. Some colors and shapes, light and dark, he could still make out in one eye, but that was about it. In the other eye, things were blurry, but slightly better. Either way, Gary was a faithful assistant who helped him navigate around the house and around Heart Lake pretty independently. She missed Tom, but Tom was living in the lap of luxury at Rosie's house, so she still saw her pretty often. That cat was glued to Rosie's twins, and Becca was already saying that she planned to sneak Tom into her future college dorm one day.

"That's all I want," Dominic replied, kissing her back. He leaned his head onto her shoulder. "Thanks for throwing me this birthday party, Amanda. It's been a really great day."

"Next year, let's not invite Marvel," Amanda joked. "I think she's trying to microdose the entire party."

Dominic lifted his hand up and there was half a brownie in it. "Wait, is that why I feel so good right now?"

Amanda laughed and grabbed the brownie from him, smelling it. "No, I think this is one of the regular ones. Maybe."

"You know the episode of my podcast where I brought her on to talk about her love affair with Mike Schmidt from the Philadelphia Phillies is still one of my highest-rated episodes?" Dominic said to her. "An entire podcast about baseball, and still the human romantic element wins out with the listeners."

"The human element is the most important thing anywhere," she replied, then leaned in to kiss him again. "I know it is for me."

Dominic lingered in their kiss for a moment before they pulled apart. "I love you, Amanda. I love our life together. I don't think I could have imagined any of this for myself a year ago. Things felt so dark back then."

"I know," she said softly, remembering how difficult the beginning of their relationship had been. Settling into a new relationship postsurgery while he was also relearning how to do a lot of things he'd previously done so independently had been incredibly difficult. It had definitely tested them on more than one occasion, and she'd even gone to some of his therapy appointments with him to talk about it. Finally, she'd agreed to get her own therapist, and now she'd been going weekly for almost six months. It had been a game changer. She was already so much more comfortable talking about emotions and communicating her needs with other people. She and Dom had weathered the worst parts of his depression, and once he finally found the right combination of antidepressants, Gary the dog, and therapy, he was doing a million times better.

"What do you think the next year has in store for us?" she asked him, musing as she thought about what they'd already accomplished in the last year. One thing was certain about her new life—she never felt even remotely lonely. "I feel like we need a vacation."

She'd moved into his house with him about eight months ago—bringing a ton of sunflowers with her, of course—and they were renting out her cottage on

Airbnb, which apparently was a huge novelty because of the sunflower theme and, of course, the view of the lake. They'd hired her mother to be the property manager for it, as well as two other properties they were looking at turning into Airbnbs on the other side of the lake.

Amanda had also finally convinced her mother to retire from full-time work, but only by offering her a part-time job with them. Not perfect, but it did mean that she was spending a lot more time with her mother. It might have been in a work-related sense, but it still meant the world to her. She looked over to where Ellen and Richard were now talking to her mother, happy that they all got along. This past Easter had been the first time both sides of the family had met, and they'd all really seemed to hit it off since then.

"We should absolutely take a vacation. Somewhere really warm, so I can feel the sun on my face and the sand in my toes," he agreed. "What about the Bahamas? Or Mexico? Ooh, wait—you know what sounds amazing?"

"What?" she asked.

"A honeymoon in the Cayman Islands," he replied. "Just you and me on the beach and a sugary cocktail in our hands. Lots of naps in the cabana and a dip in the pool—I don't know if I feel comfortable swimming in the ocean, but we'll see."

She lifted her brows. "Wait, hold up. A what?"

"Come on, Amanda," he teased. "You know we're going to get married eventually. What are we waiting for?"

"A judge to sign a piece of paper? Because I don't want a wedding," she said jokingly. "And honeymoons are just sexcapades."

Dominic shrugged like that was an easy fix. "So let's go to the courthouse on Monday, and then we'll plan ourselves the most luxurious, sexless honeymoon in the Caribbean that ever existed."

Amanda laughed loudly and kissed him again. "You are literally insane, you know that?"

"Insanely in love," he replied, kissing her back.

She gazed into his eyes, and her heart felt like it was going to explode in her chest. "I love you, too, Dominic."

Acknowledgments

Thank you so much to Junessa at Forever and Lea and Emily at et al Creative for letting me write an asexual, aromantic main character! This was such a thrill for me to be able to show different types of love and represent them to the world.

Thank you as well to my agent of over a decade, Nicole Resciniti, who continues to help push me forward and bring my books to new readers. I am excited for all we will continue to do together.

Lastly, thank you to my chosen family for stepping in when I needed you and for being the reason I can keep going every day. Your support moves mountains for me.

About the Author

Sarah Robinson (also known as SC Nealy, pronouns: they/them) first started their writing career as a published poet in high school and then continued in college, winning several poetry awards and being published in multiple local literary journals.

Never expecting to make a career of it, a freelance writing Craigslist job accidentally introduced them to the world of book publishing. Lengthening their writing from poetry to novels, Robinson published their first book through a small publisher before moving into self-publishing and then finally accepting a contract from Penguin Random House two years later. They continued to publish both traditionally and indie with more than eighteen novels to their name with publishers like Penguin, Waterhouse Press, Hachette, Forever, Grand Central Publishing, and more. They now also write under the name SC Nealy in nonfiction and children's spaces.

In their personal life, Sarah Robinson identifies as a queer, nonbinary mother of two little girls. They are happily living in Arlington, Virginia, where Robinson also works full-time as a psychotherapist with queer individuals and couples.

You can learn more at:

BooksbySarahRobinson.com
X: @scnealy
Facebook.com/BooksbySarahRobinson
Instagram: @scnealy
Pinterest.com/BooksbySarahRobinson

Book your next trip to a charming small town—and fall in love—with one of these swoony Forever contemporary romances!

THE SOULMATE PROJECT
by Reese Ryan

Emerie Roberts is tired of waiting for her best friend, Nick, to notice her. When she confesses her feelings at the town's annual New Year's Eve bonfire and he doesn't feel the same, she resolves to stop pining for him and move on. She hatches a seven-step plan to meet her love match and enlists her family and friends—including Nick—to help. So why does he seem hell-bent on sabotaging all her efforts?

HOME ON HOLLYHOCK LANE
by Heather McGovern

Though Dustin Long has been searching for a sense of home since childhood, that's not why he bought Hollyhock. He plans to flip the old miner's cottage and use the money to launch his construction business. And while every reno project comes with unexpected developments, CeCe Shipley beats them all—she's as headstrong as she is gorgeous. But as they collaborate to restore the cottage to its former glory, he realizes they're also building something new together. Could CeCe be the home Dustin's always wanted?

SUNFLOWER COTTAGE ON HEART LAKE
by Sarah Robinson

Interior designer Amanda Riverswood is thirty-two years old and has never had a boyfriend. So this summer, she's going on a bunch of blind dates. Pro baseball pitcher Dominic Gage was on top of the world—until an injury sent him into retirement. Now, in the small town of Heart Lake, his plan is to sit on his dock not talking to anyone, especially not the cute girl next door. But when they begin to bond over late-night laughter about Amanda's failed dating attempts, will they see that there's more than friendship between them?

SNOWED IN FOR CHRISTMAS
by Jaqueline Snowe

Sorority mom Becca Fairfield has everything she needs to survive the blizzard: hot cocoa, plenty of books…and the memory of a steamy kiss. Only Becca's seriously underestimated this snow-pocalypse. So when Harrison Cooper—next-door neighbor, football coach, and the guy who acted mega-awkward after said kiss—offers her shelter, it only makes sense to accept. They'll just hang out, stay safe, and maybe indulge in a little R-rated cuddling. But are they keeping warm…or playing with fire?

Follow @ReadForeverPub on X and join the conversation using #ReadForeverPub

AN AMISH CHRISTMAS MATCH
by Winnie Griggs

Phoebe Kropf knows everyone thinks she's accident-prone rather than an independent Amish woman. So she's determined to prove she's more than her shortcomings when she's asked to provide temporary Christmas help in nearby Sweetbrier Creek. Widower Seth Beiler is in over his head caring for his five motherless *brieder*. But he wasn't expecting a new housekeeper as unconventional—or lovely—as Phoebe. When the holiday season is at an end, will Seth convince her to stay…as part of their *familye*?

CHRISTMAS IN HARMONY HARBOR
by Debbie Mason

Instead of wrapping presents and decking the halls, Evangeline Christmas is worrying about saving her year-round holiday shop from powerful real estate developer Caine Elliot. She's risking everything on an unusual proposition she hopes the wickedly handsome CEO can't refuse. How hard can it be to fulfill three wishes from the Angel Tree in Evie's shop? Caine's certain he'll win and the property will be his by Christmas Eve. But a secret from Caine's childhood is about to threaten their merrily-ever-after.